HELSINKI NOIR

EDITED BY JAMES THOMPSON

AKASHIC
BOOKS

This collection is comprised of works of fiction. All names, characters, places, and incidents are the product of the authors' imaginations. Any resemblance to real events or persons, living or dead, is entirely coincidental.

Published by Akashic Books
©2014 Akashic Books

Series concept by Tim McLoughlin and Johnny Temple
Helsinki map by Aaron Petrovich

ISBN: 978-1-61775-241-4
Library of Congress Control Number: 2014938694
First printing

This work has been published with the financial assistance of FILI (Finnish Literature Exchange).

FINNISH LITERATURE EXCHANGE

Akashic Books
Twitter: @AkashicBooks
Facebook: AkashicBooks
E-mail: info@akashicbooks.com
Website: www.akashicbooks.com

ALSO IN THE AKASHIC NOIR SERIES

MUNKKINIEMI

EAST PASILA

SEURASAARENSELKÄ

HELSINKI

LAUTTASAARI

GULF OF FINLAND

ITÄKESKUS

VUOSAARI

AURINKOLAHTI

MEILAHTI

TÖÖLÖ

LINTULAHTI

KALLIO

RAUTATIEASEMA

STOCKMAHN
DEPARTMENT STORE

FABIANINKATU

ESPLANADI

HELSINKI

EIRA

TABLE OF CONTENTS

PART III: WINDS OF VIOLENCE

INTRODUCTION
A Parallel Universe

Finland, the myths and truths. Internationally, it has a reputation as perhaps the best place in the world to live. A great economy. A low crime rate. Good and nearly cost-free health care. The needy are provided for by the state and live in reasonable comfort. Finns: peaceful and quiet people, living in the perfect example of a social democracy functioning as it should. A tourist, or even a person who has lived here for a length of time, might well view Finland as such. There is some truth to this, but like every country, Finland has many truths.

Finnish literature, traditionally, with the exception of the work of a handful of authors such as Leena Lehtolainen (she has publishers in around thirty countries), a contributor to this anthology, hasn't sold well abroad, especially in the noir genre. The reason for this is likely related to the fact that Finland is a quirky country, with customs, traditions, and ways of doing things that mystify some foreigners. In certain translated books, foreign readers are often wondering: *Why would a person do or think that?* It stops readers dead in their tracks.

The problem is one of language—and Finnish is in certain ways a difficult and bizarre language. I sometimes consider something in Finnish, then again in English, and reach different conclusions. Finland is, like the theme so often explored in *Star Trek*, a parallel universe in which, on the surface, all seems normal, but under that shell lie vast differences. Finland is Oz. Like Dorothy in Kansas, Finns usually live internal lives full of dreams, of tin men and witches, lions seeking hearts and flying monkeys. And they hide their frustrations and anger—until they don't. As this book demonstrates, Finland is a noir nation.

The true Finland exists in the Finnish mind, in the Finnish soul, and without an occasional explanation as a guide, some readers can't grasp the Finnish mind. Without a glimmer of understanding of the reasons belying thoughts and actions, stories can confuse and fall flat. This book has no such difficulties.

Being chosen as the editor of *Helsinki Noir* brought me mixed emotions. I felt tremendous pride, because although I'm considered by most to be a Finnish author, I was given the honor of working with some of Finland's finest and most popular writers. I felt trepidation for the same reason. I've lived in Finland for fifteen years, but it's a fact of Finnish culture that if I live here for a hundred years, even if I take dual citizenship and become a Finn, I will never truly be considered Finnish. I'm frequently referred to as a Finnish-American. People often aren't quite sure what to make of me. Would I gain the respect of the authors in the anthology, or would they be dismissive, working under an American? Scary.

On the practical side, the stories in this volume were originally written in Finnish, English, and Swedish, whichever language the individual author saw fit to write in, so I suppose the pool of writers who are also experienced editors and able to work in those three languages was rather limited. I focus on the pride of being chosen editor in spite of this.

That duality of cultural experience gives me the ability to see things about Finns that they might take for granted, things that might never occur to them as being uniquely Finnish.

As it turned out, I had no reason to be nervous about editing *Helsinki Noir*; every author treated me and my suggestions with respect, and the process of writing and editing the book went seamlessly.

This anthology is, I believe, the best representation of Finnish noir ever offered to the international community. Every word rings true. It holds Finland up in a way that not only exposes this wonderful and fascinating country to the world, but acts as a mirror that reflects its people and culture in a way every Finn will recognize, vocalizing those truths that are so seldom spoken here amongst ourselves.

Enjoy.

James Thompson
July 2014

PART I

Deep Cuts

JENKEM

BY Pekka Hiltunen

Töölö

Translated by Owen F. Witesman

There are six of us. We fill the dark street, walking in a line. People coming the other way turn immediately. They are avoiding us.

They are avoiding fear. We are fear.

We walk the breadth of the street. All of Töölö flinched when we appeared from that big building. It was one of those old, expensive Helsinki apartment buildings with all the fancy decorations on the walls where people like us don't belong. Groups like ours never pile out of buildings like that, which is why the entire neighborhood recoiled.

We were leaving Little Dude's apartment, which we had remodeled for him. Destroyed more like. His parents aren't going to believe their eyes when they get home. Little Dude, a distant acquaintance of one of us, is edgy and insignificant. We used him. We convinced him to let us into his house for the night and then threw him out. Little Dude is so timid that he didn't dare come back to chase us out.

Rapa looks at me. Rapa, there's something too sharp in your eyes. You haven't sniffed enough. What do you want? We have Red Sun, and we have cheap-ass Bostik from the store.

Tonight we have everything. We have the whole city.

Toppe is walking in the road. Come on back over here,

Toppe. A car swerves to avoid him. Everyone swerves to avoid us.

Our voices echo off the walls and the windows of the shops. People returning from the bars downtown are still trickling through the neighborhood, but our shouts keep our path clear. The night separates out the loudest and most piercing shouts. Everyone can hear us coming half a mile away.

The six of us walk slowly. Take a good huff, boys.

We stagger and laugh. What a night.

My five boys. They were all sniffing glue together at the Little Dude's place. He didn't have much booze, but we had our own stuff with us. I didn't touch any of it. Glue and solvents and gas are for kids. Tonight I'm not even going to drink very much. But my boys huffed and laughed and huffed some more. They even hit the butane right off the bat, which always gives them wings.

My five little flying demons. I can point to what I want and they bring it. They steal it. They rip it to shreds.

"We'll choose someone soon," I say.

It takes a minute for this idea to sink in. Rapa gets it first, but still a little late. The idea wakes them all up a bit.

Toppe lets out a shout. Howl, boys, howl.

When we're on the move, sometimes we choose a victim. We take anyone, theoretically a random passerby, but in reality everything but random: we choose a person and take everything they have.

A mere facial expression is enough to justify the selection. Or clothes. Expensive clothes, and you're done for.

We've stolen everything from so many people that I don't remember all of them anymore. At first I remembered, but over time they've become a faceless mass; the excitement of grabbing someone dwindled a bit, and they've become *anyone*. Just people curled up on the ground after we were done with them, half-naked, robbed—beaten if they tried to resist.

Someone is standing on the other side of the roundabout. An old woman. She has stopped, afraid of us, waiting to see which direction we will take.

The woman tries not to look directly at us, something grotesque and crooked in her stance. We caused that.

Rapa looks at me, waiting for the word. Let the woman go.

I lead the boys onto Mechelin Street, and the woman disappears. It isn't her turn, and there isn't any fun in humiliating old women anyway. After a life on their knees, tasting of sorrow and suffering, I can never get the expression I want to see out of them.

I want to see the shock when a person realizes how random the continuation of his life really is. I can get that with a younger person, by putting them face-to-face with death.

When I choose the person who we're going to accost tonight, my boys will howl and bray and laugh, and I won't even have to raise my hand to take from that person their feeling of security. The boys will do it all.

My boys: Rapa, Toppe, Mika, Marko, and Liban. Brothers bound by booze and glue, comrades already serving their future jail sentences in their hearts. They have abandoned everything normal, everything ordinary. They are up-and-coming losers united by their shouts and euphoria and hate. Big, bad boys. Inconvenient questions that no one can answer, living and in the flesh.

I am not one of them. I'm too grown-up for that. I lied to the boys about my age. They think I am twenty-six, but really I'm thirty-three. They are just thirteen, fourteen. Rapa is sixteen. They are at the age when they can't tell the difference between twenty-six and thirty-three; to them, everyone my age is simply an adult.

Except that I'm not like the other adults, not their fathers, not their brothers. I am the leader of their group.

Fly, boys, jump on top of the cars. Slash to pieces the lives of these rich mortals, my little demons, fly. Claw marks in the sides of their cars and make these middle-aged fools weep. See the row of men at dawn standing on this street crying for their cars.

Shriek, boys, shriek. Is anything more beautiful than the guttural, mindless shriek of youth?

The night hears as we approach.

Toppe finds something and calls, his voice hoarse, from the edge of a small park along the road. I don't go to see what it is. The boys know without being told that they should bring their discoveries to me or tell me what there is to see.

A pile of dog shit. Standing over a mound of dog droppings, Toppe waves excitedly. In these parks and carefully swept streets there shouldn't be anything like that, but there it is, a big pile of crap that is sending Toppe on a tear.

"Le's make jenkem!"

Is anything more beautiful than the guttural mindlessness of youth?

"What's 'at?" Marko asks.

They gather around the pile. I don't. I keep my distance.

Jenkem is a drug made from excrement. The others' eyes go wide as Rapa explains. In the slums of Lusaka they put human shit and piss in containers to ferment and then huff the end result.

"Where da fuck is Lusaka?" Marko asks.

"Zambia," Rapa says.

His quick response surprises me. This is the first time in a long time anything has surprised me.

Rapa, when did you get so smart? Are you getting too smart maybe?

"Oh fuck!" Marko yells. "Is dat true?" he asks me.

I think for five seconds. "No."

Jenkem is mostly just an urban legend. No one really uses it much anywhere. The guys who have tried snorting it are mostly just kids living in the projects in America looking for new limits to how hard they can go. I remember a time when tricks like this spread across the world slowly, but now everyone knows about them everywhere at once. The slums of Lusaka, excrement, drugs—the combination is heavy enough to stop anyone, anywhere in his tracks. People believe jenkem exists because they want to believe.

But I simply tell the boys jenkem doesn't exist. Half of my position as their leader comes from what I decide to tell them and what I decide not to tell.

Rapa, you look unhappy. Relax.

Take a huff, boys. Not from that dog crap, from the plastic bags Toppe and Mika are carrying.

I start moving again, and the boys follow me.

On Rajasaari Street we feel the sea before it comes into view.

In the warmth of the early-morning hours, a wave of cooler air—nights this warm don't come along very often, perhaps four or five times a summer. Nights when you could lie down and curl up with the warmth.

We have to be outside on a night like this.

Summer changes boys this age. When they spend two long months free from school, they go wild like dogs put out of the house. Their coats change. Their barks change. They don't come up to be petted as quickly as before. These boys haven't let anyone pet them for years, and after a summer like this, they are dogs that bite.

As fall approaches, the boys' anxiety increases. Vacation has been their time to graze, the time when the grip of parents and neighbors and teachers and child psychologists and the police and the whole organized world loosens on them. At the end of summer, they are almost uncontrollable. The knowledge of what is ahead begins to weigh on them, the knowledge that soon they will be chained and measured again.

Howl, run, fly, my demons. How many nights like this do we have left?

What more does this night still hold?

Toppe has found something again. He is tottering in the street, carrying something in his hands. Big balls that shine strangely in the gloom.

Heads of cabbage. Spoiled heads of cabbage, their leaves already covered in slime, their stench biting from yards away.

"They's all kinds o' stuff over there," Toppe explains.

Someone threw a sack of trash on the side of the road. A discarded mound of food. Vegetables, smashed bits of someone's meal. It looks like leftovers from a restaurant. No one has that amount of vegetables at home.

"Fuck yeah!" Toppe yells and throws a head of cabbage high in the air.

It comes down in the middle of the road, pieces flying everywhere. It's a pale green artillery shell, a grenade sending shrapnel across the street, leaving only the heart.

There are at least five cabbages, but before the boys have time to throw and smash them all, I motion for them to stop.

"Practice," I say.

Rapa grins, the only one in the group who gets it from just that word. He takes out his knife. Grabbing a cabbage, he launches it into the air. When it comes down, it splits in two.

The others join in. Suddenly they all have their knives out, and Toppe is hacking Rapa's split head into ever smaller parts.

The sounds that come from them: *yahh, hiyaaa, ugh-ugh-ugh.*

Why do people always yell when they use a switchblade?

I don't carry a knife. I don't need one, and since I don't have a weapon, I could never get caught using one. Not even on a security camera.

Helsinki is full of cameras. The life of the residents is filmed from every angle like an action movie, and everyone who carries a weapon gets recorded by the government as armed and dangerous. But here there are no cameras. Here where Rajasaari Street approaches the sea, the buildings fall behind.

Are you done, boys?

The heads of cabbage are all gone. The scent of grass and sea and spoiled food with young, unwashed sweat mixed in.

The boys sound bigger than before. They have slashed themselves up a size, filling all the space given them.

Shreds of cabbage lie on the asphalt, shining an insolent white in the night.

No one comes along. Not a single man, woman, or child.

It's already past two, and despite the warmth no one is around at this hour. Perhaps the city is suffering from heat stroke, everyone lying in their beds panting and drenched in sweat. People don't even come out on nights like this because it would break from everything familiar. On weekday nights, life in Helsinki crams into the buildings to sleep, to wait, to mourn.

Toppe and Mika send the plastic bags around again. Huff it up, boys, tonight is our night.

They stand in a ring, my five boys, slender bodies getting their cheap glue high. Every breath takes them somewhere farther away from here.

Rapa breaks the line, coming over to me. He walks without stumbling, but the stuff he was just sniffing will get to his legs eventually.

He looks at me. "Which one of us?" he asks. His voice is low and flat. An earth-shattering question uttered in the most muted tones.

Rapa, how you keep surprising me. You want me to choose one of us. There isn't anyone else on the street, so why couldn't the victim be one of the boys?

Rapa, you want to rise, you want to be bigger than the other four.

The intoxication of the choice rushes through me like the glue and solvents in the boys' plastic bags.

Of course I will, Rapa, I'll choose. You want to please me, and how could I say no?

We haven't ever done this before. We've done a lot of other things as a group, but never this. Chosen one of our own and made something new of him. A person marked by us, who will carry that mark to his grave.

"Marko," I say.

The boys hear it and try to understand the meaning of what they have heard. Their consciousness is saturated with glue that normal people use for patching flat bicycle tires. And butane, which can take down any man in a matter of years, a child in months if his luck is bad.

Once the name has been uttered aloud, nothing else need be said. My boys understand.

Why do they accept the idea of assaulting one of their own? Because I chose him. Because four of them are relieved that they weren't the one. And they are afraid—all of them, except for Rapa, feel how weak they are.

They don't have the strength to oppose the world on their own. Their detachment and little capers are a flaccid protest against this world's perpetual, uniform decency. They want to follow me, the strongest-willed person they know, because in a tranquil, feeble country like this, people like me stand out. We draw to us those who have broken away from the herd.

And this is what these boys are capable of. Attacking anyone. These streets and parks are named for old composers, but my boys will never hear that music. To our right are big, fast motor boats, but none of these boys have ever ridden in one. My boys will hear other music, will drive other vehicles, and the only power they'll ever know will be in what they are about to do.

Marko himself is the last one to realize.

The boys are still in their huffing circle. Rapa rejoins the group and takes one of the plastic bags from Mika in the middle of a sniff, offering it to Marko like a condemned man's last meal, the last supper, the final breath before the end.

Marko takes the bag and stares into it. He looks at me, as confused as any fourteen-year-old can be, but he has just realized that the choice was him. He doesn't know what is going to happen—none of us know with certitude—but it is clear that Marko will suffer at their hands.

He raises the bag to his face and breathes.

Closer to the sea, the boys' voices sound different again. The deep canine growls coming from their chests disappear and their shouts become the thin, ear-splitting screeching of birds.

The others in the group shriek and yell, but Marko does not make a sound. The knowledge of what is to come silences him. He does not try to run. His fuzzy mind grasps that in his state he wouldn't get very far. And if he tries to get away, he will only feed the bloodthirst of the other boys.

We walk slowly along. Everything slows down, the glue holding the boys, this moment caressing me.

Now there is nothing around, just the street, the park to the left and the sea on the right. Tall buildings loom ahead. Apartments for rich bastards.

I remember a time before them, and I remember how this whole area changed when they were built. It changed from a place for regular people into an expensive, artificial place. Buildings constructed to maximize views of the sea brought inequality and class division. These buildings sliced out a strip of permanent happiness for the well-to-do, just like the boys slicing cabbages.

Scratching cars isn't enough right now. This night needs to be left with a more permanent mark.

I look at Rapa. I don't need to say anything. He understands the look.

Rapa, you will become a problem for me someday, but now you are closer to me than anyone.

I make a cutting motion, a hand holding a switchblade slicing a cabbage in the air, and Rapa understands: on this night a person will be cut. Marko.

Driven wild by the summer and their detachment, how well these children will do the job.

To our right in the distance looms a seaside restaurant. Marko tries lazily to move in that direction, but his attempt is futile. No one has been in the restaurant for hours, and there's no one out on the patio.

Marko gets back in line when Rapa follows him.

Why Marko? Why did I choose him?

Liban is everybody's friend, the easygoing Somali who always agrees with everyone, too helpful to want to get rid of him. Toppe is stupider than Marko, Mika more sensitive and withdrawn and thus less useful. But Marko isn't really anything. He has no personality. Cutting him will be like cutting air. The world would lose nothing if he just slipped out of it.

And in that moment I understand why I agreed to Rapa's idea to choose one of the boys. The end of summer is affecting me as well. When the boys return to school, I won't see them every day anymore. My grip on them will loosen. They will become tamer, weaker in my mind.

That is why I want to see them cut Marko.

I want to see how red the sea turns when drops fall into it from an opened boy.

I walk ahead of the group.

Marko staggers and spits, the glue making him cough, and I see that his body is seized with fear. He knows that pain is coming. Realizing that would sober anyone up, except for a teenager who's spent half a day high on glue.

He knows that crying out won't help. Our shouting has made the residents of the surrounding buildings numb—if anyone is still awake, they are undoubtedly cursing us.

The boat docks loom in the darkness. There. We will never forget what we are about to do. This we have to do in an open place, on one of these docks stretching out into the waiting sea.

Rapa hangs in the back. He is watching in case Marko tries to slip away.

Rapa, have I really taught you so much?

The giddy feeling that something big and uncontrollable is happening. That feeling quiets the boys. For a second none of us make a sound, and the loudest noise is Marko's panting. His breathing becomes labored.

As we descend the steps to the docks, the stillness of the night continues to envelop us.

But then a thin, slightly distorted sound breaks the silence. Music, from a radio. I locate it instantly. On the farthermost dock is a guard booth. In it is a man, his head sagging down. From the windows of the booth shines a yellow light that we couldn't see from the street, like the music that we couldn't hear until we headed down to the docks. The man is dozing despite his radio playing old-school pop.

The situation changes. Even Marko, who has reluctantly climbed down the stairs to the docks, realizes it.

A boat guard is acceptable.

A soft splash as Toppe enters the water. Idiot. But the man in the booth doesn't stir as Toppe paddles around the chain-link fence protecting the docks and crawls out of the water.

We hurry after him, still hardly making a sound. Marko tries to sneak off somewhere, but Rapa makes sure he stays with the group. And as we each clamber onto the dock, some sort of power flows into us.

I see the brightness in the boys' eyes, the electric charge that comes from stalking another man. Their brains are full of Red Sun and butane and everything they've sucked in today— the mesmerizing walk to this place, and the knowledge that just moments ago we were planning to cut Marko but now we have a completely new victim.

We have a new Chosen One. A man swollen by too stable a life sitting slumped in an old T-shirt. I can see the ring on his finger. Somewhere there is a family who will soon awake to a call from the police.

The guard booth is unlocked. The door stands open a crack. We surround the booth. Toppe and Rapa approach the door, and Rapa pounds on it with his fist. The man shoots out of his chair.

He isn't at all prepared for this, this slumbering boat guard. He lets out a yelp.

"Shut up," Rapa says. "Get out."

Then Rapa and Toppe are halfway into the booth, dragging the man out. He is bigger than them, but too taken by surprise to put up a fight, and with all his heavy breathing, the only thing he accomplishes is some flailing and a stream of confused sounds.

Rapa and Toppe have their switchblades out. Horror fills the fat man's eyes. He staggers out onto the dock, forced by these boys.

"Down, get down," Toppe says.

And the man collapses to his knees. We need something to bind him with. Even Toppe the idiot recognizes it and starts looking around in a nearby boat for a rope. When he finds one, he cuts pieces for the man's hands and feet.

When the guard sees how the blade cuts the rope, his face twists into a grimace. He makes a sound again, but Rapa presses his knife against the man's cheek and the sound stops.

There are four, maybe five nights like this in a Helsinki summer.

When Rapa sets his switchblade on the man's cheekbone and flicks a slice in it, I feel the warmth of the night, I feel the flow of blood pulsing in the man, the frenzy of the boys, the dregs of society, surrounding me.

A dark line trickles down the boat guard's face. He closes his eyes.

Rapa, give us a victim worthy of us. Mark this man so we will remember this night.

Rapa takes a step back and raises his hands.

In anticipation, I close my eyes.

So much happens in so little time. I hear steps: one of the boys is moving. But I don't hear the strike. Where is the strike?

I open my eyes. Rapa has stepped even further back.

The boat guard before him sways on his knees. The man is ready to accept the blow. We are all waiting for the blow, but it doesn't come.

"Get the fuck out of here," Rapa says to the man.

The man yelps again and leaps from the dock into the sea.

Struggling in the water, he moves farther off until his feet find the bottom and his movements gain strength. Then he is on the shore and on his way up to the street. The only sound coming from him is sloshing water. Something keeps him from crying out. Perhaps there is only enough air in his lungs to get away.

Rapa turns to Marko. Still with his knife.

I can't help but smile. On top of it all, the boy has a dramatic flair.

Where has this boy learned all this? From me?

Marko retreats, his eyes filled with blurry disbelief and distress. Toppe grabs and holds him tight.

Rapa, you are becoming an artist. Carve us a statue to commemorate this night.

The sea around us is black, the air unbelievably warm,

and the switchblade in Rapa's hand shines as he turns and moves toward me.

"Jenkem is real," he says.

He sticks the knife in me, over and over again.

I have taught you too well, Rapa. Groping at my throat and belly, I see myself erupting in a torrent, not of drops but waves. I flow into the water.

And have just enough time to see how I make the sea turn red.

KISS OF SANTA

BY LEENA LEHTOLAINEN
Stockmann Department Store

Translated by Jill G. Timbers

1.

It was a bitter-cold December evening. The wind whipped sleet into my face as I crossed Mannerheimintie Street. The lights changed and I barely managed to whisk a half-blind old woman safely out of the way of an approaching streetcar. The conductor rang the warning bells and the old woman thanked me effusively in Swedish. She called me "young man."

Stockmann Department Store was festively lit, as always in the weeks before Christmas. The employee entrance was on the Mannerheimintie side. A man was waiting for me at the elevators. He was about four inches shorter than me. His Boss suit fit elegantly. The frames of his glasses were the latest thing, straight out of *Vogue*.

"Miss New York?" he asked. On the phone he had insisted we use no names.

I nodded. The man summoned the elevator and took me to the basement level.

"The employee lounge is on the eighth floor, but there's a secret conference room down here where we'll be left alone." He opened a four-inch-thick steel door. Behind it was an interior reminiscent of a Töölö drawing room in the center of old Helsinki: a deep cushiony sofa, two classic Le Corbusier armchairs, a glass table with an orchid arrangement on it. The windows opening onto a park were of course just artful photo-realistic paintings. My sleet-drenched parka and worn boots did not fit the setting at all.

"Please sit down." The man used the formal form of address, rarely used in Finland. "May I bring you coffee or tea?"

"Neither, thank you." I steered clear of unnecessary stimulants while working. They just clouded my focus.

The man pulled a file from his briefcase and flipped through the papers inside it. His face was pasty and pale, his black hair oiled into place. His eyebrows had been plucked into narrow streaks. His voice was low and expressionless.

"Hilja Ilveskero, age twenty-eight. Graduated from the Queens Security Academy in New York with excellent marks three years ago. Employed privately by Finnish individuals after graduation, but currently unemployed. Why?"

"My former employer moved to a company in Tokyo that provides security services to its key employees. You'll find his letter of recommendation among my papers."

The man smiled. "Of course, I have checked your background. In today's world one cannot be too cautious."

I snorted. It appeared that Stockmann Department Store Security Chief Henrik Bruun and I spoke the same language.

"You are accustomed to carrying a weapon in your work and employing direct physical force when necessary," he stated. "Precisely the man . . . the person . . . we need. We are looking for an extra guard for the Christmas season. I did not wish to say more than that to the employment authorities. The job is not quite the normal lying in wait for shoplifters and removing troublemakers. It's a question of in-house scrutiny. Thieves have infiltrated our staff. Your job is to expose them.

You will need a suitable disguise: you will thus become one of the house Santa Clauses."

2.

It tickled terribly under my nose. I was accustomed to using mustache glue to dress as my male alter ego Reiska Räsänen, but the Santa Claus disguise also involved a beard down my chest. I glued the eyebrows over my own; they shaded my bespectacled eyes. I rouged my nose to a drunkard's red and added a few moles with makeup. Long white hair covered my ears. I wore a fat suit under the red Santa Claus coat, overalls that added about forty pounds and also hid my meager maidenly curves. It felt strange to sit, because the suit's stomach and chest squeezed together and the thighs bulged to the sides. My walk became more ponderous and imposing than my usual spring. I stretched often so I'd be ready for action when I needed to be quick. I slipped the gun and spare cartridge under my left arm, between the fat suit and the Santa coat. I opened a seam and attached it with Velcro. I was used to do-it-yourself repairs and sewing from a childhood spent on the remote island of Hevonpersiinsaari, a backwoods locale whose very name means Horse's Ass Island, far removed from department stores like Stockmann.

I pulled on thin red mittens edged with fur, because my bare hands looked feminine even though I kept the nails short and unpolished. I entered the elevator on the lowest level of the parking garage. Bruun and I had agreed that I would get into costume in the secret room. That way I could best hide my identity.

"When the employees leave the building, they have to exit through this well-lit corridor," Bruun had explained to me after the department store closed. The security measures appeared sound: employees carrying anything from the store would have to show a receipt. No system was 100 percent sure, but Bruun and the guards had been checking the exits for over a month now and no one would have been able to smuggle through the large amounts of expensive goods that had been disappearing from the store: cameras, phones, PDAs, expensive jewelry, as well as cosmetics worth hundreds of euros. Design cutlery had been taken from the housewares department. All together, the losses had already climbed to nearly 30,000 euros.

The missing items were all small in size. They would have been easy to conceal in clothes or under a bag's false bottom. But how had the alarms been deactivated and the locked cases opened? These were the questions that had turned the security chief's suspicions toward the staff.

I started with routine work, running the data on any new hires in the past several months and checking the security camera tapes. I had worked earlier as a store detective at a shopping center in Vantaa. The kleptomaniacs and candy snatchers didn't interest me, but since I was a foot soldier in the security field, I had done everything they paid me for. One of the compulsive thieves I'd caught, an R&D director for a big corporation, had tried to bribe me not to report his crime, swearing it was a sickness. I'd refused; he didn't offer me enough.

After the foundation, it was time to pull on Santa's boots. My grandfather had made them; he had been the village shoemaker. My late Uncle Jari had added roughness to the soles.

The leather boots with their upturned tips gave a Finnish stamp to the corny Coca-Cola Santa's red garb, and they made it easy for Bruun to distinguish me from the store's other Santas, of which there were five, working in two shifts. I didn't envy them: to listen to spoiled brats' overblown wishes and pose with tots on their laps, careful not to take hold of the wrong place and send the parents screaming pedophilia. I had a bag of candy in my pocket to give the kids when necessary, but I'd tell them to send their wish lists straight to the North Pole.

People stared when I stepped into the department store's elevator, even though Santa was an everyday sight in Finnish stores in December. A little boy about two stepped back into his mother's coat. I tried to smile, since my purpose was not to arouse attention but to observe. The mustache tickled more than ever.

The cosmetics department was still quite empty. I made my way over to the counter from which the most products had been taken. The most expensive cream, a gold-toned fifty-milliliter bottle of night cream promising eternal youth, cost over 500 euros. Six bottles of that had been stolen from the display shelf over the last few weeks. The security camera had not disclosed the guilty.

A woman in her fifties with pleasant laugh lines approached me. "Is Santa thinking of a present for Mrs. Claus?" Her name tag read, *Merja*.

"The lady's already 300 years old but I love her old too," I quipped back, and the woman gave a warm laugh. She was the brand's dedicated consultant. She of everyone would have had it easiest to pinch the creams. Even if she sold them under the store price, the profit would be considerable. But who would recognize the value of a 500-euro night cream? It made more sense to steal things with a market ready and waiting.

Mike Virtue, founder and director of the Queens Security Academy, had repeated that the greatest security threats often come from within organizations, from their trusted employees. The cosmetologist named Merja was one I resolved to watch. Santa could pretend to be interested in her. Flirting with women didn't bother me, I'd done it before, both dressed as a man and as myself. Not likely I'd manage to break Merja's heart.

The Stockmann Department Store contained nine floors of dreams. It was a downtown Helsinki institution. Next I headed down to the basement-level entertainment and electronics department.

The gender distribution of customers here was different than one level up: teenage boys playing hooky were at the game displays while middle-aged men focused on the phones. Santa Claus did not interest them. Real men don't believe in fairy tales.

I picked out the junkie instantly. The man's age was hard to guess, could have been anywhere from twenty to forty. His nondescript brown hair hung to his shoulders and a black ski cap was pulled down to his eyebrows. He had last shaved a month ago. He'd wrapped himself in an oversized black wool overcoat he'd managed to grab from an Uff secondhand store or recycling center. His body twitched and trembled. I knew the symptoms from my Manhattan landlady's body language. Mary had used every substance in existence that could screw with her head. I had saved her life a couple times, though I wondered why on earth I'd bothered. I was just postponing the inevitable.

I slipped nearer to the man. The phone display was an open shelf where the devices were attached at the base with a metal coil that couldn't be cut with ordinary scissors. The druggie was fooling around with the latest Nokia model. I waited for his next move. Not many addicts were clever thieves. They'd just pocket anything easy to snatch and then sell it cheap to pay for their next hit. The professional leagues were a differ-ent story: they calculated the potential supply and then cre-ated a demand for it. At Tallinn's Mustamäe Market no one asked where the bargains came from.

When I approached the junkie I saw that his left little fin-ger was cut off above the top joint. So the chap hadn't paid his debts. I slipped forward slowly, like a cat stalking a mole. The man kept looking around nervously. Both nearby salespeople were keeping an eye on him and I also saw one of the store detectives appear at the back left. Damn. I would have liked to see the man try to steal.

He put the phone back on the stand and moved over to the next. I could smell the sweat of fear on him. Evidently he needed to get the next payment to the dealer ASAP. The store detectives didn't know I was hunting the same prey they were. I tried to figure out how to warn them to stay back.

I snuck over to the other side of the phone display, and this time the junkie noticed me.

He lurched and bumped against the phone shelf, and a cell phone hurtled from his pocket and slid across the floor. I managed to grab it before he could, even though my fat suit made it hard for me to bend over.

"I'm thinking you haven't been a good boy," I murmured as he tried in vain to yank the phone from my hand. He was my height, about five-nine, but seemed shorter, sunken down, as if his bones had been softened by the drugs. He didn't have enough meat on him to feed a hungry dog.

"Give me my phone!" he rasped. I noted that the guard had taken off. Evidently he had more important tasks.

"Don't even try. You swiped it, anyway."

"I did not! Just look at the screen! It's mine! That's Paula's gravestone . . ."

The phone was Nokia's granny model. It wouldn't have brought more than twenty euros on the street and the screen was cracked. I brushed the scroll key and a photo appeared. The gravestone was dark gray with an image of a swan flying away and a simple bit of text: *Paula Johanna Salo, 1985–2012.*

"What business does Santa Claus have with my phone?" The man's voice had a stronger ring now.

"How else can Santa figure out who's been naughty and nice? May I see your ID?"

"You don't have any right, you're not the police—"

"I can get the cops here in a flash if you want them. I'm guessing you're an old buddy of theirs."

The man wiped the sweat from his brow and claimed that he'd left his wallet and papers at home. I asked him if he wanted me to pat him down right there in front of everyone or in the back room. He tried to whine something about me not having the authority, but I grabbed hold of his broken-off finger with a grip that a bit tighter would have dislocated the remaining stump. The junkie was right: I did not have any authority to do this. I just needed to act as if I did.

"I guess my wallet is in my pocket after all. Hang on." Fear was making him sweat, and the younger of the salesclerks, a girl of twenty-five at most, was gaping at me in astonishment. The forty-something male clerk was pretending not to notice the whole incident.

The junkie's wallet was as flat as a sick flounder. No sign of plastic, of course; the unfortunate did not even have a Stockmann loyalty card. The health insurance card had a photo and the name Veli-Pekka Virtanen. The birth date listed meant the man was twenty-eight years old. Place of birth, Vantaa.

"Now listen up, Virtanen. If you're hoping Santa brings you even one gift this Christmas, you'd better not show your ugly mug here again. Tell your boss that this source has dried up." I let go of the man's finger. "Looks like the white Christmas you wanted isn't coming. You're not getting money for snow from here, in any case."

Virtanen grimaced at me like a snared wolverine and vanished. He was such a pathetic case that he'd hardly have been capable of the thefts that had taken place, but at least I'd driven away one disturbance to the gentlefolk's gift-purchasing orgies. That's what they were paying me for.

3.

Virtanen was the most dramatic thing that happened in the store the first week of my gig. The Christmas crush grew worse each day and the sugary carols I heard dozens of times a shift hurt my ears. I tried to stay far from the guards as well as from the other Santas, because the child customers mustn't see two redcoats at the same time. Might lose their belief altogether. My own I had lost at the age of five when I had seen my uncle, who'd raised me, leave to be the sports club's Santa Claus. I had confronted him and he confessed that Santa Claus was make-believe. Uncle Jari said everyone needed miracles. But you couldn't expect miracles on the slush-covered streets of early December.

I did not place my hopes in anything but my own efforts. I had lost enough loved ones not to rely on anyone but myself, but to achieve my wishes I might disguise myself as anyone, even Santa Claus.

Merja of the cosmetics department told me that the thefts from her shelves had stopped. She sounded relieved.

"Must be Santa's miracle-working powers," she smiled, and then told me that some of the products were good for men's skin too. Santa must need makeup remover, at the very least. I flirted back; it reinforced my identity as a man. Was Merja sharp enough to see behind disguises? Perhaps she sensed that I wasn't an ordinary Santa Claus, but rather keeping an eye out for thieves.

By Saturday evening I was so beat I decided to stop at a bar. I changed clothes in the secret room as usual. Security Chief Bruun had assured me no one knew of its existence besides the store management and him, not even the house detectives. It wasn't even marked on the building's official floor plan. I checked the security camera to make sure no one would see me leaving the secret room. I circled the parking garage so it looked as if I'd come by car and then I entered the elevator. I was myself again, a tall blond woman who looked like a white version of Grace Jones. My jeans and black suede jacket offered little protection from the wind that blasted in from the Mannerheimintie Street doors. I darted across the street to the Hotel Marski bar and ordered a tequila. That would get my blood flowing. There was old-time jazz playing, soothing as a bubble bath after listening to endless Christmas carols. I pretended to read the free newspaper while I played with my phone. I was used to sitting alone in bars and chasing away any unwelcome company.

A familiar-looking man was seated beside the window. He had an athletic build, and black hair cut very short and spiked with gel. The thick-rimmed glasses confused me for a moment before I realized that he was the Stockmann store detective who had been in the electronics department when I'd confronted the junkie. On the job, the guy didn't wear glasses and dressed in bargain-basement jeans that bagged at the knees and butt and a sweatshirt with tattered sleeves. Finer ladies averted their eyes from him. The man's civilian clothes were more stylish, and I noticed that the young women sitting at the table next to him were trying their best to attract his attention. He wore no wedding band, but I knew from experience how easy that was to remove.

I shifted my position at the bar counter just enough to be able to watch the women's attention-drawing rituals without turning. The man did not appear interested in them. He was nice-looking in a safe, ordinary way, and men like that did not turn me on. I didn't look for bums, either, and had zero interest in wasting time on whiners, for I was not the sympathetic sort.

To the pair's disappointment, the store detective folded the paper, in which he had already finished the crossword, and rose. He had to pass me on his way to the men's room. He smelled of musk and lemon, a pleasant scent. I noticed it again when he walked past me to the bar and ordered another Christmas ale. He sat at the bar to drink it. Since he had evidently not come to the bar in search of female company, I stayed silent. I ordered another tequila.

"Outside of Mexican restaurants I've never seen a woman who liked those," the store cop said.

"To the best of my knowledge liquor bottles don't state gender restrictions." I looked at him scornfully. Moron. That had an effect.

"Drink whatever you want. Just usually women drink sparkling wine or cider."

"I'm not any *just usually* woman." I appended a small smile to my retort.

The man asked if I had ever visited Mexico. I confessed never to have made it farther south than New Mexico, though I had spent several years in New York. I told him the same false story as usual, that I was in the restaurant field and had worked as a guard for the organic gourmet oasis Chez Monique, among other places. The man introduced himself as Petri and explained he was in the security business and could say no more about his work. I told him my name was Kanerva, which is actually my middle name. Petri thought the name lovely.

The women on the hunt left. The dyed-blond boob bomb threw me a knife-sharp look and deliberately bumped my back with her bag. She didn't even bother with what serves as the typical Finnish apology, *O-ho!* We both knew what was in question and I didn't have the energy to teach the young miss her manners. It was best to conceal my true nature from my prey.

Petri was talkative, which suited me fine. He mostly talked about his travels. He enjoyed windsurfing and snowboarding and his work appeared to be merely a means to fund his hobbies. He lived in a small rental in Kallio and owned only a bicycle. His whole salary went to traveling.

By the time I'd finished my second shot I was mulling over whether Petri was attractive enough for me to take the risk of exposure and sleep with him. Of course I couldn't take him to the place I shared in Käpylä, but what if I went home with him? In the end I nixed the thought—not because I was shy of one-night flings but because the danger of being caught was just too great. My security guard ID and driver's license were both in my wallet, and I for one would riffle through someone's wallet if given the chance.

The man, in contrast, was ridiculously trusting. When he went to the men's room he left his phone on the bar counter. The bartender was occupied mixing cosmopolitans for a trio of girls full of holiday cheer, so I took a quick peek at the gizmo, a simple Oyster Nokia no longer even sold.

Not a single message. Just first names in the address book,

like *Mom* and *Boss*. Maybe Petri had left the phone on the counter because it didn't contain any secrets anyway.

Almost by accident I opened the picture gallery. The first shot showed a snow-covered mountain scene. The next was considerably darker. It showed a gravestone. A swan flying away, and the words, *Paula Johanna Salo, 1985–2012*.

Santa Claus must indeed have magic powers.

4.

Although I didn't have to, I went in to work on Saturday too. The temperature had dropped to minus 14° Fahrenheit during the night, and pale stars still strove to be seen on the horizon when I awoke at six. Petri had not given his last name, but I'd get that from the Stockmann employee directory. I had two guesses: Virtanen or Salo. The night before I had pleaded exhaustion and when I left I had given a false Facebook address with the name Kanerva Hakkarainen.

I pulled on a sweat suit and walked to Stockmann. The sun had not shown itself for weeks, but now it rose over the Vanhankaupunginselkä Bay to the east, red as a Christmas tree ornament. The world was silver white, dogs lifted their paws quickly in the snow and tried to fluff out their fur against the biting cold. I tightened my parka hood, pulled on an extra brown ski hat over it, and donned sunglasses to hide my face from the cameras when I punched in the alarm code. I walked behind the Old Student House to reach the elevator to the parking garage. It was always possible that Petri was watching the security cameras.

A store detective and a junkie—was that the team of thieves? Though a burglar alarm deactivator was not part of a store cop's regular equipment, it would have been easy enough for Petri to obtain. Maybe he had also gotten his col-

leagues to see Veli-Pekka Virtanen as harmless. Or had the
men perhaps figured that a junkie was too obvious a suspect
to fall under suspicion?

In the secret room I opened the employee directory Bruun
had given me. Petri's full name was Petri Ilmari Aalto, address
Pengerkatu Street, as he had said. Military rank, reserve second lieutenant; age, thirty-one. I googled Paula Johanna Salo
but didn't find anything to help with the gravestone woman. It
would have been useful to have access to the police database.

Fortunately, I had connections. Tommy H. and I had been
in the army together and in our spare time we had trained together for the police academy entrance exams. Tommy H. had
been in love with me and imagined we'd build a career together,
but in the end I didn't apply to the police academy. They'd
hardly have accepted a murderer's daughter. On our last long
march, Tommy H. had sprained his back, but he wouldn't let
himself quit. I had carried his pack as well as mine for the last
part of the trip, and the resultant debt of gratitude had already
provided me with some information I'd needed. Tommy H.
had gotten married a year ago, so I could no longer repay his
services au naturel. His marital status wouldn't have stopped
me, but for the time being Tommy H. had shown himself to be
the faithful type.

"Hello, Tommy H.!" I tried for a syrupy voice, though I
doubted I could bullshit my old buddy. After a minute of small
talk I got straight to the point: "I have three names I need
data on fast: Veli-Pekka Virtanen, Paula Johanna Salo, and
Petri Ilmari Aalto."

I'd barely gotten into the fat suit, Santa coat, and beard
when Tommy H. called back. Petri was totally clean, nothing
on him in the police files. Virtanen had done two short stints
for drug dealing, and before that there'd been a pile of fines for

the same thing. Paula Johanna Salo's charges stopped at one. She'd driven into a truck in the middle of the night on busy Kustaa Vaasa Street. The blood tests had found alcohol, benzodiazepines, and strong pain medicine. Salo had left behind a three-year-old daughter.

"Who's the father?"

"The papers give only the mother's name. The child is currently in her grandmother's care."

"I'll spring for the next round."

"We'll see. Jenna's pregnant and she feels lost without me."

I congratulated Tommy H. He'd been a satisfactory bedmate, if uselessly romantic at times. It was better for him to spend his emotions on his wife.

Merja waved at me from behind her counter. I blew her a kiss and left to do my security rounds. Petri was nowhere to be seen that day. I caught a pair of teenage girls trying to snatch some push-up bras. I threatened no gifts for the rest of their lives unless the young ladies straightened out their ways. Their response would have made gang members in the Kerava Juvenile Prison blush. Long live gender equality. I left them waiting for the police in the store detectives' room.

On Sunday the sleet blew horizontally. The storm winds brought down one of the Christmas light garlands over the store's main entrance and it knocked a passerby unconscious. From the coffee shop window next to the cosmetics department, I watched as Petri called an ambulance for the old woman. After it had come, he stayed standing on the sidewalk even though the sleet had soaked his light-blue Oxford shirt so thoroughly his nipples showed through it. I turned away when he changed position. His profession required him to be able to distinguish one from another among us Santas. I drew back into the shadows beside the escalator and watched him come inside. He walked straight over to Merja's counter and took some tissue.

"Goodness, you're wet," Merja said. "Wait a minute, I'll get you a whole package."

She turned and opened the case where jars were kept. The package of tissue was bulging; it looked as if someone had tried to stuff it with extra paper. Petri thanked her and began to wipe off his hair.

"Don't much want to be seen this way," he said with a grateful smile to Merja. Then he resumed his path toward the watch department. I waited a short while before I walked over to Merja.

"You're cheating on me with that handsome youngster," I teased. Merja jumped but recovered quickly.

"Him?" she giggled as if delighted. "Don't be silly. I've known Petri since he was a little boy. He was one of my daughter's best friends."

"Was?"

There was no time for an answer before I felt someone tugging at my coat.

The child was at most three. Thick overalls and a sleet-drenched fur cap concealed the gender. The kid wanted a pellet gun because Julius at day care had one. The mother standing beside her shot me looks indicating that was not a present she favored. I told the kid we'd see what Santa could do. By the time the child was gone, Merja was busy showing face packs to a customer. Had she realized I'd seen everything? I couldn't be sure.

During my break I glanced at the employee directory. I was not even surprised when I saw Merja's last name. It was Salo-Virtanen.

5.

Sunday night I tossed and turned in bed wondering whether to mention my suspicions to Henrik Bruun. I did not have any concrete proof against Merja and Petri. Giving him the package of tissue had taken place carefully outside the range of the security camera. On the face of it there was nothing peculiar in the occurrence other than that Petri was not wearing an overcoat. Usually the store detectives dressed like the customers for the season at hand.

But were there more involved than Merja, Petri, and Veli-Pekka? Someone in the watch or electronics department? The regular salespeople knew that Petri was a store detective, but wouldn't they become suspicious if items disappeared each time he pretended to be a customer looking at them? I must have fallen asleep for a short time, because I dreamed that half the Stockmann staff belonged to a league of store thieves and Bruun was shouting that he'd hired me just so he could set me up as guilty. They'd punish me by suffocating me with my Santa Claus beard. I woke up to find I'd stuffed the corner of my sheet into my mouth.

Monday was quiet. Merja wasn't at work and I circulated for over an hour before I saw Petri in the menswear department half a floor up. He was looking at bathrobes. A dyed-blond silicon babe crept up beside him. When I looked more closely I saw that it was the same woman who had slammed me with her purse in the bar Friday evening. Was she following Petri?

Petri pushed his hand into the pocket of a luxuriously thick terry bathrobe. I saw that his hand was closed in a fist. When he pulled it out his palm was open. He shook his head as if to indicate that the robe did not suit him and moved over to look at the next. The blonde moved along with him to the bathrobe he'd just left and she, too, pushed her hand into the pocket. Then she raised her purse in such a way that she could drop into it whatever object she had taken from the pocket. Petri had already left the bathrobes and moved on to the underwear. The blonde, in contrast, set off purposefully toward the exit on the Esplanade side. No exit alarms sounded when she headed outside into the storm gales.

I stepped onto the escalator. Petri was fingering long underwear patterned with hockey sticks. I walked over to him and murmured, "Tasteless. Wouldn't allow those in my pack. I've been keeping an eye on you. Seem to have left the path of good children."

Petri did not lift his eyes from the long johns but he hissed, "What the hell are you babbling about?"

"I know how you stole the stuff. That blond bird is one of your mules and junkie Virtanen is another. He's apparently Merja Salo-Virtanen's son. Are you in debt for Paula Salo's gravestone? Or just looking for the good life?"

The color drained from Petri's face. "What do you know about Paula?" He was clearly struggling not to yell.

I bent over to whisper into his ear: "Paula chose death over life."

"Who are you? Did Jansson send you? You can see I'm sticking to our deal. Another thousand euros' worth of cameras just left in Milla's bag. The debt will be paid off by Christmas. Then Jansson can go to hell. Tell him I said so!" Petri glared at me, his eyes burning with hatred.

"Hey, Santa, can I have some candy?" I was again surrounded by creatures the height of fire extinguishers, there were at least four of them. I said Captain Cavity had forbidden me from handing out candy and that no one wanted false teeth for Christmas when they grew up, anyway. That got the crowd of mothers giggling.

"Could we at least take a picture?" one mother asked, and I couldn't refuse. By the time that was done, Petri had disappeared. I, too, vanished to my secret place. Time for Tommy H. again.

"Jansson?" he sighed when he heard my question. "Sometimes I think Jansson's as mythical as Santa Claus. In any case, no one's been able to catch him at anything, though it's general knowledge that he deals drugs and sells stolen goods. But Jansson's vassals won't talk. Quite a number of them have just happened to get their fingers caught in a saw or their toes run over by a lawn mower. Be careful with him. He takes no pity on women, either."

I reminded Tommy H. that I was not just any woman, and I promised to let him know as soon as I got more information on Jansson's doings. I straightened my beard and returned to work. There were rarely children in the furniture department, so I headed there to think things through. I had accomplished my assignment; I just needed proof. Who would be easier to break, Petri or Merja? Women were often tougher, especially when it concerned their children. What if I were to approach Merja as my real self, Hilja?

I waited to see if she'd come in for the night shift, but she did not appear. A pretty young coworker said she would be back at work the next day. "So Santa's fallen for Merja?" she teased, and I clutched my hands to my heart dramatically. This wasn't the first time I'd acted at acting.

In the final weeks before Christmas the department store stayed open till nine. It was quarter past nine when I took the elevator toward the ground floor. The customers had already left and the elevator was empty. I was terribly tempted to take off my hot wig right there. Luckily I didn't, because at the P2 level the elevator stopped. Petri stepped in.

"So, Santa Claus," he said, as the elevator jerked and came to a stop, "looks like we're stuck between floors. My, my, after closing it can take quite awhile before they get the elevator running again. I hope you aren't claustrophobic. Now take off the stupid disguise and we'll have a face-to-face talk, man to man. Or shall I take it off myself?" Petri whipped a knife from his pocket, one from the souvenir department. I backed to the corner of the elevator, trying to feign fear.

"For God's sake, don't wave the knife around. I'll take it off . . ." I raised my hand toward my beard and trusted myself to my luck. I had practiced the move many times, and I was quick enough. Petri's menacing expression vanished when he saw the Glock in my hand.

"Scissors beat paper, and guns beat blades. Fine with me to chat, but I pose the questions. Santa's not taking wish lists right now."

Of course my gun was not loaded, but how would Petri know that? He evidently hadn't the slightest idea whose sack I was bagging prey for.

"Drop the knife. Hands clasped behind your neck. On your knees. Santa expects respect."

Slowly Petri obeyed.

I kicked the knife to the side and demanded, "How'd a boy with clean papers like you and Merja Salo-Virtanen get mixed up with Jansson's gang? Who joined first, Paula or Veli-Pekka?"

"So you don't know the whole story?" A glimmer of hope flickered in Petri's eyes but dimmed when I held the gun closer to his temple.

"I know enough. Now I want to hear the rest."

"There's not much to tell. I've known VP since we were kids, even before his mother remarried and had Paula. VP was always in trouble and I couldn't do anything about it. Paula . . . It was too bad we ended up in bed together, sometimes that just happens. We had fuckin' bad luck, she got pregnant. She wanted to keep the kid and Merja, her mother, was excited too. We agreed to raise it together even though we weren't in love."

Petri had fastened his gaze on the floor and was blinking away tears. "But Paula had postpartum depression. VP, the goddamn idiot, gave her speed to help. And it did. Merja and I tried to get her to stop, but what can you do when someone's hooked? Paula fell into debt to Jansson's gang. She saw what they did to Veli-Pekka and she couldn't take the fear. She killed herself. But you don't skip out on a debt to Jansson. He knew Paula had left a kid. He sent Veli-Pekka to pay a visit to Merja: if she didn't pay off Paula's debt, he'd take the kid and sell her to the highest buyer. The world has plenty of markets for cute four-year-olds."

"Why didn't you go to the police?"

"He said that Petriikka would die instantly if we went. That he had eyes everywhere."

Petri might be an experienced store detective, but the role of father trumped the professional. It was a mistake to take anyone into your life whom you'd start to care about.

"And the blonde? Is that your current girlfriend?"

"Milla? No. She works for Jansson. Sometimes picks up the payments."

"Do you ever hand things directly to Jansson?"

"Tomorrow it's his turn to come again. But please don't get the police mixed up with this. I beg you—" Petri raised his clasped hands over his head for a moment—"this is about my child! Merja's already lost one and VP is more or less gone. Needs a new liver, but with what money?"

I faked a Santa's ho-ho-ho. "Let the elevator move again now. Back to the first floor. Don't try to follow me. Leave a message at Merja's counter where and how you're meeting Jansson. How much does he still need?"

"Three thousand. Can I get up to press the code?"

"No tricks."

"Who are you, really?" Petri asked when the elevator door opened.

"I'm Santa Claus. You'd better believe in me."

I did not dare go to the secret room. I went out by a different elevator and walked to the streetcar stop. I took the Number 6 to St. Paul's Church and walked the last part, though the wind whipped my beard and blew my coat hem over my ears. For God's sake, why hadn't I left well enough alone? Why did I want to help Merja and Petri? And above all—*how* could I do so?

6.

Merja tried her best to keep up the usual flirting, although we both knew it was fake.

"Here's my list for Santa," she said coquettishly, extending a folded piece of paper to me. *Twelve fifteen at the men's overcoats. Hope you know what you're doing. P*

I wasn't sure I did. That's why I had turned to Tommy H. for help. Because Jansson had long been under police observation, Tommy H. had been eager to work with me. He'd gotten me the needed three thousand from the snitch fund. It was in my coat pocket, wrapped as a gift.

Petri was waiting for me at the time we'd agreed on. I gave him the package and moved aside. Tommy H. and two other plainclothes police were in the store watching what would happen.

Jansson arrived at the prearranged time. He was an unremarkable-looking man a little over thirty with no distinguishing features. He stood looking at the overcoats. Petri for his part watched him as a store detective should. Jansson took one of the coats into a dressing room. Petri followed him. The package would change owner under the stall divider.

A few minutes passed. Petri returned to the men's clothing department, perspiration on his brow. Would Jansson fall for the trap? The bills had been marked with ink, visible only under ultraviolet light. The police would track their use. It could take years, and in the best case scenario Jansson wouldn't even know which money had finally caused the demise of his money-laundering operation. The foundation of the plan was that once Jansson got the debt payment in full he would leave Paula Salo's family alone. Petri and Merja had not earned a cent from their thefts, and though they had committed crimes, it was not my place to judge them.

The next morning I told Bruun that the thief had been an external one after all and that I had frightened him so thoroughly that the game would end there.

"But the penalty? The damages?" he asked.

"The police are on his trail, but because of the investigation they can't disclose any more. Nor can I. And you of course want to keep your own secret—the secret room."

I could see that Bruun was seething, but I didn't care. Even if I didn't get a job reference, the important thing was that I got my final paycheck. I told him I'd be gone at the end of the shift.

As the afternoon wore on, the crowds in the store became unbearable. Merja left after the morning shift, but Petri was doing a long day. Later, after closing time, I saw Petri waving at me from an escalator heading to the ground floor. I set off after him as fast as my fat suit permitted. Most of the staff had already left the store; only the cashiers remained counting their sales. Petri entered a door that read, *Employees Only*, and beckoned me to follow him. His face was pale, his eyes red, and his skin peeling.

"I got a message from Jansson that the debt's been paid. I can't believe it. Are the police really going to get him without dragging us into it? Will we get off scot-free?"

"Let's try our best."

"Why did you do this? Weren't you supposed to rat on us to Bruun?"

"Does it matter?" I didn't know the answer myself. I seized him by the shoulders and kissed him on the mouth. The surprise was so great that it took a minute before he wrenched free and stepped back, gasping.

"Who *are* you? Are you police too?"

I pulled off my Santa hat and tore off the beard and mustache. Petri gaped at me in disbelief.

"You're a woman?! You have to be kidding. Are you the . . . Did I meet you in the bar that time Milla was trying to get away from her friend?"

"We may have met."

"But Kanerva Hakkarainen isn't your real name. At least, I couldn't find you on Facebook."

"My name isn't important." I stepped closer to Petri again. He reached out his hand and tried in vain to feel my shape under the fat suit. We kissed again, and there was a moment when I thought I'd go all the way and take the man right there on the spot. Then I came to my senses and pulled away from his embrace.

"Present distribution ends here. Time to head back to the North Pole."

I picked up my things and took off. I left the Santa gear in the secret room, walked up the stairs from the parking garage to the Old Student House and through the underground tunnels to Forum and from there to Yrjönkatu Street. I rode to the Hotel Torni's Ateljee Bar and ordered tequila-spiked cocoa. I watched the snow blowing in over the sea from the southeast, and I savored Santa's kiss, still on my lips.

THE HAND OF AI

BY JAMES THOMPSON

Kallio

I rest my feet on Mama. I don't feel much, but when I stretch out in my leather wingback chair with a cup of coffee and a cigarette and put my feet up on Mama, I feel a touch of satisfaction. She was sick, very sick and for a very long time, and I made her wel.

I light one Marlboro off another and stub out the last in the ashtray on the stand at the left side of my wingback throne. My lungs wheeze and I cough like I have tuberculosis plus asthma from my three-pack-a-day habit, but it doesn't concern me. My dead hand stays cold, has almost no blood flow. Sooner or later, gangrene will set in and blood poisoning may come with it. Depending on whether it's wet or dry gangrene, they'll want to take it.

My hand may be dead, twisted and gnarled, scarred; it may sicken people to look at, but it's mine, and I'm keeping it or going out with it.

It happened on the day after my fourth birthday. My birthday present was a bomber-style down jacket. The collar turned up and it was thick and fluffy, but tight at the waist. I suffered from malnutrition—my bones jutted out and my stomach was distended. Mama wasn't much interested in eating and I suppose she thought I wasn't either. I knew being so skinny made me look gruesome and ugly, and I thought the jacket helped hide that. I was proud of it.

I still look gruesome and ugly. My dead hand revolts people. I've made it worse. I put out cigarettes on it to make people think I'm tough. I don't feel the burn, but after using my parlor trick hundreds of times, the already disgusting hand is now just a deformed lump of scar tissue and scabs. The sight and smell of the cigarette burns, and the fact that I don't even flinch when I do it, causes an attitude adjustment when I sense that people are considering fucking with me.

Aside from my hand, I never recovered from malnutrition, and I'm paper thin and my face is scarred from beatings, both from Mama and bullies; I'm so weak that I feel as if I'm made of bubble wrap and Styrofoam instead of flesh and blood.

My hand got ruined on the day after my birthday. Mama had been sweet, even made me a birthday cake, but she was about as predictable as a heart attack—she didn't feel well because she hadn't taken her medicine, and she was getting angry with me.

She taught me to play a game. She taught me that men in stores in uniforms were playing the game too. We didn't know them, but we knew they were playing. The object of the game was to go to stores and get treats and goodies. If we got out unnoticed, we won the game, but it we were seen, we would lose and the men would be mean and take us to bad places.

Mama didn't work. She was on permanent disability because of her illness, and her medicine cost almost all her money, like injecting liquid cash into a hole in her arm, so I liked the game, even if it was scary, because we always had something good to eat after we won. If we didn't play, sometimes dinner, if she bothered at all, was soup made out of ketchup and hot water.

Mama gave me my nice jacket to help me play the game. One time she wrote, *naudan sisäfilet*—beef inner filet—on the palm of my hand. I couldn't read or write, of course, but all I had to do was match the letters on the palm of my hand with the writing on the package, then slip the meat inside my coat.

The man in the uniform passed by me; I was afraid to lose the game and afraid of him and afraid of Mama, my palms got sweaty and the writing blurred. *Sisä* turned into a smudge and I got something called *naudan ulkofilet*—beef outer filet.

When we left the store and walked away from it, I gave her the beef, and she turned furious. *Ulkofilet* isn't as tender as *sisäfilet*. Her boyfriend—she had a lot of boyfriends, and when she didn't have one, I would watch out the window as she walked up and down Flemari, getting into cars. When she came home, her hair was a mess and her lipstick smeared all over her face. Say what you want about Mama, even though she was sick, she was pretty.

Her boyfriend was coming and bringing her medicine, and she was making him a nice meal. Beef and mashed potatoes. She was pounding the *ulkofilet* with a meat hammer to tenderize it. A pot of water was boiling, waiting for the potatoes. My cake from the day before was on the counter near her. I reached up and took a slice. I thought it would be all right. It was my cake.

Mama went crazy. She grabbed my wrist and the cake fell back onto the plate. She forced my left hand flat onto the counter and started smashing it with the wooden meat hammer. I felt bones crackle and pop. I started screaming in pain: *Ai! Ai! Ai! Ai!* This further enraged her, she flipped the hammer and kept smashing my fingers and hand with the pyramid-shaped spikes on the back of it. Bones snapped and blood flew. I shrieked and cried and kept screaming, *Ai! Ai! Ai! Ai!* I was in so much pain that I couldn't even form words to beg her to stop. I bawled and shrieked at the top of my lungs. She kept my hand pinned to the counter and wouldn't stop hitting it. She told me to shut up and quit my crying or she would give me something to cry about.

I couldn't stop. My hand didn't look like a hand anymore. It looked like a tiny piece of the *ulkofilet*, just bloody red meat, thoroughly tenderized. In some kind of dope-sick twisted logic, to stop my crying, she jammed my hand and arm almost up to my elbow in the boiling potato water. I've never, before or since, experienced anything approaching that agony, but in a way, it was a kindness. I blacked out.

I woke up in darkness, folded into the cramped space of the bedroom closet. Mama said she didn't like me to see her take her medicine, and that her boyfriends weren't interested in children. She always jammed a chair under the outside handle to make sure I stayed put. She expected me to stay silent, to give no clue that I was there.

It was cool and quiet in the closet and I didn't mind, except for the times she forgot I was there and left the apartment. Then, I measured time by when light peeked into the thin space below the door. Except in winter, when there was no light. Then, life was timeless. Mama's medicine usually made her pass out or at least left her on the nod, and I could usually count on spending the night there.

When I woke, I tried to be quiet, but the pain was so awful that I couldn't stop mewling. She must not have wanted to make a scene in front of her boyfriend, so the first time, she tried to gag me quiet by taping my mouth shut, but they could still hear me. The second time, she gave me a pill. It was a blessing. I slept for a long time.

I woke up when Uncle Jukka opened the door and lifted me up in his arms, like he would a baby. He carried me to the couch and laid me down. The boyfriend was gone, but the evidence of medicine was on the coffee table: a scorched spoon, white dust, syringes, and needles. He didn't say a word to Mama, just started slapping the shit out of her. Before, I would have thrown myself on him to try to protect her. But at that moment, my own pain was of more concern than hers and I didn't care. Agony killed my emotions. It wasn't that I didn't care about her, I just couldn't care about anything at all. Watching her take a beating sparked nothing in me.

Jukka carried me to his car and took me home. He and his wife Anni had a powwow: what to do with me and Mama. I could hear them talking. Jukka always stopped by our apartment a couple times a week. I thought it was because he liked Mama, but it wasn't. He came to make sure nothing like this had happened to me. He called Mama a "filthy-piece-of-shit junkie whore." Mama used those words a lot. I wasn't exactly sure what they meant, but I knew it was something bad.

The options. Call child services, have me taken away from her; but Mama would be in terrible trouble too. Keep me here until I healed, and tell Mama that if she didn't become a good mother, and now, they would see that she was punished for hurting me. They chose the second option. Jukka couldn't stand putting his sister in jail. She would get one more chance.

They said the hand was ruined. No amount of surgery would correct it. More than likely, it would be amputated. They needed to invent a story. I didn't know the word *amputate*. Jukka explained. I screamed, cried, and begged. Finally, he relented, provided that as it healed, it didn't start rotting and endanger my life. Strange that I understood so little of this but remember so much of it. Every last word.

Since a doctor couldn't become involved, as certainly the police would become involved too, they slathered my arm and hand with burn ointment, wrapped them in gauze and bandages, and hoped for the best. And the best that could be hoped for, given the devastation heaped upon me, is what I got. One day, Jukka changed my bandages, and a thick layer of dead skin was loose. It peeled away like a long and thin white glove a woman might wear to a night of ballroom dancing. Muscles were visible in spots, under the blood, scabs, and dreck.

Neither of us said anything. Jukka just wrapped it up again. I healed over time, even though the result was a horror show. Probably because I was so young, the hand adapted to its devastation and didn't putrify, just atrophied into a useless, twisted, and mangled mess.

For a time, I stayed with Jukka and Anni and their two boys, both a few years older than me. Jukka was big and had a reputation for being mean and he drank a lot. He had no compunctions about backhanding his boys or even Anni, but he never hit me. He was good to me.

After about a month, Jukka talked to me. Mama was coming to take me home. He pressed twenty euros into my good hand and told me it was secret emergency money. There were lots of little kiosks around our apartment on Flemari. He told me to hide it and use it to eat if Mama didn't feed me. He said he was going to visit often, and we would have secret talks, and I was to tell him if something bad happened to me again.

Mama showed up, medicated, and he told her to explain herself and to tell him exactly what she had done. They sat at the kitchen table and the medicine made her giggle while she told him the scripture pure truth. When she got to the part about me screaming *Ai!* over and over again, she started laughing and couldn't stop. Jukka just sipped coffee and stared at her.

Over the years, naturally enough, her boyfriends and fellow medicants asked her what had happened to me. She would tell the story like it was nothing and laugh her way through it. And *Ai!* made her laugh the hardest. Eventually, my real name was forgotten, everyone called me Ai, and so I remain.

When Mama was done and stopped laughing, Jukka laid down the law. She was never to hurt me again. She was never to lock me in the closet again. She was to see that I was fed and cared for. She was to treat me like a human being. Any infraction of these rules would be punished. He would heap whatever harm she caused me upon her tenfold. Then he would report her to the police. They would both go to jail: her for hurting me, him for hurting her. When they got out of jail, he would do to her exactly what she had done to me, and she could spend the rest of her life with a withered and deformed hand as well.

She laughed in his face. "Fuck you. You can't tell me how to raise my kid."

He swung his fist across the table and broke her nose. She wasn't laughing anymore.

When she came back from the hospital after having her nose set, she took me home.

Everything changed. Mama was afraid of me now. My influence with Jukka gave me power over her. She dealt with it by ignoring me. I considered this a significant improvement in our relationship. She kept food in the house, which she mostly shoplifted herself. She whored when she had to.

I was still unhappy. Kids at school bullied and beat me. I was a soft target. I made a friend once, a boy who had been mauled by a dog. The stitches made his face look like a patchwork quilt, and he couldn't cry because his tear ducts were gone. His companionship made things worse. Bullies got two for the price of one. We parted ways. He even started picking on me, thinking it would raise his status in the eyes of the bullies, and diminish their affection for beating him. He was wrong. They beat him worse. Those tear ducts would have come in handy.

I was about twelve when Mama met Jari, a midlevel drug dealer. Their relationship stuck. He more or less lived with us. Mama was happy. Jari kept her supplied with medicine. He used drugs too, but liked to go up, not down. Mama hadn't worn too badly over time. Her teeth had fallen out and she wore dentures. Jari didn't mind. He said she gave better head toothless.

Jari had intelligence and a sense of humor. He treated me with decency, even seemed to like me. He had the street smarts not to flash his cash and drove junk cars which he changed frequently. He ran a daily route and sold dope in the parks around Kallio, the district we lived in: Karhupuisto (Bear Park), the dog parks in Torkkelinmäki and Lintulahti, Vaasanaukio (often called Piritori), Speed Square, the little park down the street from it that bordered Aleksiskivenkatu, and a couple of other places. He changed his route schedule every couple weeks. Sometimes he took me with him after I got out of school.

I liked to go with him. It changed my status. Jari's pride and joy was a Remington .12-gauge tactical shotgun. It looked like something from *Star Wars*. It was short, had pistol grips instead of a butt. Extra ammo hung off the left side and it had a magazine extension.

Jari taught me about guns, and I like technical things. I like to memorize things. TacStar offers a variety of tactical shotgun accessories for Mossberg Maverick 88, Remington 870, Benelli Nova as well as M1/M2, and Winchester 1300 shotguns. TacStar shotgun accessories allow the professional operator to personalize a tactical shotgun to meet specific mission needs. Adding the TacStar shotgun pistol grips reduces the overall size for close combat quarters, while the addition of the side saddle and magazine extension assure sufficient ammunition for any given circumstance. High-tech flashlights under the barrel and on the top allow it to be used in the dark and blind whoever you are going to kill with it.

Jari's precautions—the shitbox cars and route changes, and his shotgun, which he said he kept because it caused a lot more fear than a pistol, and he was right—kept him from getting busted. Business thrived. He let me keep the Remington in my lap sometimes. A lot of the bullies liked drugs, and seeing me with Jari and that gun made them think twice before beating me. He tried to teach me to use it, but I wasn't strong enough to cock it. The bullies didn't know that. Life got better.

I looked up to Jari and thought he liked me. Often, he patted my knee or rested his hand on it while we were in the car, running his route. I even let myself think it a sort of fatherly affection.

I stayed away from people. I turned into a bookworm and read a whole book almost every day. I learned how to use computers at school and stole one at Rautatientori—the main railway station. One afternoon a guy in a suit had a few bags beside him, must have spent the day shopping. He was taking money from a cash machine while talking on the phone, attention diverted. I was a habitual thief, had stolen almost everything I owned. After a lifetime of practice, I was expert at it. One big bag was from Verkkokauppa, the mega-IT store.

I could read *Apple* on a box at the top of the bag. I picked up the bag and strolled off to an Internet café just a few minutes away.

Jackpot. The receipt was in the bag. He had bought a Mac computer and paid cash for it one hour and twenty-seven minutes earlier. He hadn't filled out the registration or warrantee yet. I filled out the forms right then and there. It was a gamble. The guy I boosted it from could report it to Verkko-kauppa, Apple could eventually trace it through the internal registration code. I banked on him being too lazy—took the chance that he would just try to get insurance to pay for it and forget about it. Maybe even think he lost it.

But for now, it was mine. If any questions came up, I would dump it and steal another. I couldn't envision the police getting a search warrant and raiding our apartment over one lousy computer. I took it home, plugged it in, and immediately found an unprotected Wi-Fi connection. The Internet was my oyster. I began envisioning all the cool games I would shoplift. I won the bet. There were no questions. I could keep the computer.

It was summer. The sun felt good, even just beaming through the windows. Now, looking back over my sixteen years, it was the best time of my life. I was no longer beaten up. I had discovered books and lived vicariously through them. I had a computer, and soon learned the joys of social networking, mostly on literary sites, like Goodreads. People online couldn't see me for the ugly, misshapen creature I was. Jukka still visited us on a regular basis. Since Mama had Jari, she kept food in the house. When Jukka and Anni bought new clothes for their own boys, they bought for me too. Jukka gave me twenty euros a week.

* * *

I was fourteen when the world came crashing down again. Jari came home drunk one Monday evening. He and Mama sat on the couch, both toasted on their drugs of choice, watching a porn film. It was one of Jari's favorites, *Fuck Her in the Ass IV*. I walked by, on the way to my bedroom. Mama still didn't care for my presence, and although she no longer locked me in the closet, she made it clear that I was to make myself scarce when Jari was there. She didn't like me. Never had. Never would.

Jari opened a beer bottle with his teeth. I walked past him. He leaned forward and grabbed my butt. "You know, Ai, you got a sweet little ass. We slap some lipstick on you, you'll be prettier than your mama. Too bad you still got your teeth though."

He yucked and elbowed Mama in the ribs. He expected us to laugh at his joke. It all came reeling in a lightning flash of understanding. The hand brushing my leg or resting on my knee. The occasional unexpected drunken hugs and kisses. This was no joke. I was certain, absolutely without doubt, that Jari was going to rape me. I wished Mama would lock me in the closet again, hide me there, so I could be safe.

I managed a little hee-haw to placate Jari, then scurried off to my bedroom and had a panic attack.

I didn't sleep that night. Even once the panic ended, I was afraid of what might happen if I slept and got caught unawares while Jari crept in. But I couldn't stay awake forever.

I thought about telling Jukka. He would try to defend me, but tough as he was, he was no match for Jari. Jukka would end up in the hospital, maybe even dead. I couldn't do that to him, and both Jari and Mama would take out their anger on me. I would be in a worse position than I was now. Once again I had two options: run away from home or kill Jari.

I mulled it over. I only had enough money to last for a few days. I would have to live on the street. Bullies would go back to having field days with the ugly disfigured kid again. I would starve, and eventually, someone else would get around to raping the defenseless street urchin. That wasn't an option, so that left me with only one course of action.

I needed something to kill him with. Since I was kitten weak, I couldn't cock his shotgun. He slept with it propped up next to the bed anyway. I needed poison or a weapon that he couldn't take away from me before I could use it. I could stab him to death in his sleep. Hold the kitchen knife with a rag so only Mama's fingerprints were on it, to keep me out of jail. But then Mama wouldn't have her medicine. She would take it out on me. Maybe even ruin my other hand. Jukka be damned.

I needed a gun.

I searched the Internet, read gun laws, tried to figure out some way I could get one. I also needed ammo. Jari had a box of .12-gauge shells, so I should get a .12-gauge shotgun. Guns and ammo are hard to steal. Stores keep them locked up in display cases or behind the counter. I hadn't learned to pick locks yet.

I hunkered down with the computer overnight. I found a gap in the law. A firearm over a hundred years old is no longer technically a weapon; it's an antique. I checked antique auctions on the Internet. I found a piece-of-shit shotgun. A Crescent, made in 1904. It was beat to pieces, looked like somebody used it to drive nails. It was hammerless. I didn't have to be strong enough to cock it. Opening bid, sixty euros. I had saved about a hundred euros from the money Jukka gave me.

Two sleepless days later, I went to the auction and got it for the opening bid. Nobody else wanted such a piece of trash.

They were hesitant to sell it to me. I made up some song and dance about my grandpa wanting a shotgun for his birthday. The pricks knew my grandpa wouldn't even try to fire the thing—it looked like it might explode—but they didn't want it sitting in inventory forever either, so they sold it to me. I asked them to put it in a couple garbage bags. Most likely, the bus driver would call the police, and one way or another, I would be stopped by the cops about ten times before I could get home with it. So they hid it for me with a bag on each end and taped them together.

When I got home, I threw it in a junk pile in back—worn-out tires, stuff like that—then went out and bought a hacksaw and a short handsaw, and some oil. I didn't have enough money for an electric carving knife, so I shoplifted one. When I returned, the house was empty. I laid my backpack on a tire, and the gun on the backpack, cut the butt down to a pistol grip, and sawed the barrels down just enough so that the gun fit in my backpack. It left me exhausted, but the lever to open the breech squeaked and so did the breech when I opened it to load it. I oiled them, and worked the lever and breech back and forth until they were almost silent. I put the gun in the backpack with my schoolbooks. No one would suspect it was there.

The following day, Jari took me on his afternoon run. His hand was brushing against my thigh and closer to my privates even more than usual. Time was short. It was now or never. He kept a box of shells in his glove compartment.

When he got out of his vehicle of the moment—an object of ridicule, a Lada, a dented Russian rust bucket—to sell some meth and heroin with shaking hands, I took two shells out of the glove box, slid my shotgun out of my backpack, and loaded it. I laid it down in the floor space between my seat and the door. Jari had his shotgun between the driver's and passenger's seats. I wondered if, when I killed him, the gun would blow apart and take off my good hand.

Jari pulled back out onto the road, and when his attention was diverted, I pulled out my shotgun. It was heavy, so I rested the barrels on his crotch and kept my fingers on the triggers.

I thought he might go for his own gun, but he just laughed. "What the fuck do you think you're doing?"

"I'm protecting myself from being victimized by a pedophile."

He saw I was serious, and nervous, and might accidentally blow his balls off. "I'm not a pedophile. I've treated you not like a son, but like a friend. I've taken care of you and your mother. And you're gonna pull some crazy stunt like this on me. Are you fucking crazy?"

I told the truth: "Yeah."

He didn't know what to do. He was king of the hill, and all of a sudden, a disabled teenage boy had a cannon in his crotch. He radiated bewilderment. "What now?"

"Drive over to Lintulahti, and park where they keep the rental vehicles, behind the gas station."

Most of the vehicles were moving trucks. Parking between two of them made for zero visibility into the little Lada, and not a lot of people came and went anyway. It was just a few minutes away. We rode in silence. I could smell fear-sweat roll off him.

"Cock your shotgun, put the safety on, and put it on the backseat," I said.

"Why?" he asked.

"Because I might need it later. Empty your pockets and put everything in the glove box." His dope was already there. He put in his fat cash roll with a rubber band around it—a lot of money—and then his wallet. He asked if he could have a smoke.

"No. Drive to your supplier's place," I said.

"You're getting in way over your head," he said.

"It's *my* head, just drive."

We went back up the hill to an apartment building on Vaasankatu. I didn't even try to hide the guns. Just tucked the tactical shotgun in the crook of my bad arm and held the sawed-off in both hands, pointed at him, but just out of his reach, in case he tried to take it away from me. People in that neighborhood tend to not want to get involved.

He rang the buzzer, a voice answered, and Jari said, "It's me."

The front door unlocked. We took an elevator up. The apartment door was open for us when we got there. We went to the living room. A pretty woman in her twenties was smoking a joint and watching TV. She didn't even bother to glance at us. "What's up?" she asked.

Jari said, "We're being ripped off by a child."

She looked up and showed no emotion. "Put the guns down and I'll let you live."

I set the sawed-off at my feet. The tactical shotgun was actually lighter, despite the bells and whistles and big magazine. I flipped the safety off. An air rifle was propped against the wall, next to an open window. A box of pellets on the sill. It looked like a nice gun, was scoped and everything. "What's that for?" I asked.

"I shoot pigeons when I'm bored."

"Jari, use it to shoot her eye out."

"You're making a mistake," she said.

"Your stash and cash, or your eye," I answered, though it was a lie. I had already decided that she would track me down and kill me, probably torture me first. I had already decided to kill them both.

I pointed his shotgun at him. He looked at her and shrugged, as if to say, *What can I do?*

It was a powerful kind of air rifle that runs on nitro cylinders, not the pump-up kind. He stuck a pellet in it.

"If I give you my dope," she said, "I'll be killed for it. No one will believe this story. Don't do this."

"With just one eye left, and the possibility of Jari shooting out the other, you might decide to take your chances." I aimed at Jari's head. "Shoot," I said.

She closed her eyes. He put the muzzle to her left eye and pulled the trigger. Her head slumped back against the couch. Jari checked her pulse. "She's dead," he said.

Damn. The projectile penetrated all the way into her brain cavity. I didn't know a pellet gun could do that. "Reload it," I said.

He was soaked with sweat, stunk, didn't say a word, just stuck another pellet in it and propped it against the wall, where it was when we came in.

I told him to sit beside her on the couch. "Where is her dope and money?"

"I don't know. She keeps it in another room. She only brings it out here so I can watch her weigh it." He's talking about her in the present tense. Reality hasn't set in yet.

"Last chance," I said.

Panic showed in his eyes, and a tear ran down and dripped off his nose.

"Lay on the floor, facedown, arms and legs spread eagle."

"Please," he said.

"Like you said, you've been good to me and Mama. I'm not going to kill you. Just stay put while I search the place."

This calmed him a bit. It was difficult to hold two weapons, but I took the pellet gun and shot him in the temple with it. Motherfucker. I wished I could have killed him ten more times.

Now I had all the time in the world. I turned the place upside down. She hadn't hidden anything well, but she was organized. All the drugs were in big freezer bags and clearly marked: *heroin, cocaine, methedrine, marijuana, ecstasy.* I also came up with three handguns.

Jari had taught me to drive. I took it all downstairs and put it in the Lada. Including her set of scales. My future had become clear.

I bagged it all up and took it home. Mama was on the nod. Had overdone it a bit. Her dope and rig were there on the table. I shot her up. She moaned. Her eyes closed. I shot her up again. And then once more, just to make sure. I brought everything inside while she was dying.

It was hard, but she was skinny. I dragged her to the bathroom and left her on the floor. I laid her on her stomach with her face down and neck over the shower drain. The electric carving knife went through her throat like butter and the blood flowed. No muss, no fuss.

I went through the IKEA online catalog and ordered a coffee table sort of like a coffin. The top opened and there was a lot of space inside. And I ordered two hundred kilos of lime, paid them a big delivery charge. And another tip for the guys from IKEA to assemble the coffee table in front of my throne. I can't manage a hammer and nails, so I bought the local grocery out of Krazy Glue.

Mama went into the table, a piece at a time, each chunk covered with a generous portion of lime. I glued the top down with as much care as if I was handling nuclear waste. Mama finally got cured, and makes a nice footrest as well.

* * *

I bought myself a cool bicycle, and have a little route that I run around Kallio every day after school. No one picks on me because I have what they want, and a snub-nosed .357 Magnum further convinces them that there are plenty of other people they would rather bully.

This story was originally written in English.

ST. PETER'S STREET

BY RIIKKA ALA-HARJA

Eira

Translated by Kristian London

Water is flooding out of the bathroom.

Klaus has been here.

I shut off the valve to the washing machine and throw my sweater on the hallway floor. The heavy wool soaks up the water. I throw the bedspread on the kitchen floor. I walk over to the bed, lie with my head against the wall the way Klaus always does. I listen to a truck backing up on St. Peter's Street.

I saw Klaus this morning on my way to the island. He turned in the direction of St. Peter's Street and disappeared. I was in a hurry, my shift was about to start. I jumped onto the ice, walked across its foot-thick lid until I made it to the island. I opened the door to the sauna, checked that the janitor had cleaned the showers, and then I clicked on the electric sauna stove. I went into the coffee shop, tied on my apron, and put the cinnamon rolls in the oven. I sold hot coffee and cocoa for eight hours.

I toss the soaking, heavy blanket and sweater into the bathtub. I get the sleeping bag from the cupboard and crawl into it. I can't sleep. I take off my nightshirt. The light is on in the bathroom; Klaus forgot to turn it off again. Klaus never flushes the toilet, Klaus flicks Q-tips onto the bathroom floor, Klaus munches on Finn Crisps, Klaus doesn't let me sleep.

Klaus and I are always cooking together, making love, surfing our phones, laughing at our mutual friends' updates. In the summertime, we sail an old-fashioned wooden boat, we walk, and we breathe. People who live in our neighborhood are active and well-balanced, people who live in our neighborhood don't do bad things to each other, people who live in our neighborhood know what they want.

At night we lie in our double bed. My feet are pointed toward the wall, Klaus's feet are pointed at the window. One time when we were arguing about our sleeping arrangements, he asked if I had ever thought about the name of the street we lived on.

No, I answered.

St. Peter's Street, Klaus explained. Peter, who said that if he was going to be killed, he wanted to die a more horrible death than Jesus.

Peter was crucified upside down.

Stupid Peter. What did he achieve by hanging there?

I doze off for a moment, then snap back awake.

Is Klaus staring at me from over by the stove?

I bend my knees inside the sleeping bag and stare at the ceiling. It's clean, white, and dry. The floor is already dry too.

Does the floor really dry this fast? Is the incident over this fast?

In the morning I head out onto the ice. I pass the island but I don't go into the café. Today is my day off, today they don't need me at the café, someone else gets to bake the cinnamon rolls. The island cinnamon roll oven heats up every morning, the island sauna stove heats up every morning.

* * *

Two women in swimsuits run down the wooden planks to the hole chainsawed into the ice. The women take steady strokes in the ice-cold water; I walk toward the low-hanging sun, the snow crunches under my winter boots. I walk up to the edge of the ice. I'm never the one who goes out the farthest. Klaus is, though.

When I return to the island, I glance in the sauna. The sauna is empty, the women have left. I take off my clothes, climb onto the bench, and toss water onto the stones.

Once, Klaus and I reserved the entire sauna for ourselves; money had come in from the ad agency, the sauna was just for the two of us.

I put on my swimsuit and walk along the wooden planks to the hole in the ice. The sea is frozen, but a hole has been sawed in it. The de-icer keeps water circulating so that the hole doesn't freeze over. I lower myself into the sea one step at a time, the water is ice-cold but my toes can't feel a thing. I lower myself in up to my waist. I slide out, my heart pounding. It's a hundred yards to the shore, but there's ice in between, you can't swim there from here. The shoreline of the city's most expensive neighborhood is full of free swimming spots: public beaches and ice holes.

I climb out of the water. I'm instantly bitten by the cold. I walk along the wooden planks toward the warmth. I open the door, I take a hot shower, the water sprays, my toes start to melt, I let the water from the shower flow. I drop my swimsuit to the tiles, turn off the shower, and step into the sauna.

Klaus, can you turn on the tap so I can get some more water for the sauna, will you let it run? Klaus, come sit next to me on the top bench. I slap more water onto the stones. I lean into you, Klaus. Klaus, say something to me, you have something to say. Tell me about Peter, tell me about the crazy disciple or whatever you want, you know how. It makes me laugh when your mother says that you live in London now, that you moved back there in November. That's what your dad says too and your best friend Pete, but why would I believe them, since I see you every day. That's what I tell Klaus's mother over the phone, but Klaus's mother hangs up.

Klaus, if I change the locks at St. Peter's Street, will you climb the ladder to the second floor?

No, no, I won't change the locks, you can always use the door. You can come whenever you want, as long as you come. When you leave the tap on, I'll throw the mattress onto the floor to soak up the water, and in the morning everything will be dry again.

At home, I drop my bag on the hallway floor and hang my swimsuit up to dry. Heat is rising from the radiators, the air crackles.

Klaus, are you coming?

Klaus, are you coming right now?

Yes, Klaus comes, Klaus comes and turns on the faucet, Klaus lets the water flow, Klaus is the one who runs the show.

We lie in the dry bed, Klaus's head is on the wall side and my head is toward the window. Water streams across the floor.

HARD RAIN

BY TAPANI BAGGE
Esplanadi

Translated by Kristian London

T he entire rail line was an enormous graveyard: tomb-
stones of concrete, steel, glass, of people standing at
stations, of scrubland trees and bushes. As fall went
on, people fattened with clothes, trees and bushes stripped
naked. The rain stripped them.

First thing at the station, a bald young monk in an orange
robe walked up and tried to pass off some book with a bright
cover. Tried to pull a fast one. Just wanted to talk, he said,
but wouldn't stop plugging his Buddha. Said there was a meal
in it too, some shitty vegetarian crap way the fuck out in the
middle of nowhere.

Marko didn't say anything, he just crushed the monk's
windpipe with a flick of his fingertips as he walked past. The
guy dropped his books and flyers and stood there, windmill-
ing and hacking. So much for that conversation. Marko kept
moving with the crowd. No one noticed anything.

Marko may have had blue eyes, but he could see when
people were trying to pull a fast one. He saw it every morning
in the square between the station and the department store.
They lay there on the pavement with a plastic cup in front of
them—crippled or old or otherwise humble—some tortured
a note or two out of a broken-down accordion or a beat-up

sax, acting jolly. And every evening he watched as young, less humble men came around to collect the day's take and carry it over to the mustached man sitting in the Benz with tinted windows outside the post office. There wasn't an ounce of humility in that old bastard. The tiniest traces of humility had been scraped off with a steel grater. You could see it in his face, the cheeks like raw hamburger. You couldn't see the eyes, his eyes were covered with mirrored shades. Maybe he was a blind old-timer, a panhandler who had risen to this preeminent status after having begged on the streets for years.

Maybe, but not likely.

It pissed Marko off, but what were you going to do? You couldn't whack them, or you were a racist. You couldn't whack drunks or junkies either, no matter how belligerent they were or how much they spat on you or mouthed off or waved their bottles and bloody needles at you. Besides, it was easier to take bullshit from them than from kids, and Marko remembered how just a few years ago he had talked back to security guards and rent-a-cops. And then got the hell out of there.

But Marko had to earn a living somehow, since he didn't feel like sitting at college till his ass got numb or begging for scraps from the unemployment office or welfare. A week's training was all it took to become a guard. The job was so shitty that there weren't a lot of people who felt like doing it for long.

On Saturday, a scum of grease and crap had flooded out of the sewers of the department store and into the square, where the human scum also accumulated. People had slipped and fallen in the shit. Even after the square had been cordoned off with red-and-yellow barriers and tape. People had been determined to go and soil themselves in shit-scum.

And although sewage trucks had sucked the sludge into

their tanks and the maintenance men had rinsed and scrubbed the sidewalks and a street cleaner had done the same, it wasn't until the Sunday rain came that the stench had been washed away.

Someday there was going to be a real rain. A hard rain, like in that song. So hard that it would wash away all the beggars, drunks, junkies, whores, and punks. And fags and trannies and foreigners. All the filth. They would wash out to sea and stay there.

Until then, Marko was going to be pissed off.

The thing I hate most is everything. Now that was a good title for a book, even though Marko didn't read books.

It was raining now too. Hard, but not hard enough. You could smell the stench of human scum in the air.

Normally when it rained, Marko took the tunnels. There were plenty in downtown Helsinki, and it meant you didn't have to smell the outdoors so much. Despite the fact that it smelled worse underground. Like piss and shit and vomit and jizz and blood. The whole spectrum of life. And death. Death is the best time in life, after all.

Now Marko walked down the street, didn't care when his mohawked head and trench coat got wet. The rain cooled his scalp but not his thoughts.

Usually when Marko ranged the downtown streets it was in his company coveralls, with his nightstick, pepper spray, and handcuffs at his waist and combat boots on his feet. He was wearing them now too, but he was also wearing a long leather trench coat. His gestapo coat. He had confiscated it from some junkie, stolen goods anyway. It was perfect for concealing weapons. He had stood in front of the mirror and shaved the mohawk with an electric razor before he left, it was just like in that movie—*Taxi Driver.*

"You talkin' to me? You talkin' to me?"

A young fundraiser holding a light-blue Unicef folder got spooked at the corner and turned around, didn't walk up to ask Marko, *Do you have a minute?*

Good. Marko didn't have time today. Marko had a destination.

"Marko? What's the Suburban Stud doing here?"

Marko snapped out of it. Marina was standing at the stoplight in her loose black coveralls, standing there radiating light. Her hair was spiked too, but it was short and black. He felt like stroking it. He had to shove his hands deeper into his coat pockets.

"I thought you never came downtown. Nice coat, new hair too! You got a date?"

Marko mumbled something even he couldn't make out. He was careful not to look into Marina's dark eyes. It was so easy to get drawn in by them. Marina was his only coworker with any brains, the rest were complete tools. A few shots short of a full round.

Across the street, the pairs of stone men stood stiffly on either side of the station doors—abandoned there, holding their glass spheres as if they didn't know what to do with them and were in constant fear of dropping them.

Marina ruffled Marko's mohawk. The *karateka*'s hard hand felt soft.

"Where'd you get this from, you an old punk rocker or something?"

"Punk rocker, my ass. Indian."

The light changed, Marina started on her way. "All right, you behave now, so I don't have to come use my stick on you."

Marko almost forgot his destination as he stood there

watching the swishing of Marina's ass in her coveralls. So light.

At the corner, some brand-new ex-drunk was timidly hawking *The Big Number*, holding his newspapers under his arms as if they were full of X-rated photos. They weren't; the dirty pictures were up on the billboards for the whole world to see. The only things forbidden on billboards were images of poverty or marginalization.

The paper seller had slouched shoulders and a beer belly; you could tell how he had spent his time. Marko was a brick shithouse and proud of it. Kept himself in good shape. Spent at least an hour at the gym every day, a few hours on his days off. His job was easier when you had a little mass, a little muscle. He didn't go to the bars or walk the streets at night. If he did, someone would always come up and start something up. First a fight, and then a court case after Marko kicked the guy's ass. Or the cops would pick up both of them, but Marko always took the fall.

Besides, Marko had plenty of chicks, one-night stands. He would have liked something permanent, but the chicks didn't. They were either bimbos, which he had no interest in, or students of sociology or philosophy who just wanted to try out what it felt like with a big guy. Then they'd get scared and wouldn't dare answer their phones anymore or say hi if he ran into them; they'd cross over to the other side of the street and slip onto the first bus or tram that rolled past. Maybe they'd heard somewhere that Marko had a girlfriend.

He had never dared to try anything with Marina. They were just coworkers. Marina was small but solid, you could sense it somehow. It would take a lot to break her. Unlike Marko, who was built but fragile.

Fucking fragile. No, he was also strong. Fucking strong. He would never break. Nothing could break him.

* * *

The Academic Bookstore. Academic, my ass. As if your average working man couldn't buy a book. Or rip one off. If he felt like it. Marko didn't feel like it. What the fuck was he going to do with a book?

And that fucking millionaire there on the stand in the bookstore, sucking in his pale gray mustache as he spewed out his truths, a smile on his lips and blue eyes flashing behind his tinted glasses. His baby shit–yellow tie fluffed and a matching handkerchief in his breast pocket like the swollen tongue of a hanged man. And the interviewer, a slick young guy, all he did was simper, lick the millionaire's ass there on the stand. What the fuck did either of them know about life?

"People need to stop complaining and go to work. I didn't become a millionaire by twiddling my thumbs and whining."

Work, huh? What work had that douchebag ever done? Played with other people's money at the bank, that was the extent of his work history. Pulling in sick amounts of cash the whole time. Born with a silver spoon in his mouth.

It pissed Marko off, but what were you going to do? You couldn't whack millionaires, that would mean jail time.

From the shelves, *A Message from the Angels* struck Marko in the eye like a dart hitting a dartboard. Message, my ass. A black angel was going to come and claim the hero of the moment, like in that song. This black angel was wearing the black coveralls of the security company. It was going to drag the guest of honor around the corner and whack him behind the knees first, then in the kidneys. Maybe boot him in the nuts and the ribs. But not in the face—that was only for drunks. You can kick them wherever you want, no one will say anything. Drunks and hippies and alterna-fruits and all the fucking fundraisers and sprout-eaters and sand-niggers. All the fucking bastards with nothing better to do.

Marko had nothing better to do now either. He'd gotten the boot from his boss and his lady. He had stuck it to a drunk, even though it was against the rules, and some fucking idiot had filmed it with his cell phone and posted it online. He had stuck it to another woman, not even a stranger, his lady's sister, but that was against the rules too. No one had filmed it or put it online, but his lady's sister had gotten a bad conscience and sent a text message to her sister. So, he got the boot from both, once his boss caught wind of the first bit of intel and his old lady the second.

"I don't know what I ever saw in you . . . You've always been an asshole, but this time you crossed the line. With my own sister?! I'd kill that fucking whore, but I'd have to go to prison and she's not worth it. Neither are you. So get your shit and get out of here."

"You've been a good guard and showed up for all of your shifts, but these overreactions are starting to get out of hand. The guy's in ICU, and we don't know if he's going to make it. That's bad PR for the company. We can't turn a blind eye to this . . . Bring your ID and keys to the office on Monday."

Marko wasn't sure which had said which, his boss or his bitch. Who gave a shit? The boss had been yakking over the phone, the bitch at arm's length. The boss he had told to fuck off with a promise to kick his ass; the bitch had lunged at him with the bread knife, but missed. He'd slammed her into the wall and she'd slid to the floor, her skirt rising up to her waist. For old time's sakes he had fucked her there in the entryway, from the front and the back among the grit and the dust and the shoes, blown his load in her eyes and then grabbed his shit and tried to leave. The bitch started waving the knife again and calling him names, but she ended up tripping onto her own blade. The blood had spattered all over, but luckily not on Marko. He had watched her twitch for a while, then headed out. The entryway smelled of lust and blood, the stairwell of piss and microwave pizza. Hard to say which was more disgusting.

All his crap was in a gym bag at the station now. It'd be safe there until evening; at night, the railway company would empty the lockers. Or actually, the guards would.

How the fuck would this whole shitty society stay standing without guards these days? There was no fucking way. Normal people wouldn't dare to go to the train station if there weren't guards there. Or walk around downtown or in those fucking malls from hell. Nowhere. Cops were being cut all the time, guards were being bumped up.

Except Marko. Marko had been cut.

Should he go to the police academy? No. He had tried right after completing high school and his military service, but they wouldn't take you if you were color blind. You had to be able to tell a red light from a green one. Or was it the other way around? Maybe both.

"A market economy is better or at least nicer than a democracy, in that, in a market economy minorities aren't left to fend for themselves," the millionaire was saying. "Is it fair that Parliament gets to mandate income redistribution?"

The crowd was as heavy as an overcoat, though not that many people were wearing theirs. They would have been sweating; Marko was sweating in his trench coat. He was standing near the Esplanade entrance, but there was no way he'd get closer to the stand without using force. And it wasn't time for that yet.

"How would you summarize the message of your book?" the interviewer asked.

"The core issue is, of course, freedom. Freedom of choice. In my book, I develop a vision of the future in which people—and companies—vote more and more often with their feet, as they say."

"Why?"

The millionaire shrugged. "Voting with your feet is far more common than voting at the ballot box. We see it in consumer choices, investment decisions, and the places people choose to live and study. If taxes rise too much, who's going to want to live here anymore?"

He was damn right about that. But what was an unemployed guard going to live on abroad? And what taxes did an unemployed person pay in the first place? Fuck! No, the guy was wrong. He was just thinking about things from his own perspective. And there weren't exactly a lot of fucking millionaires in Finland.

"The tyranny of the majority must come to an end. When it comes to decision-making, instead of level-headed politicians, we need visionaries with new ideas for the future. From a financial perspective as well."

"Do you see yourself as one of these visionaries?"

The millionaire laughed. "Well, of course I possess the necessary competence, but I prefer my current job. And life isn't solely about work. It's also important to be able to enjoy a change of scenery when you feel like it. Aside from my manor, I have several homes around the world."

Blow me, asshole. Easy to talk when you have the dough to do whatever you want. Otherwise every guy in the world would head for Thailand to screw slant-eyed bitches and toss back beers under the palms.

But there was something to what he said before that. They needed a new leader. Someone who would bring a real hard rain to clear the unfit out from their midst. Someone who knew who needed to go and stop polluting the air.

Some Marko.

Marko tried to move closer to the millionaire, shoved people to the right and left out of his way. People grumbled, but no one said anything to him. At least not after they saw him.

The interview ended, and the millionaire began to sign books. Marko picked one up from the stack and stopped shoving, moved along politely with the line. The blood vessel in his right temple was throbbing, but he calmed himself. There was no point calling pointless attention to himself yet. There would be time for that later.

A little before it would have been his turn, Marko looked around and realized that there were too many people left in the store. A burly guard in black coveralls was hanging around the edge of the line, thumbs in his belt loops, and near the stage there was a broad-shouldered guy in a dark suit, maybe a bodyguard. Marko might not have time to carry out everything he had planned. Better to wait for the right opportunity.

The millionaire continued signing for about half an hour. Eventually the line petered out, and he and the women from the bookstore and the publishing house and the guy in the suit went up to the third floor for coffee. Marko flipped through the travel books near the café, wondered where he would travel if he could afford it. Came to the conclusion that it made no fucking difference. He had a trip coming up real fast anyway.

After finishing his coffee, the millionaire shook hands with the others and stepped into the elevator with the guy in the suit. Marko put on his gloves and rushed in after them, noted that the button for *P3* was already lit, and nodded at the men.

The elevator jerked into motion and began its descent.

The bodyguard in the dark suit was big, just a little smaller than Marko. He'd have to take him out first. He was clearly wary, eyed Marko like he was a shoplifter. Marko was still carrying the book under his arm.

"Could I get your autograph?" Marko asked, holding the book out to the millionaire.

"Of course," the man smiled, pulling out a gold ballpoint pen from the breast pocket of his dove-gray suit. "To whom shall I dedicate it?"

"For Mar . . . tti." Giving his real name might not be a smart idea. There was a camera on the ceiling.

"For Mar . . . tti, huh?" The millionaire smirked, opened the book, and began scribbling. The bodyguard relaxed a little. "You did pay for this, didn't you?"

"Sure, I can show you the receipt . . ." Marko said, and started digging around his trench coat pockets with both hands. With his left he pulled out a department store receipt, saw the bodyguard tense up for a moment and relax again. Then with his right, he pulled out a sturdy yellow-handled Solingen meat knife that he had just bought from the department store and sank it into the bodyguard's stomach.

The bodyguard tried to grab the knife but fell to his knees, the blade tore through the white shirt and the flesh and into the breastbone. The guy had shaved his chest. His guts struggled to escape. He tried to hold them in, sliced his hand as Marko pulled out the knife. Marko immediately severed the guy's carotid artery, blood sprayed onto the millionaire's pants and all over the elevator. Like in the movies.

As the shower of blood sputtered out and the bodyguard toppled over onto his stomach, the elevator doors opened onto the first floor.

A horrified woman stared from the bookstore lobby, dropped her bags, and screamed. She looked like Mom that time she was fucked up and had knifed Dad for the zillionth time and the old man had actually croaked.

The millionaire snapped to and tried to get out. Marko tossed him against the back wall and pressed *P3* again with his gloved hand. The doors shut in front of all the idiots who had stopped at the elevators to gawk. No one had time to try and enter.

"What . . . what do you want?" the millionaire asked surprisingly calmly. He was more thrown off than terrified.

"What do I want?" Marko said. "I want to talk to you for a minute. Your basic theses are okay, but you're totally fucked when it comes to some other stuff. I want to give you some advice."

"Advice? Me?" The millionaire looked almost amused, even though the bodyguard was emitting a death rattle at his feet and blood had sprayed onto the millionaire's suit and glasses and cheek.

"Yeah," Marko said, yanking the glasses from the millionaire's head and stomping them to shards with his combat boots. It pissed him off when the other person didn't show him the proper respect. "We need a hard rain. You know that song, *a haa-haa-haa-hard rain is gonna fall?* That's what we need. And I'm the rainmaker. It's raining blood, as you can see."

The millionaire sobered and fell silent. Marko shoved his left hand into the bodyguard's armpit, found a matte-black pistol there. Looked like a Glock. He dropped the meat knife from his right hand and switched to the gun. It wasn't exactly an Uzi, but it offered a little more range than a knife.

The elevator doors opened onto the parking garage. There was no one in sight.

"Where's your car?" Marko said, dragging the man along by his tie. He almost tripped over his bodyguard.

"I don't know . . ." the millionaire started, banged the corner of his eye on the edge of the elevator door, and continued in confusion: "I don't know. Koskela is . . . was my chauffeur. He looked after the Jag . . ."

"How many Jags can there be down here?" Marko asked, pausing to look around.

There wasn't a single Jag in sight. The parking garage was shared with the neighboring department store and had three levels. It held six hundred cars. If the millionaire's chauffeur had pressed the right button, they had two hundred cars to check. Or a hundred and fifty, not all the spots were full. How much time did they have? A minute? Thirty seconds?

Marko pulled the guy along. He didn't resist or cry out for help, he must have been at least a little shocked about his chauffeur's fate.

"Where . . . Where are you taking me?" the millionaire asked in a strangled voice. His tie must have been pressing against his windpipe.

"What fucking business is it of yours?" Marko gave the tie a tug. "What fucking business is it of anyone's? Shut the fuck up!"

As they rounded the next corner, they saw the Jag, a burgundy XJ, an extra-long luxury model, of course. Marko yanked the millionaire by the tie headfirst into the back of the car so hard that his head slammed against the metal; it looked like he'd put a dent in the trunk. The man grunted and dropped to his knees.

"Give me the key, I want to get out of here."

"I don't have—"

Marko shoved the pistol back into his pocket, a gunshot

would arouse too much attention. He took the nightstick out from under his coat and whacked the millionaire in the temple. There was a rewarding thud, and the guy hit his nose against the back bumper. The blood sprayed.

The first drops of rain.

"What the hell are you talking about? You don't have the keys to your own car?"

The millionaire was holding his nose with both hands and looked at Marko as if he were a primitive life form. "You don't think I carry my car keys around, do you, if I have a chauffeur?"

Marko realized that things had gotten out of hand. It was a couple of hundred yards back to the elevator, and it had zoomed back up as soon as they stepped out. The same elevator doors were already opening now, as well as those of the other elevator, and then the steel door to the stairwell popped open. Urgent footfalls approached from two directions.

"Your game's up, rainmaker," the millionaire said. "It'd be smartest to give yourself up right away. There's not going to be any more rain."

Something in Marko's head snapped. He heard it clearly, as if a dry branch had cracked in two. He pulled out his pepper spray and misted the guy's eyes with it.

"No rain, maybe, but plenty of fog. How do you like that?"

The millionaire bawled like a little baby. Marko began to smack the little baby with all his might, just like Dad had smacked him. Dad only had a belt but Marko had a nightstick, he was able to achieve serious results. The man's arrogant expression melted into tears, Marko's eyes were blurry with rage and then pepper spray, someone was spraying him in his eyes; he turned and sprayed back, someone yelled something but he didn't hear what and couldn't see anything. He just waved his nightstick around until it was knocked out of his hands, someone jumped on his back but he threw the person off, some little piece of fluff, he pulled the pistol out of his pocket and fired at them, then a few bigger pieces of fluff jumped on his back, knocked him to the ground, and wrenched the pistol out of his hand; he managed to fire it once more before easing his grip, the bullet headed in the wrong direction.

The final shot cleared his field of vision, the mist and the spray and the tears melted in the gun smoke, and he saw everything clearly. Too clearly.

The millionaire was wiping the corners of his eyes between the cars; he had a few bumps and bruises but they'd heal and he'd forget about them before long—his millions would take the edge off both. The guy would walk out of this whole shit-show without a scratch.

A small figure in black coveralls was lying on its side, face toward the Jag, black hair spiked up. When a cop touched the guard's shoulder, the guard rolled over and lay there, staring into Marko's eyes. The torso of the coveralls had darkened and was growing darker and darker, the guard was gasping for breath and trying to say something, she probably would have asked why, but Marko didn't have an answer. Nor did the question ever come, blood just trickled onto her cheek from the corner of her mouth. Then Marina was no longer breathing, and the light in her bright eyes went out.

The final shot had hit Marko in the ribs, angling down from above. He could feel the life flowing out of him into the parking garage drain, could feel the concrete and iron grate cold and hard beneath him. Darkness awaited him too. He still struggled against it, rolled onto his back flailing with his fists and feet, rose up to his knees for a moment even though at least four large men with nightsticks were on him.

He didn't feel the blows anymore. In the end, the men let

go, and the electric probes of a Taser punched into him. The first wasn't enough to stop him, neither was the second. The third one dropped him to the concrete. He couldn't feel that, either.

The light had already gone out.

PART II

Broken Blades

THE SILENT WOMAN

BY JOE L. MURR

Munkkiniemi

Kati sways on the balcony to rhythms that only she can hear. Question marks of smoke curl from her cigarette in the cool night air. I stand right next to her, but I might as well be alone. I have no fucking idea what she's thinking. She hasn't said more than ten words to me since I arrived at her flat. It doesn't mean she's upset with me. This is a Finnish silence. She'll break it when she has something to say. I've become used to it, living in Helsinki.

So we smoke and drink wine, both of us in our own headspace. That's fine. I'm happy to just watch her groove. She's a stunner, the kind of girl who belongs on a catwalk.

But she's not at her best now. Staggering on coltish legs, she grips the balcony railing to steady herself. Red wine sloshes down the front of her blouse. She curses, spitting out, "*Vittu saatana perkele.*"

Cigarette between her lips, she hands me her wineglass and unbuttons the wet shirt. Her skin is creamy and goosepimpled, her bra a very bright white. One last puff from the cigarette and she flicks it over the railing. She leans over to watch it spin three stories down, spark against the tarmac.

Then she breaks her silence. "Splat. That's what I want to do to Daddy."

Like most Finns, she speaks English in a monotone, and that came out sounding like a deadpan joke. But I've never heard her tell one. I'm the funny one, apparently. Her funny Englishman.

"What, toss him off? That's disgusting."

She doesn't react to that. Probably not familiar with the idiom. Her eyes on the pavement, she says, "Bastard might not even die from this height. End up cripple instead."

"What did he do?"

"He said no."

It's probably the first time in her twenty-three years that her father has refused her anything. "No to what?"

"I don't want to talk about it."

She turns her back to me. I follow her into her cramped flat. It's only thirty-odd square meters, but I wouldn't be able to afford it in a hundred years—not even renting. Prices in Helsinki are on par with London. This place is worth around three hundred thousand euros. Her father owns it. He also has two six-room flats in the building, valued at around a million each. I know this because property prices are one of the few things that Kati loves to discuss.

"Refill," she says.

I top up our glasses from the bottle of expensive Australian Shiraz in the kitchenette. She does all her shopping with Daddy's credit card. When I'm with her, I eat and drink like a rock star.

She sprawls on the living room sofa, feet on a glass table. When I give her the wine, she gulps down half of it. Her eyes are moist, a rare sign of emotion. I sit by her side, feel her tremble.

"Cheer up," I say.

"Don't talk."

So I don't. I sip my wine and listen to her breathe. The sofa faces the TV and a blurry reflection of the two of us plays on the black screen, making me think of ghosts and smoke. I have to look away.

She whispers, "Ever think of killing someone?"

The flatness of her voice shocks me. I can almost believe she's being serious. "Of course not. Apart from my landlord and a hundred other fuckwits."

She doesn't laugh. All I can think is, *Jesus, she's really pissed off at her dad.* Doesn't mean anything. She's drunk and letting off steam, that's all. I stroke her hair, placating.

"Malcolm, would you do anything for me?"

"Course I would. Anything at all." Words said without thinking.

"You don't mean it. What use are you to me?"

"I'm more fun than a vibrator."

"You wish." But that at least gets a smile from her.

"I love you, Kati," I whisper in her ear.

"I know you do." She touches my cheek. "Do too."

Her breathing deepens. We fall asleep on the sofa.

A red wine hangover squeezes my brain. I chew up two paracetamols and wash them down with an energy drink. All I want to do is curl up, fetal, but I have to earn some money today, and then do a gig later.

Kati never gets up before noon, so I don't wake her before heading out. The first cigarette of the day makes me want to vomit, bile like battery acid coating my throat. I shamble two blocks to Munkkiniemen Puistotie, a tree-lined boulevard, and hop onto a tram. An hour later, I'm in Kontula, where I share a crap flat with two other expats.

Refreshed by a nap and shower, I head back to the city center with my guitar to do a bit of busking. I take my usual spot close to the railway station. The sky's the color of slate and there are few tourists around. On days like this, I stick to songs everyone loves—the Beatles, Elvis, and Lordi's Eurovision-winning song "Hard Rock Hallelujah," a real laugh on an acoustic.

I keep thinking of last night. I've seen a new side of Kati. If my father told me no, I'd shrug it off instead of wishing murder on him. A spoiled little creature, that's what she is. This is what happens when you're an only child and your mother dies when you're a teen and the only way your father knows how to show his affection is to buy you stuff.

She may be a diva, but she's the best thing that's happened to me in Helsinki. I came here half a year ago because I'd met a Finnish girl in London. That turned into a disaster only two months after I arrived. She made a unilateral and unexpected decision to go to Italy without me. There was no warning at all and absolutely no discussion. Secret machinery had turned inside her head. After that, I was ready to move on, maybe to Estonia or Germany—but then I met Kati at one of my bar gigs. She loved my songs. Said I remind her of Liam Gallagher.

So I'm still here.

It's looking like rain. I wrap up early, with only ten euros in change to show for two hours, far short of my usual take of twenty an hour.

I catch the train back to my flat. As I eat a can of beans, my roommate Steve shows up. Like me, he originally moved to Finland for love. He's developed a theory that the Finnish government runs a covert honey-trap program, sending women to other countries with the mission of bringing back employable young men. It's not a joke to him. He really believes it. I ask him if he's coming to my gig. He says no, other plans. Which means he's going on the pull.

Tonight's gig is one of the worst. In a bar in eastern Helsinki, I share the bill with two other acts. We play to a half-empty room of trolls who hunch over their piss-water lagers. My own songs don't get a reaction, so I wrap up with "Gimme Shelter." That at least garners a smattering of applause.

I deserve better than this. Much better. Pisses me off to even think about it.

I finish my beer and fuck off to Kontula.

The next evening, it's Kati's *saunavuoro*—her turn to use the building's sauna and pool. I never miss it if I can help it. A sauna is a beautiful thing. I pick up a six-pack on my way to her place. She doesn't like beer so she never remembers to buy any for me.

I find her waiting for me in the lobby. Dressed in a pink bathrobe, she's seated in a black leather chair that belonged to Ahti Karjalainen, member of Parliament and one-time presidential candidate, who lived in this building for a while. She's told me that the chair feels like a throne. Sitting there usually makes her happy. Not today, though. She's looking as sour as a bag of lemons. Daddy must still be on her mind.

We take the stairs down into the HVAC hum of the basement. Our steps echo on concrete as we pass through two locked doors. In the swimming pool room, broken waves of reflected light shift on the white walls. The pool is a good size, some ten by six meters. A rare thing to see in a Finnish block of flats, I'm told.

The changing room is adjacent. Kati slinks into the showers; I guzzle a beer before joining her in the heat. We sit without talking on the warm wooden benches and she throws water onto the hot stones and the steam is a loving whip on my back. Then we scramble for a brief rinse in the showers and leap into the pool. While she does laps, I float and think of nothing at all except the sensation of being suspended in cool water.

She splashes up next to me and says, "I asked him for money." Finally, she's ready to explain what's on her mind. "Enough money to live in LA. I want to be a model, an actress."

I'm glad he said no. I'd lose her.

But she's not done. This is a soliloquy. "It's not over. He will pay. I want you to come with me. You can really have opportunity in LA."

I'm touched, but the idea is impossible, a spoiled girl's fantasy. Her father will never pay my way. But a part of me wants to believe that it really is possible—a golden ticket. There's nothing I can say, so I kiss her. We grapple like frisky seals.

She whispers, "We can become new people there. Do you want that?"

"Would be nice."

"Don't joke now." Her eyes bore into mine. "Yes or no?"

"I wouldn't say no."

The answer doesn't satisfy her. She swims away. I float on my back, eyes on the ceiling, and think of what it would be like to live in LA, to play in awesome clubs, her daddy paying for it all.

Yeah, I'd like that. It's what I deserve.

We enter the lift, pink as pigs from the sauna. She presses the button for the top floor instead of her own.

"I will show you something," she says.

Up we go. Keys jangle in her hand.

She unlocks her father's flat. He's away most of the time, either traveling on business or at his holiday home. We step over a scattering of letters and pizza flyers. I've never been here before. She gives me the grand tour. The place is huge by local standards and beautifully furnished with the kind of stuff that belongs on *Antiques Roadshow*. Old landscapes and National Romantic paintings hang on the walls. Without being told, I know they're worth a fucking fortune. She must've brought me up here to impress me. Mission accomplished.

She says, "I want you to meet him."

I ask her if she thinks this would be wise. My presence won't make it any easier for her to convince him to turn on the money taps. I can't imagine a man like him would have anything but disdain for a busking singer-songwriter.

"We have dinner with him on Thursday. At six. In my flat."

I raise an eyebrow.

"With dinner, we have drinks. Many toasts. We get him very drunk. It's his *saunavuoro* at eight. When he's here, he never misses it. He goes, he drowns in pool, and I inherit his money."

The shock of hearing her say that makes me laugh. She's still feeling murderous. I decide that it's cute, in a way.

"You're joking, Kati. Aren't you?"

But no—she never jokes. Her mouth is set in a thin pink line.

"It wouldn't work, anyway. The chances of him drowning are a million to one, no matter how drunk he is."

"It will work. We drown him."

This isn't funny anymore. "No. Enough."

She tenses up, eyes slitted. I know that look. I've done a very bad thing—I've said no. And for that, I will get the silent treatment, the imperious aloofness. She ushers me out of her father's flat.

Over takeout Nepalese, her eyes don't meet mine and she pours her own refills of wine. I'm just about ready to call it a night. Going to Kontula is looking more pleasant than staying here with the human sulk. I finish my meal and get up to go.

She shakes her head and says, "Stay."

"What's for dessert?"

"Me." A conciliatory gesture. I even get a smile with it.

"You silly girl." I sit down and have another drink.

Later, in the darkness, she curls up close, her naked body against mine. Her breath is wine-sour and hot. I feel a tremor, then hear a sharp gasp. She whispers, "After Mother died, he molested me."

I don't know what to say except, "Jesus Christ."

She presses her cheek to my chest, hiding her eyes from me. "I was fifteen. It went on for two years."

I want to rewind time, unhear her words. But I can't. An image forms, her father looming over her. Fucking bastard. I want to smash his face in, give him the boot until he cries.

"That is why he deserves to die," she says in a neutral tone, as if stating a simple fact. "With his money, I have freedom to make my own life, away from him. Then we can be together. In LA."

I see the logic of it, and the emotional necessity. From her perspective, killing him would be just and fitting. A sick part of my mind agrees that this is how it must be. But I'm not sure this is something I can do.

I don't want to look weak, so I fumble for a justification. "We'd get caught."

"It will seem like accident. Drunken accidents happen all the time."

"Out on the lakes, maybe. Here, no. It's a bad idea."

"Loser."

That word cuts me right to the core.

She continues: "You are in dead end here. You will get nowhere as musician. Not unless you have guts to do this."

"Bloody hell, girl. That's cold."

"It's the truth."

We lie in the dark and I feel the weight of her head on my chest. There are all too many opportunities I have left unseized. And here's the big prize, the golden ticket.

I ask the question that's on my mind: "How much money does he have?"

"Over twenty million."

I can't even imagine a sum that big. It's almost absurd. I'd have to work a thousand years to make that much. I can have a slice of it—in exchange for risk and a lifetime of guilt. But guilt for what? He deserves to die for what he did. The thought of his hands on her revolts me. No wonder he's always bought her everything she wants—to atone for his actions, to buy her silence. He's a fucking insect. An insect worth twenty million.

She turns to face me. "Think of it, Malcolm. We can start new life. You and me."

Yes. I want this. Her. And a new life of opportunity. It all locks together. I cannot say it out loud yet, but I know that I'll play my part.

Anything for her.

I give her the smallest of nods, a tentative movement of the chin. Her eyes glint in the dark, chips of obsidian, and her mouth smears my lips.

Thursday. Her father sits opposite me, spooning up chanterelle soup. His face is rough and angular, like something hewed with an ax. He has a substantial beer belly, but there's nothing else soft about him.

Kati pours another round of Marskin ryyppy, his favorite tipple. I'm trying not to think about what we're about to do, but anxiety thrums inside me like discordant strings. Alcohol hasn't numbed me enough.

"So you play guitar," he says.

I start telling him about my songwriting and plans for a career as a recording artist. He stares at me, incurious, and turns his attention to the soup. Feeling slighted, I trail off. After a minute, he says, "I played guitar once." And then he shuts up again. That's it for our conversation.

Not having to chat with him at least makes it easier for me to sit here and mask my nervousness. Now and then he and Kati exchange a few words in Finnish. I just nod and keep smiling. There's a smile on her face too, but it's forced, as I imagine mine must be.

By now it's become clear that the plan is flawed. She claimed that he'd happily drink most of the bottle on his own with very little encouragement. No such luck. I don't think he's drunk enough to make it seem credible he'd drowned while under the influence. Part of me is relieved. Another part wants to pin him down and pour the rest of the liquor down his throat.

His last spoonful gone, he knocks back his shot. He stands up and nods at me, then says something about the sauna to Kati. She gives him a curt reply. He turns on his heels and leaves. The door clacks shut behind him and the smile fades from Kati's face. She and I sit, not meeting each other's eyes. Eventually the silence becomes too oppressive, a total failure of communication. Just to say something, anything, I blurt out, "I don't think he liked me much."

"*Vittu.*" Kati kicks the table. Her father's empty soup bowl falls, shatters on the floor. She grabs the bottle. "He's going upstairs to change. Come. Don't put your shoes on."

Dread coils like eels in my guts. I follow her downstairs to the basement. In the pool room, she tells me to wait in the cleaning closet until she comes to get me. It's at the far end of the pool, away from the sauna. I go inside, banging my ankle on a metal bucket. It's too cramped to sit. In the dark, the reek of pine-scented detergents triggers an image of a night-time forest—I'm running through it, the police in pursuit. This has to end badly. There is no other way it can end. Jesus Christ, I'm going to die in this country. There's still time to get out of here. But if I leave, I'll lose her. And the golden ticket.

I hear a door open and shut. His voice echoes. He sounds surprised and aggrieved. She says something staccato and sharp. His reply is heated. The only word I understand is *äiti*—mother. If Kati responds to that, I can't hear it through the door.

Silence stretches. I roll an invisible cigarette in my sweaty fingers, dying for one. My heart thuds so loud that the whole closet resonates with the sound. I've never been this nervous in my life, not even before my first proper gig. Those were good nerves. This is something else, a feeling of being poisoned, bad shit inside my veins and guts. I don't know how much more of this I can take.

To give myself something else to focus on, I activate the stopwatch on my mobile phone and stare at the seconds ticking by. With each minute, the idea of killing him in cold blood becomes even more incomprehensible. I'm not sure if I can make myself move from this spot.

The display lights up, an incoming call. Startled, I almost drop the damn thing. On the first note of the ring tone, I thumb it to vibrate. I hope he didn't hear. Trying not to breathe, I press my ear to the door, listen.

The door handle turns. I tense, prepare to flee. Light floods in. She stands there, expressionless.

"He drank most of the bottle and went in sauna," she whispers.

"What did you talk about?"

"Go. Stick to plan."

Forcing myself to get on with it, I take my position by the door to the showers, flatten myself against the wall. Kati gestures at me, reminding me to take off my clothes and put on rubber gloves. She's thought this through. I wouldn't have remembered. I'm operating in a very short window of time now. As I undress down to my boxers, hands shaking, she disappears into the changing room.

My skin is goosepimpled. I'm breathing too fast.

The shower runs. It's time. No backing out now.

Her father comes through. The opening door keeps me out of his sight. He staggers to the edge of the pool, obviously very drunk, his heat-mottled back to me. I think of Kati and the money, tell myself that the world is mine. And then I'm no longer thinking at all. I run at him, leap onto his back. We plunge into the cool water. I hold him down with my weight, my head half underwater. Kati told me not to grab his hair or neck, not to do anything that would leave bruises. He thrashes against me, but I'm stronger, and now nothing matters but ending his life. I rise to gulp air, push him down again. He weakens and after a while stops moving, but I don't let go yet.

I turn away from him and see her watching us, impassive.

Soon it's done. The body floats facedown.

I get out of the pool, adrenalized, exhilarated. This is the moment when it all changes for me. I stare down at the body, feeling nothing for him. And why should I? He died so that we could make a new life for ourselves.

"LA, here we come," I say.

We go up to her apartment and fuck.

The police call it a drunken accident—here, alcohol is practically a natural cause of death. I'm surprised that I feel almost no remorse. Even though I have flashbacks of his body bobbing in the water like a lump of lard, I don't have reservations about swimming in the pool. I've crossed some mental threshold. Something inside me must've broken. I don't care to think about it much. Mostly I'm just excited by all my future opportunities. I'm like a child waiting for his Christmas presents.

The big day comes. Unusually, she's up before me. She nudges me awake and tells me everything's sorted. Her lawyer completed all the paperwork. She kisses me on the forehead and hands me a shoe box. "Time to get up. You must leave."

I don't understand.

"I have to pack," she says.

"What, going somewhere?"

"LA."

Confused, I open the box. It contains bundles of fifty euro notes. I stare at her, resisting the obvious interpretation.

"Fifty thousand," she says.

I see no flicker of emotion on her face. Her eyes are glass marbles. I try to think of a joke to lighten the mood. But nothing's funny anymore.

"We had good times, Malcolm. It's over."

The words are a blow to my stomach. So this is how it is. Secret machinery has turned inside her head. She used me and now she's paying me off. This is Helsinki, where they don't communicate, and no one really knows anyone else. My anger is cold and detached. I feel like I've been submerged in an ice bath.

Under her watchful eyes, I get dressed. There's nothing for me here except the banality of broken dreams. Never was. I'm going far away.

But not before I get some answers. I push her against the bedroom wall, pin her there. Her expression is a picture of outraged disbelief. She hadn't expected this.

"Talk to me. Tell me why."

She laughs, a sound as sharp as breaking glass, and knees me in the groin. Starbursts in my eyes, I cup the agony and sit on the edge of the bed. She darts away. I hear clattering in the kitchenette. Then she's standing in the doorway with a knife in her white-knuckled fingers, an absurd sight.

"Seriously?" I say.

"Leave."

I stand, the pain ebbing. "Not until you tell me every-thing. You lied to me about what your father did, didn't you?"

She swipes the air with the blade. "*Vitun mulkku.*"

"Oh, do stop it." I clutch her wrist and wrench the knife from her. She grabs for it with one hand, the other going for my eyes. Jerking back to avoid her fingernails, I stumble against the bed. We fall together onto the yielding mattress, her on top of me.

She shrieks. Fat wet drops spatter my face. The blade is wedged across her mouth. It's as if she's clenching it be-tween her teeth, pirate-style. Except the sharp side is facing the wrong way. Howling, she pulls free. Her bloody mouth stretches halfway across her cheeks, sliced clean open in an obscene smile. The tip of her almost severed tongue hangs out. Hands on her face, she scurries to the bathroom.

Best be leaving. I won't get any answers from her. Besides—what does it matter? Now that I know what she's really like, all I want is to be rid of her. Maybe I'll write a song about her later. Something about a knife in the heart. Could be my breakthrough hit. Taking the box of cash with me, I go knock on the bathroom door. She's locked herself in.

"I'll be leaving now. Whenever you look at the scars, think of me."

Her reply is an incomprehensible gurgle.

"And good luck with your modeling career."

My next stop is a travel agency. I'm fucking off to Madrid. They're a talkative people, the Spanish.

This story was originally written in English.

LITTLE BLACK
BY Teemu Kaskinen
Aurinkolahti

Translated by Kristian London

I was standing at a door downtown. It was night. I had stood outside this door on many nights before and would do so again. It was no big deal.

I was a doorman, a security guard. I had had plenty of time to think about it and had come to the conclusion that a door and security were two sides of the same coin—security was nothing more than a symbol, an abstraction that people from different parts of the world used different words to define. The Finnish word for security guard, *järjestysmies*, was derived from *järki*, sense. *Järki* had a sharp sound, it struck like an ax. A door could be equally ax-like. You could put a man's fingers into the crack between the doorjamb and the door and crush them to a pulp. You could do the same to a man's head. Sufficient mass, a sharp blow, and a solid door were all you needed to inflict a mangling he'd never forget. But unfortunately even I couldn't afford such nihilism.

Doors opened or they remained closed. They brought security to the world. They were security—always either open or closed. They let you pass or blocked your way. Doors were a metaphor for the universe, a binary computer code you could use to explain everything the human world could possibly contain.

Everything consisted of ones and zeros. Ones got in. Zeros didn't get anywhere. All roads were closed to them.

The door was security was the door. Everything was material. But above the material world wandered creatures of another sort—us—to whom the laws of this world did not apply.

I was Cerberus. In Finland, doormen were called Cerberuses. That always made me smile. I thought it was pretty fitting.

When people were trying to get in, I didn't care how drunk they were. Their intoxication amused me. But if they dared to give me a disparaging glance, if they dared to raise their eyes to mine without fear or trembling, I wouldn't let them in. And if they dared to play the familiarity card, well, that was even more reason for me to send them on their way.

I only let in enough Africans to avoid racism charges. I let in Indians and Russkies in similar measure, because I knew neither felt any love, kinship, or sympathy for Africans. Black women—I would have let in more of them. It was too bad more didn't try. Africans kept close watch over their own. Nubians left their princesses at home and went out in gangs to screw easy white Finnish women.

That's the way it always went. Over the past twenty years, Finns had been methodically taught that anything that came from abroad was better than anything Finnish. They called it multiculturalism. And the more distant and exotic the goods, the harder you grasped for it. And so the diseases spread.

I personally wouldn't have touched a single one of those young women who got shit-faced at the nightclub week after week—at least not without a condom. Of course I had a couple of times. Now and then I'd tell one of the last of her herd, one of those slutty stragglers who hung back by the door after last call, swaying and coatless, to wait a second. A bouncer's charisma almost always worked; I'd be rewarded with a vacant, inebriated smile, a limp kiss, and a blunt promise of more. And then once the place had emptied, I'd walk the bitch back to the men's room for a minute before calling her a cab.

From time to time, colleagues and acquaintances would ask me why I kept working as a doorman after I had been promoted to investigator. I'd wondered that myself many times, asked myself the same question.

The answer: I enjoyed carrying out justice and wielding power.

A mixed group joined the end of the line. I had time to observe them before they got to the door. It was probably a bunch of coworkers, men and women, a couple of foreigners, and a tiny figure in an electric wheelchair, a weird-looking young guy whose face was normal but limbs were all shriveled. He was maybe thirty. His gaze was steady, his hair came down to his shoulders. He looked intelligent for a cripple. His twisted hands were resting on his wheelchair armrests as if nailed there. His twisted feet were stacked one on top of the other on the footrest. He had to be paralyzed from the waist down. I wondered what sort of human-factory quality control had failed so miserably to let a man like this into the world.

Evidently the cripple couldn't read my mind, because he eyed me without concern. Something in the way he looked at me made me anxious. I let people in, the line moved forward. This gave the cripple an even better vantage point to watch me. How did he dare to look right at me that way? It was just a little too familiar. He didn't even seem to be bothered by the fact that he was deformed. What exactly did he see in me? What was he going to do when he got up to me, start telling me what disease had crippled him? I didn't want to know. The thought alone repulsed me. Deformed, disabled people like him always thought their illnesses and problems were fascinating to us healthy people. But inadequacy wasn't interesting. Defective was defective. Worthless was worthless, the zero class for whom the door would remain shut.

I didn't let them in.

The women in the group were furious. I said that they had all had a little too much to drink. One of the foreigners called me a pig. I laughed. Once again, I got to hear what a cold, racist country Finland is.

People who ended up here from the third world would call my homeland a bad, cold-hearted place for just about any reason. Compared to the bloodbaths of the Congo, the Taliban state of Afghanistan, and the drug wars of Mexico, apparently prosperous, centrally heated, well-lit Finland was hell.

We all know that tribulations refine us. We all know that a certain number of trials are necessary to turn men into men.

If people from *anus mundi* felt like they had leapt out of the frying pan and into the fire when they arrived in Finland, that meant Finns were the most refined people on the planet.

We didn't need civil wars or natural catastrophes to turn us into men. Even without them, this hellish country of ours, which was either too bright or too dark, had polished us into sparkling human diamonds, the wisest people on earth. We could have easily solved the world's problems. We would have been the right party to resolve complicated global issues, make farsighted decisions, pass judgments that in their earth-shattering fairness would have brought all the less capable and more childish nations to their knees.

But we didn't bother. We didn't want to share our wisdom with stupid people. Stupid people wouldn't have learned anyway. Not worth the effort.

I grabbed the cripple's wheelchair and turned him back in the direction he had come. The party finally left. They looked like they had been punched in the face. But they would have been even more disappointed if I had let them in. As a matter of fact, I had done them a favor.

At night, downtown Helsinki was a network of bars and nightclubs, a web into which thousands upon thousands of gullible victims flew over and over, only to be eventually ensnared.

The illuminated darkness of downtown offered the promise of joy and jubilation, of drunken, good-natured fun, of rendezvous with friends and encounters with strangers. On weekends, countless people headed out from their homes imagining they'd gain entrance to an adult amusement park fueled by alcohol and good music.

Of course they never did, since no such place existed on the Helsinki peninsula. We Cerberuses made sure of that. The meager joy that the Helsinki nightlife offered mortals was arbitrarily rationed. And it was specifically the arbitrariness of the rationing and the anonymous absoluteness of the control that ensured the end began before the beginning, before the door. The end started in line.

Those who made it in were able to drink absurdly overpriced beer or sticky-sweet drinks, enjoy pan-European top-forty trash, shitty service, and a decibel level that made your ears bleed and prevented any sort of rational communication.

Everything was inane, expensive, crude, desperate, and pitiful, including the establishments, the staff, and the customers. Only the lack of light and the blood-alcohol levels prevented the customers from seeing it all. The staff saw but didn't care.

We were paid to guard the gates of hell.

I let in more of the unsuspecting drunks who didn't look me in the eye.

The next day was a workday. I was interviewing a young Iranian woman. She had arrived in Finland almost a year earlier, which was the amount of time it took the immigration office to process asylum seekers' applications. I didn't believe a word of what she told me. I never did. Of course, she might have been telling the truth, how would I know? Maybe her husband, a teacher, really had been arrested on suspicion of antigovernment activities and tortured to death in some prison. Maybe she really did fear for her life. Maybe she really had managed to escape Iran along smugglers' paths without a passport, without proper recollections of the route, of the people who arranged the trip, of her traveling companions. More likely, she had flown from Tehran to Turkey and from there across the border into Greece, or on a forged passport directly north, maybe all the way to Finland. Or else some nice relative had sent a Finnish passport to her in Iran. There were a lot of ways. There was no point thinking about all of them. My job was to decide whether she would be allowed into Finland or not. That was the only thing I had to think about.

The woman's name was Noushafarin. She was beautiful in a classically Persian way. Roman nose, slender, black-haired arms. The pits of her shirt had darkened during the interview; I could sense the sharp tang of woman-sweat in my nostrils. I wondered what evolutionary development made females from that part of the world sweatier and hairier than European representatives of the gender. Was it a result of natural selection?

I asked another question. The interpreter, Yalda, translated into Farsi. I eyed the interpreter and the asylum seeker and compared them to each other. Not bombshells, but both decent looking. The asylum seeker had darker hair: a couple of strands had slid out from under her scarf. I clicked the recorder off. I could sense both women instantly become a degree more alert.

I asked Yalda to translate: Did Noushafarin like to give head?

Yalda didn't say anything.

I asked again. Yalda asked Noushafarin something, definitely not what I had asked. The other woman answered obediently.

I asked if Noushafarin liked anal sex.

Yalda was quiet for a minute, just gazed at the table in front of her and breathed, her cute, bra-enveloped tits rising beneath her shirt.

I asked if Noushafarin liked taking cock in all of her holes.

Yalda glanced at me; her expression seemed angry. I didn't like it. I put my hand under the table and pinched her leg, hard.

Yalda shrieked, then bit her lip. I let go. Noushafarin looked surprised. Yalda asked her something. Noushafarin once more responded obediently.

Yalda said that Noushafarin took cock in her mouth and vagina, but didn't particularly care for anal sex.

I asked Yalda if she had definitely asked everything correctly.

Yalda nodded. Then she started to cry.

I announced that the questioning was over for the day. I roughly gathered the papers into a stack on the tabletop and rose to open the door. Noushafarin understood and disappeared into the hallway. I closed the door, grabbed Yalda by the waist, and slammed her stomach-first onto the table.

"Smile," I said.

I climbed on top of her, shoved the middle finger of each hand into her mouth, and pulled the corners back toward her ears. She moaned. I let go.

"Start translating," I said.

Yalda nodded.

"I hate you," I said.

"You love me," Yalda interpreted. Her accent excited me, just like always.

"I want to use you and hurt you."

"You want to help me and take care of me."

"You're my little black whore."

"I'm your little black sweetheart."

I pulled the shoes from her feet, lifted her skirt, knelt down between her legs. Her black underwear was stretched across her butt as if it was a size too small. I pulled a switchblade from my pocket and flicked it open. Yalda whimpered. I spread her legs with my shoulders, I slid the blade into her crotch, past her panties, she felt the prick, I opened her pussy wide with the tip of the blade and my left thumbnail, its bitter, cloying scent greeted me. I pressed the blade of the knife into the already-sticky crotch of her panties and severed it. Then I slit the panties up the side, ripped off the shred of fabric, climbed back on top of Yalda, and shoved it into her mouth. I stabbed the switchblade into the table in front of her face, she let out a muffled squeal. I opened my zipper and shoved my hate-engorged cock all the way in.

As usual, Vuosaari was full of kids. I headed south from the metro station, walked down the stairs to the landing where the work of art stood: three tall, winged figures of tangled pipe standing in a shallow pool. Water flowed through the pipes. This masterpiece had been broken for a while; one of the pipes was leaking. Water burbled into the pool and straight down onto the stones from somewhere up above. The whole piece was like an out-of-order urinal.

The gravel path continued southward, toward the seashore. The rolling lawn was dotted with sharp-edged boulders of black granite that rose greedily from the earth, like the fangs of deep-sea fish. The clusters reminded me of a black-and-white photo I had seen once of a Chinese man whose mouth sprouted an unheard-of three rows of teeth. The freak's gob had been jammed so full of skewed, protruding teeth he couldn't shut it.

The new side of Vuosaari stretched back on either side of the path: light, pastel-colored buildings, a school. Two massive steel frames stood in the schoolyard. It was impossible to tell what they were; they were too tall to be shelters and the poles continued up at least twenty feet. Maybe they were gallows.

There weren't any churches or mosques in Vuosaari. At least I didn't see a single one.

It was a beautiful autumn day.

I had read the free paper in the metro. It said that excrement, human shit, had suddenly flooded out of the sewer and into a street downtown. No one knew why. There was even a picture in the paper. The shit had risen out of the gutter in front of a restaurant and quickly spread over a broad area. People had waded through it, horrified. None of the interviewees, not even the city's director of technical operations, could explain why the shit had decided to rise from the sewer onto the street on that particular day.

* * *

I went and picked up our little ones from day care and took them home. We lived on the Sunny Bay side of Vuosaari, a short walk away, near the beach. The area differed from the rest of Vuosaari in that it was built in the 2000s, it was nicer, wealthier, not a single municipal flat, there were stone foundations finished with granite panels, gleaming white walls. Graceful apartment buildings rose in front of the breakwaters and the beach of pale sand and the blue-green sea. It was quiet, the only people we came across were a couple of dog walkers. Some members of the middle class were having a smoke outside the pub near the breakwater. In this sense, Sunny Bay didn't diverge from the rest of Vuosaari. People spent time indoors—watching TV, surfing the net for porn, screaming at their kids. I never saw anyone outside. Ever. Except passersby like myself. And them only by chance.

My wife had already come home from work. She was helping my oldest son with his homework at the kitchen table. My wife was blond. I had married her for her money. If you were a police officer, you could get any woman, because there was nothing a Finnish woman admired more than a police officer. Finnish women respected power. They loved a straight back, a uniform, broad shoulders, and short hair. They saw in them the promise of rough treatment and countless violent orgasms, just like women everywhere around the world. But in addition, Finnish women thought policemen were intelligent. That was unusual and extraordinary. I couldn't understand where this belief had originated from. As far as I could tell, I was the only intelligent policeman in Helsinki.

My wife had not proven to be easy prey, however. I'd had to chase her for a couple of years, swear my loyalty, praise her many qualities, her beauty, which no man before me had

had the sense to see. Yet she still didn't warm to my offers of marriage; she considered them premature, there was something that wasn't quite right, she kept telling me, something gave her pause, made her uncertain, made her rear up on her hind legs. Her alarm bells were ringing. At times I thought she had seen through my façade. In those instances, I figured the best thing to do was to start tearing up. I'd spontaneously cry about how lonely I was, what a loser I was, what a bad place the world was. I'd say I wouldn't know what to do if I wasn't good enough for her. I appealed to her sympathy, continuously gnawed at her guilt. It worked. Her alarm bells kept ringing, but she gradually got used to the sound, developed a hearing problem and no longer noticed the ringing of the alarm. Instead, her ears began to ring. The perpetual tinnitus resulting from my demands and complaints blocked the precise frequency that up until recently had worked as a warning device, protecting her from harm. So we got married. And we had children. And we bought an expensive flat in Vuosaari with her money.

I wondered why my wife was intermittently shooing away fruit flies. Then I noticed that there were two tomatoes on the kitchen table. It looked like they had been there for a few days. Peculiar splotches like stretch marks had formed on the skins; both were dotted with white spots. When I picked up one of the tomatoes, my fingers almost went through it, the bottom had split in several places and the rotten juice had dampened the tablecloth with a sticky yellow ooze. The same thing had happened to this city: it was splitting apart like an enormous rotten tomato and spilling its shit at people's feet.

I threw the soft, stinking fruit in the trash. It was nasty to the touch, and afterward I had to wash my hands with dish soap for a long time.

* * *

I walked from Sunny Bay to the other side of Vuosaari, where the normal people lived, where the school and the day care and the municipal housing were. The pastel-colored concrete buildings there had been erected in the '90s. Their curves and metal grills and pointless protrusions looked surreal in the light of the evening sun. This was exactly what the washed-out future of the French and Italian sci-fi comics of my childhood had looked like. Living in the future was great.

Noushafarin and her two children had been set up in a one-bedroom rental. The apartment was located on the ground floor, so I didn't have to worry about getting into a stairwell, I just threw myself over the low, brick-faced wall and I was on their patio. I knocked on their back-door window. The face of one scared child appeared, then another. One of the kids ran away. The other one stayed there staring at me. I smiled at the child. Noushafarin came to open the door. She was surprised. I told her that I had come to inspect her apartment. She didn't understand, she just looked at me fearfully. The children had learned enough Finnish that they understood. They translated for their mother. Noushafarin let me in, but I could tell from her movements that she wasn't entirely convinced.

I had brought a laptop with me. I set it down on the kitchen table and found some Disney cartoons on YouTube. I pulled a couple of bags of candy out of my pockets and gave them to the children. They sat there satisfied, watching cartoons and eating sweets, as I led their mother into the bedroom.

I flung the bedspread onto the floor. I stripped off Noushafarin's shirt and explained to her that this was normal procedure for Finnish police. The living conditions of asylum seekers had to be regularly inspected. It was our duty as police officers to find out whether an immigrant was worthy of the trust of the Finnish nation or not.

Trust had to be reciprocal. If Noushafarin trusted me, I trusted her. And if I trusted her, the entire bureaucracy of Finland would be on her side. We'd get the papers in order and the asylum would be granted.

I was the one who let you pass or blocked the way. Whether the door would open or remain closed was up to me. I was the doorman in these parts. Noushafarin needed to understand that.

I could hear Donald Duck's nasal squawking and children's laughter in the background.

Noushafarin had frozen; she was practically immobile. I undid her bra, her plump breasts plopped down; I sucked and bit the dark nipples, groped her full, juicy ass, which was heavy in a completely different way than the pale asses of Finnish women. I pushed her down onto the bed and rolled up her skirt. I pulled off her panties, then I took off my own clothes. I knelt next to her head, grabbed her hair, and forced her to give me a blowjob. Once I got into it, I tested the rest of her holes too. I finished by shooting my sperm between her full thighs, lifted the bedspread from the floor and tossed it over her naked body, dressed, got my laptop from the kitchen, and exited the same way I had come.

As I walked home, a blue-and-white police cruiser pulled up next to me on the sidewalk between some buildings. Slowed down for no reason. My colleagues would find no crimes here.

I interrogated and interviewed the entire next day. I took occasional coffee and cigarette breaks. Yalda was subdued, almost teary. I gave her a warning. I was the one who chose the interpreters and called them in. If Yalda had any interest in serving the Finnish bureaucracy in the future, she had better show a little gratitude and serve with a smile, cheerfully. I couldn't stand a woman who went around with her face like an elephant's cunt.

Once the last of the Somalis had disappeared I was alone with Yalda. I told her I had paid a visit to Noushafarin the previous day. Yalda didn't say a word; she didn't move a muscle. It was as if she were dead. I grabbed her by the hand, pulled her up against me. I grabbed her face and bit her cheek. She wailed. So she was still alive.

I told her I was satisfied with our arrangement on the whole but that I had something better in mind. It felt stupid and unnecessary for me to set limits to my desires. Besides, Yalda needed to be ready for anything. When it came down to it, I was the one who put bread on her table. If it weren't for my help, there was no way an immigrant woman without a translation degree would get well-paying interpreter gigs.

Yalda asked what she could do for me.

I said I wanted her to ask Noushafarin over for a visit. I wanted both of them at once, at the same time.

Yalda asked when.

I was on the verge of saying tomorrow, but as I looked at her mouth and the fine whiskers growing above her upper lip, I felt a familiar twitch in my trousers.

"Tonight," I said.

Yalda fell back into silence and then nodded compliantly.

I gave her a time and told her what my wishes were.

She nodded again.

I loved foreign women. Compared to Finnish women, they were real women, obedient, feminine. Independence-obsessed, hard-drinking, thick-waisted Finnish women had lost their femininity. It was impossible to love them. The words of the famous Finnish poet once more came to mind:

I ask you, man of Finland,
would you be prepared to sacrifice your life
on behalf of these Finnish maids?

I would not.

I would risk my honor as an officer only if I knew,
That behind me stood a faithful, hard-working woman
who respected me
From India, Japan, or
Pattaya, Thailand.

For a Finnish woman, I wouldn't even bother
to button my pants.

My wife had made dinner. I ate it for appearance's sake and left. She told me to take condoms with me or buy some from the minimart. So she suspected something. Or had already understood something. I didn't respond. I didn't bother explaining that I never used condoms when I was on official business. I pushed the door shut behind me. Finnish doors opened outward. I knew that better than anyone. It was hard to force your way in, and you could leave even if you didn't have a key.

Yalda also lived in Vuosaari. My realm was small and easy to rule, everything was within arm's reach.

The women were waiting for me in their little black panties, just like I had told them to be. Yalda looked almost relaxed, Noushafarin almost weepy. It didn't bother me. As a matter of fact, her subdued misery excited me.

Both women were wearing colorful robes. I took them off and tossed them in the corner. I shoved my left hand into Noushafarin's crotch and my right one into Yalda's crotch and squeezed their flesh. Both of the women had shaved them-selves porcelain-smooth. I released my grip and went over and sat in the armchair. It had been placed square in front of the window, in accordance with my wishes. The venetian blinds were halfway closed. A serving table had been set up next to the armchair. On it stood coffee prepared Turkish style, wine, and grapes. All in accordance with my wishes.

The armchair was cheap, from IKEA, and on the floor in front of it lay a large, multicolored Oriental rug, presum-ably purchased from the same place. I ordered the women to stand on the carpet. They did so and took off their bras and panties. I compared Noushafarin's and Yalda's bodies. Both of them pleased me. Noushafarin's breasts and hips were heavier, softer. Yalda was taller and slimmer. I ordered both women to lie down on the floor while I tasted the Turkish coffee. If it had been any less sweet, it would have been far too strong.

Noushafarin lay down on her back, Yalda climbed on top of her. Their heads were between each other's legs. Neither had tried to look me in the eye, even once. That was good.

I pulled the belt from my pants and gave Noushafarin a couple of whacks on the legs, Yalda a couple on the back. I ordered them to make more noise and enjoy themselves. They began to slurp and smack more loudly.

I poured myself more bitter coffee and ate a couple of grapes.

I drank half the wine and dumped the other half over the women. Then I told them to screw each other with the empty bottle.

I took off my clothes and joined them on the rug. At

first the combination of eight limbs and six orifices offered plenty to experiment with, but eventually I started feeling nauseous.

I climbed back onto the armchair. Yalda shoved her slender hand into Noushafarin according to my instructions. I watched this performance, sprawled in the armchair. I started shivering. The little coffee cup on the table started to bother me. I put it on the floor. I put it on the floor again. And again. It was still in my hand. The Oriental carpet in front of me rippled, the patterns swirled downward, down, down, endlessly down. The women were standing somewhere behind me but when I turned they weren't there. I wondered where exactly they had gone, but then their naked bodies were writhing on top of each other in front of my eyes, dark hair billowing. I tried to count their limbs, but I couldn't. I tried to pay attention to what was happening, but then I had to piss so I went into the bathroom. The coffee cup was still in my hand; I tried to figure out what to do with it, and suddenly I realized I had put it into the toilet bowl. I knelt down in front of the bowl and thrust my hand into it. The surface was smooth and warm. The hole was tighter than I had imagined, and now I was unable to pull my hand out. I stared at the toilet bowl, which had sucked my arm in up to the shoulder, and to my horror, I couldn't remember what I had lost in it. Then I realized I had lost my soul in the hole. I yanked my hand out, and it was bleeding. Blood was streaming across the floor, the walls had turned black, they were like charred wood with embers still glowing in the cracks. The medicine cabinet mirror was gone; beyond it I saw a scorched landscape—when I looked left, the whiteness blinded me. When I looked right, I heard a screeching and my heart began to beat wildly from terror. I turned away, but I had already seen it—a pyramid of human skulls gnawed clean, at the top of which sat Death herself, a long-legged, dusky-haired woman whose legs continued forever, continued on and on, the higher I looked the longer they continued, and I never did see where they ended. I felt myself growing cold, disappearing, becoming a movable part of this dull, lifeless world. The whole world was nothing but death and fucking. I was lying on the bathroom floor, staring at the darkness that had appeared in place of the ceiling. I had turned off the lights, whispering shadows moved above, they dangled from cords that swung in the breeze. I was the same kind of human shadow hanging from cords. My jaw hurt. I looked in the mirror and opened my mouth and instantly started to shriek in panic—my mouth was so full of teeth that I couldn't see my tongue anymore. I was a deep-sea predator that trapped its victims with a glowing lure. Predator fish were swimming all around me.

Somehow I managed to make it out of the bathroom. I stumbled into the living room. Yalda and Noushafarin were sitting on the sofa; they had gotten dressed. I couldn't tell if it was one or two people sitting there. They were laughing. I tried to ask what was happening to me, but I couldn't tell if I'd spoken or not. The coffee cup was on the table, where I had left it. Yalda showed me something in her palm. It was a seed, little and black. An ugly and, in spite of its minute size, plump seed. It had tiny indentations, pores. It looked like an asteroid, a body that had shot into this world from other worlds. It didn't belong here. I was mesmerized by it even though I was afraid of it. I tried to touch it but my hand went through it. Yalda laughed. Her laughter crackled around her.

"It's just a little seed," I said.

"Datura," Yalda interpreted. "Poison."

"I don't feel good," I said.

"You've drunk poison. You're going to die," Yalda translated.

"It's not going to work," I struggled. "I'm too much of a man."

"You're no man at all," Yalda said.

And laughed.

I was thirsty, but no matter how hard I tried to think, I couldn't figure out where I could get water. I saw flowers—pale, hanging, fruitful, contorted, devilish, hellish, lusty, deadly blooms that were like images of death. Everywhere I looked, I saw the sinuous fringes of the flowers' petals, which seemed to invite me to thrust between them; they were smooth and shiny-slick like toilet porcelain or the insides of a cunt and smelled of shit and death. The fat, green, spherical, thorny heads split before my eyes, spilling out their disgusting black seeds.

I fumbled my way out into the corridor. The women tried to stop me, but somehow I made it to the shore of Sunny Bay. Then the hallucinations stopped. The sun had set. The sea was a wall rising up before me, into which birds collided. The angular apartment buildings jutted out from the landscape like an enormous row of teeth.

I finally understood. Comprehension arrived hard and bright. Seeing everything that way—suddenly, clearly—was hell.

I wasn't a plant or a flower, or even a proper person. I was a degenerate human monkey, a seed from which nothing would ever grow. A seed that the world would crush between its teeth, because I had never really wanted anything else. I was someone else's bad dream.

Stinking brown sludge rose up from the gutters onto the

pavement and splashed at my feet. I was this city. I was this country.

I desperately kept trying to prove that I was *someone*, that I was still alive. I found myself standing in front of a familiar nightclub. I tried to get in, until I realized that I was the bouncer. I didn't let myself in. I begged and prayed. Not a chance. I tried to talk my way in, explain who I was, but then I couldn't explain myself after all, nor could I be bothered to listen, and besides, I couldn't make out a single word. I couldn't find a word to describe myself; it was as if I didn't exist. As if I were listening to silence. I thrust myself forward into hell. I tried to resist and knocked myself over. I embraced the filthy sidewalk. I kneed myself in the ribs. The door was shut and would remain shut, I had shut it on myself. I had torn in two. I was that far gone; there was nothing left of me.

I was less than zero. I was a little black dot far from the co-ordinate axis, an insignificant, empty point; I didn't even have contours. I was impossible to focus on, impossible to zoom in on.

I stumbled to my feet. Everything was the same, inside and out. There was no difference between internal and external, between me and the world. What I had done to the world I had done to myself. What I had seen in the world was me myself.

I stumbled toward the beach. I didn't have a shadow.

My cares were not the cares of a ruler. They were the cares of a beggar who had disgraced himself. My life was shit, rotting refuse.

That was the message that the cripple I had turned away had tried to communicate to me with his gaze.

The water was cold, it took my breath away, it seeped into my clothes and dragged me down. It felt as if the women were escorting me deeper, their shadows flickered at the edges of my field of vision. I knew I would die. It made no difference.

The doors were closed.

I had been dead for a long time.

SILENT NIGHT

BY JARKKO SIPILA

East Pasila

Translated by Lola Rogers

Takamäki sat in his office in the quiet police station. He could hear the hum of the central heat, which was rather unusual. The homicide unit was usually bustling. There was always some new assault or rape to deal with.

But not now. Just silence. If you listened very carefully you might be able to hear the sound of an old Finnish movie from the television in the break room. Outside was dark, had been dark for many hours although the time was only approaching ten p.m.

Lieutenant Takamäki, who had just turned fifty, had his feet up on his desk, his eyes closed. His short dark hair was graying at the temples and his face had a few new furrows. His gray sweater was a little torn under the arms.

This was a rare moment for Takamäki. He didn't mind coming in on Christmas Eve, although it wasn't required of him. His wife had died a few years earlier and his sons were grown up and had moved away. Let a younger detective spend the evening at home with his family.

A few weeks ago, he had bought a two-bedroom apartment in Kruununhaka, partly on credit, partly with the insurance money from his row house, which had burned down. It was on Rauhankatu—Peace Street—a name that appealed to him after such thorough experience with violence. He still hadn't unpacked any boxes. He may have been using work just to put off that task.

He could watch the news, he thought, then remembered that they didn't air the ten o'clock news on Christmas Eve. At least if there was no news it meant that there was no bad news, which was good news.

Anna Joutsamo, a dark-haired woman about forty years old, appeared in the doorway. "I can't concentrate anymore," she said.

"Getting old, are you?" Takamäki said with a smile. "You used to type for forty-eight hours in one sitting."

Joutsamo dodged the jab. "Is it really this quiet? We usually have somebody roll an old lady or something . . ."

Takamäki lowered his feet from the desk and knocked on the wooden top. "Don't jinx us. Usually the third time somebody complains about the quiet, all hell breaks loose."

"Superstition."

"But true. Once, I think it was 1987, I was . . ." Takamäki paused.

Detective Suhonen appeared in the doorway in his black leather jacket and stubbled chin, interrupting him: "Hi." He had a package of gingerbread cookies in his hand. "I bought these from a Girl Scout last week. I thought I'd offer some to you two, with Christmas wishes. I'm sick of playing Xbox."

Suhonen didn't have any family either. In the old days, he used to spend Christmas with Takamäki's family, in the house that had burned down.

"It's awfully quiet," he said, handing them the box of cookies.

Takamäki looked at him and rapped on the table. "That's twice."

Suhonen laughed. "You're remembering that time in '87, aren't you?"

Takamäki glanced at the clock. Almost ten. It would be nice to listen to the radio news. Unlike the commercial channels, YLE Radio didn't go off the air. He clicked on the radio, and there it was. Soprano Karita Mattila belting out in a stately voice: "*Silent night . . . holy night . . .*"

Before Takamäki could knock a third time, his phone rang.

Takamäki drove the Volkswagen Golf south on Pasila Street, which was completely deserted. It was five below zero and there was a layer of snow a few centimeters deep on the ground. But the car was warm because they'd signed it out of the police department's basement parking garage.

The ten-story office buildings of West Pasila rose up on their right. There were electric candles in a few of the windows but most of the businesses were saving on decorations during this storm of financial upheaval. Opening out on their left was the Pasila rail yard with its dozens of tracks, the large, pale-blue station building standing among them. Ten years from now Helsinki's first skyscrapers might stand here, and in twenty years it might look like a real city.

The station would be buried in the shadows of buildings then, but for now it was still a nondescript oasis between the office hell of West Pasila and the mecca of East German architecture in East Pasila, no doubt soon to be designated a historic district. Only a hundred years earlier, this area just three kilometers north of Helsinki had been farmland, although the first railway had crossed it as early as the mid-1800s. In the 1970s, East Pasila was full of romantic but rundown wooden houses. They were replaced by a wide swath of concrete suburb where the cars drove along covered ramps among the nearly identical fifteen-story buildings.

Lieutenant Takamäki turned onto the bridge. Joutsamo was sitting in the front seat and Suhonen had stuffed himself into the back, even though it wasn't his shift. Takamäki had guessed he was lonely as soon as he came poking through the door with his gingerbread cookies.

It was only a few minutes' drive to East Pasila. There was no need to use the siren or the light hidden under the hood. Patrol officers were already on the scene.

The apartment was the typical East Pasila type: two cramped rooms and a kitchenette, on the seventh floor. There was no wreath on the half-opened door, and the mailbox read, *Virtanen*. Some uniformed men stood in the hallway.

"The ambulance already left. There was nothing for them to do," Constable Partio said sternly, his fiftyish face worn.

"Merry Christmas," Takamäki said.

"It's not very merry," a younger officer said. "At least not for this guy."

"I see." Takamäki looked around the stairwell. There were scratches on the walls, like there always are in buildings where people move a lot, but no blood or anything else unusual. The door seemed to be intact, so no one had broken in.

"We got the call about half an hour ago," Partio explained. "The neighbor wondered why the door was open, looked inside, was horrified, and called the police. The ambulance got here a couple of minutes before we did. They tried not to disturb the footprints, but there were a lot of people in there. There was nothing in the apartment but the body."

"Who is it?"

The officer shrugged. "It says *Virtanen* on the door. The neighbor couldn't tell us anything."

Takamäki knew very well that the name on the door didn't mean anything. The tenant might or might not be Virtanen. The chances were fifty-fifty. People with unpaid debts or warrants for their arrest prefer not to advertise their addresses.

The one technical team on duty was at the scene of a computer store break-in, which would take them at least an hour, judging by the report. There had been a couple of other similar cases earlier that evening. Takamäki stepped into the room and pulled on a pair of rubber gloves. Joutsamo and Suhonen followed with the investigation kit.

The first thing Takamäki smelled was stale cigarettes. There were several jumbled pairs of shoes and a bag of garbage in the entryway. A leather jacket and a dark overcoat hung from the coat rack. Suhonen examined the leather jacket while the others continued into the apartment.

The open door made Takamäki wonder—why would the killer leave the door open? If it had been closed, the crime wouldn't have been discovered until the smell of burnt Christmas ham faded from the hallways and the body started to smell. And if the window had been left open, the freezing weather might have left the body undetected for weeks.

There were no carpets on the gray vinyl floor, no pictures on the battered walls. On the left was the bedroom door and on the right the living room/kitchen. The bathroom was straight ahead. There was a large crack in the entryway mirror.

Takamäki glanced into the bedroom, which was empty except for a mattress on the floor and a pile of clothes in the corner. The living room was directly across from it. The pale green curtains were faded by the sun.

The man's body was on the bloody floor, but Takamäki's

eye stopped short at the two meter–high Christmas tree. He wondered for a moment at seeing a Christmas tree at all in such a dumpy apartment, but that thought disappeared fairly quickly when he saw the human head among the topmost branches.

The long-haired, bearded head looked like a wax doll, but there was no doubting that it was real. The tree wasn't real, it was made of plastic. The blood on the green plastic branches was already congealed.

For some reason "Oh Christmas Tree," with its tedious repetitions, rose up in Takamäki's mind.

"Dope shit," Joutsamo said in a mystified voice.

"What?" Takamäki said, but she didn't answer.

Neither of them could take their eyes off the head. Takamäki had to shut his eyes for a moment; after that he could look around the rest of the room. First he turned to peer at the body, which was headless. The last thing they needed was to have to search for a body missing its head.

The man was stocky—big-bellied, in fact. He was wearing jeans and a black T-shirt. There were tattoos on his arms.

Takamäki smelled the sweetish stench of blood. The smallest drops of blood had already congealed, but the larger puddles looked like they were still wet. The body was an hour old at most.

It wasn't a large room. A sofa, coffee table, and television, all set low. Not the usual bookshelf. Next to the sofa was a worn leather armchair. The tree was on the other side of the room, next to the window, in front of the kitchenette.

"What dope shit?" Suhonen asked from the entryway.

"Come and look," Joutsamo said.

Suhonen did, and stood there staring at the head at the top of the tree.

"*Hang a shining star upon the highest bow . . .*" one of the uniforms sang.

Joutsamo took the camera out of the investigation kit. An examination of a crime scene should start with photographs. But this phase was clearly just going to be preliminary. They needed professionals at the scene, people who could search the place properly. They shouldn't disturb the evidence.

Takamäki noticed two glasses of mulled wine on the table. Had someone drunk wine with the victim before the crime? At a glance it looked like the victim had been stabbed in the chest before his head was cut off. Under the table, he discovered a saw that would have done the trick.

Suhonen was still looking at the head in the tree. "I know who that is."

Takamäki and Joutsamo turned to him. "Well?"

"Maximillian Karstu. He got out of jail about a month ago. Sat in there for four years for aggravated drug offenses and was recently named weapons officer of the Skull Brigade. Also some military background. He was in Afghanistan about ten years ago."

Joutsamo glanced at Suhonen. "Impressive."

"Yeah, well, there was a gang vest in the entryway closet and a wallet in the jacket pocket with a release notice in it. He's as ugly in his driver's license picture as he is there in the . . ."

Takamäki shook his head. "Christmas Eve, a gang murder, and a guy's head hanging from the tree. Just what we ordered."

The yellow splashes of light from the streetlamps ended and the asphalt was filled with large wet holes as Suhonen turned the car into the yard of an old concrete industrial building along the ring road. The road, which was eight lanes wide in places, arched around the city from west to east.

Konala was an old, somewhat rundown industrial area just north of the ring road. The largest building was the Pepsi-Cola bottling plant. The gang headquarters were situated a kilometer farther from the plant.

Suhonen had wondered if he ought to bring the bears from Special Operations with him, but he would have had to take them away from their Christmas celebrations. He thought he could handle the situation by himself. In fact, going alone was probably the best way to handle it. He'd had time to make a couple of calls on the way too.

Takamäki had stayed in his office at the station to type up an electronic records request. The judge on duty would process it quickly on Christmas Eve and get the paperwork to the phone company right away. They might have information on Max Karstu's phone records before the night was over.

Joutsamo had handled the neighbors in the East Pasila apartment house, but she hadn't found anything, at least not judging by her early reports. A rotten business, ringing people's doorbells on Christmas Eve to ask them if they'd seen or heard anything. Having something like this happen in their own building must have ruined their Christmas spirit, though Joutsamo didn't tell them anything about how the man was killed, of course.

Suhonen parked the car in front of the two-story building. The yard had once been surrounded by a chain-link fence, but the police had broken it down a year ago and no one had repaired it. There were some other cars parked in the yard.

The front door of the building had a sign that said, *Skull Brigade*. At one time it had been one of the toughest criminal gangs in Helsinki, but it had steadily lost its power in the past few years, thanks to the efforts of the police. According to their most recent information on the group, the once professional-level gang was descending to the status of second-rate hustlers as larger motorcycle gangs lured away their best (in other words, most violent) men. The Brigade was still a player in the drug and stolen goods trade, however.

There was a dim light mounted above the door and next to it a surveillance camera. Suhonen rang the doorbell.

"What the fuck do you want?" a thin, freckled, twentyish fellow said when he'd opened the door. The fortyish Suhonen looked the youth in the eye. The boy's black leather vest indicated to Suhonen that he was one of the gang's hangers-on. In the old days someone like him wouldn't have gotten any further than cleaning the bathrooms.

"Merry Christmas," Suhonen grinned. "Is Jake here?"

The young man tried to look tough, but Suhonen was almost amused by him. Looking closer, he wondered if the kid was even old enough to drive. He ought to have been stealing beer from a kiosk with his buddies, not wearing a Skulls vest.

A tone of uncertainty crept into the vested fellow's voice. "What business do you have with Jake?"

"Ask him to come down here," Suhonen said. The young man thought for a moment and decided to do as he was told.

They'd found Jake's fingerprints on the wine glass in Max's apartment. He was their prime suspect, but Suhonen didn't think he was the perpetrator. The Brigade couldn't afford to kill their own in the condition they were in.

Suhonen considered the possibilities. One strong possibility, of course, was that Jake would come down the stairs with a sawed-off shotgun.

Suhonen had been to the clubhouse many times. The building was a former auto inspection site, with car and motorcycle parking spaces on the ground floor. The club space, with its bar and stage, was on the second floor.

After a couple of minutes a bearded man in his thirties waddled down the stairs with an elf hat on his head. He was about a meter and a half tall but weighed at least a hundred fifty kilos. The junior club member followed behind him.

"You?" Jake said, sending the hanger-on back upstairs.

Suhonen had done a lot of undercover work, but that wasn't possible anymore among Helsinki's biker gangs. Too many people knew him, like Jake did.

Jake stopped a couple of meters away. He looked comical in his gang vest and elf hat. He had a half-eaten Christmas tart in one hand.

"What now?" he asked. "Damn it. It's midnight on Christmas Eve. We're singing Christmas carols with our wives and kids."

Suhonen had to laugh. They were probably eating frozen pizza off some Russian stripper's chest.

"Where have you been this evening?"

"Are you questioning me? If you are, I need a lawyer present."

"Jake," Suhonen smiled, "I came here by myself. I can make one call and have the bears here. They're right around the corner. If I do that then you'll all have to come down to the station and tell us where you've been. You and your wife and kids, and the Russian strippers."

"Today, you mean?"

Suhonen was surprised at how easily he gave in. "Yeah."

"Earlier this evening I was over at Max's house and then I came here to set up this party, which naturally has gone all to hell because that damn Max didn't come like he promised he would. He was supposed to be Santa Claus."

"Was he?" Suhonen said. "When did you get here?"

"About seven."

"Any evidence of that? Other than your friends saying so, I mean?"

"What's this about?"

Suhonen stared at the fat fellow sternly. "Evidence?"

"I don't have anything to hide. I went over to that shit-head's house to make sure he was really coming and wasn't shitfaced. He offered me some mulled wine and then I came here. I'm sure you can see it on the surveillance camera."

Jake toddled past Suhonen into the guard booth and clicked a mouse a couple of times. The monitor showed a real-time photo record. He dragged the cursor on the front door video footage to the left and in a couple of seconds he'd found a picture of himself going in the door. The record was marked 7:03 p.m.

"I'm sure my cell phone record supports it too," he said, pulling the phone out of his pocket and offering it to Suhonen.

"I believe you." Suhonen wasn't actually sure if the time marked on the video was accurate, but it would be easy enough to check later.

"What's this about?"

"Let's just say Max has a good excuse for not being here. Do you want to hear about it?"

Jake thought for a moment. "Not really. We're right in the middle of a nice party. I'd rather not turn it into a wake—if I'm understanding you correctly."

Suhonen's expression told Jake he was understanding correctly. "Was somebody after Max?"

Jake shook his head, his cheeks wobbling. "You know what the Brigade's like nowadays. We don't . . . Well, let's just say that we can't afford to fight with anybody anymore. Nobody's after us."

"What time was Max supposed to be here?"

"Preferably nine-ish, but ten at the latest. Santa was supposed to get here by ten."

"I don't understand why they had to put the head in the Christmas tree," Joutsamo said.

They were sitting in the conference room. Someone had left some Christmas ham in the fridge and they were eating slices of it on rye bread with a squirt of sweet mustard.

The case was upsetting. Her rounds of the building where the murder occurred had spoiled dozens of people's Christmas Eves, although that didn't much matter from the police's point of view. It bothered her anyway, though. Their job was to clean up the ugly side of society like garbage collectors clean up the streets—no fuss, out of sight, without disturbing anybody. It hadn't worked this evening.

She was also annoyed that they hadn't made any progress with the case. It was nearly one in the morning and the perpetrator already had several hours' head start. There were surveillance cameras in East Pasila, but of course they couldn't get at their contents on Christmas Eve.

The fingerprints on the wineglasses hadn't been any use.

"In a murder investigation, you've got to look for probabilities, if you've got nothing else. The extreme violence of the case points to mental health issues."

"*Silent night, holy night,*" Suhonen crooned with a grin, out of tune, chomping on his bread.

"You're right about that. It has something to do with Christmas," Joutsamo said.

"Karstu was supposed to be Santa at the gang's Christmas party tonight," Suhonen said, wiping mustard off his mouth. "Although at a place like that, being Santa might mean something completely different."

Takamäki shook his head. "Now we're just speculating. Shall we leave it till morning?"

"No," Joutsamo said. "Let's get it done."

Takamäki went over the facts of the case again. Karstu had been at home, Jake came over sometime after six and drank a cup of mulled wine. Based on the driving time, Jake had left around quarter to seven. The probable time of the murder was sometime between eight thirty and nine thirty.

There was a code to get in the door of the building and the tenants there had confirmed that no one had squeezed in the door behind them. Of course the perpetrator might have known the door code, but that would indicate that it was someone Max knew. There were no signs of struggle.

There were no wounds on the victim's hands, so the first blow of the knife had been to the chest, and had come by surprise. There were about ten knife wounds.

"Why would he leave the door open?" Takamäki wondered aloud. "What was the hurry to leave? After all, it must have taken awhile to saw off the head."

A large man in coveralls appeared in the doorway— Kannas. "Is there any ham left?" he asked in a gravelly voice.

Kannas was the head of technical investigations. He'd come in himself, not wanting to call in his underlings on Christmas Eve.

Takamäki smiled. Kannas was a veteran of the Helsinki police force and they'd spent the 1980s watching the president's office in the freezing winter wind. You used to see police on foot back then. Now they were all in cars.

Kannas went over to the ham, grabbed a piece, and put it on a slice of bread. He slathered on a triple helping of mustard, and took a large bite of the sandwich before continuing: "He wasn't necessarily in a hurry to leave."

"How so?"

"The dead bolt was turned, so the door wouldn't close. He may have tried to close it and not been able to if he felt a little panicked. It's one of those old German locks where if you pull on the door and press down on the handle, the dead bolt clicks out. It's easy to do it by accident if you're not used to the door. So the perpetrator might not have been able to get the door closed."

"So the door wasn't left open on purpose," Joutsamo said. "There were no fingerprints on the lock . . ."

"No. We found a clumsily concealed false back to the wardrobe and there was a Colt .45 pistol and four grams of cocaine behind it . . . So Max wasn't expecting any uninvited guests. We're still in the middle of DNA tests, and there's no sense in speculating about that."

Kannas took another bite of his sandwich. "Pretty thin stuff. We're not going to solve this case tonight. But there's one thing I keep wondering about." In his typical manner, he finished his sandwich before continuing.

Takamäki knew it was his turn to ask: "What?"

"There was a perfectly good Sony TV, a high-quality DVD player, and an Xbox, but no movies or games. It made me think there must have been some there before."

Takamäki was about to speak, then decided to wait. Kannas had something else to say. It was his style to hold back.

He took another bite of sandwich. "Now, I'm not sure about this, but there was something odd about the burglaries earlier in the evening. Three break-ins, but apparently nothing was taken. In one of them the men from the security company were on the scene in three minutes, but the burglar was already gone. It was as if he was looking for something and didn't find it. He dropped his wallet at one of the stores. The lieutenant on duty thought they'd get him tomorrow, but now I'm not so sure . . ."

"Not so sure about what?" Takamäki asked.

"Johan Svensson was his name. I checked his background. It seems he got out of Sörkkä this morning."

"Pickax Svensson?" Suhonen said.

Kannas nodded. The nickname was from the crime that had gotten Svensson sentenced to ten years in prison. His victim had been a friend of his. They'd had a fight over the last can of beer.

Suhonen pulled out his phone and stepped away. A couple of minutes later he came back. "Someone I know at the jail says that Pickax Svensson shared a cell with Karstu for a few months this summer and that Karstu came to visit him just last week."

The ex-convicts' apartment house was in a condemned two-story brick building next to the rail yard. It was soon to be demolished, but until then a convict aid organization had found lodging there for guys who had nowhere else to go.

The building was only a couple of kilometers from the police station, so the three of them got there in just a few minutes. The light in the yard was dim but the black text on the white sign next to the door was clearly visible: *No alcohol, no drugs. All bags will be searched.*

Joutsamo glanced instinctively at her shoulder holster. She preferred not to carry it, but this time she'd even made Takamäki bring his revolver with him. Suhonen didn't need to be reminded—he routinely carried a weapon.

Takamäki tried the door. It was locked. There had once

been a window in the door but it was covered with plywood. Takamäki knocked on the wood.

He waited and then knocked again before a sleepy long-haired man came to open the door. "What the hell's the emergency?"

"Police," Takamäki said grimly, and pushed inside.

The watchman, who was wearing gray sweatpants and a worn New York Giants cap, backed up into the hallway. "Room eight. Second floor," he said, and stepped aside.

"Merry Christmas," Suhonen said as he passed, grabbing the master key from the rack behind the guard's desk.

The building had once been housing for railroad employees. The hallway was narrow and the staircase curved and steep. The apartments were all single rooms. The kitchens, toilets, and showers were in the hall. Religious posters were glued to the walls, warning of the curse of liquor.

Takamäki went first, up to the second floor. At the top of the stairs was a black sign with yellow letters: *Don't drink. Don't fight. Believe in yourself.*

There was good reason for a sign like that. Nine out of ten prison inmates had a drinking problem and just-released prisoners like these were in great danger of backsliding. They had no homes, no family, no jobs. All they had were old friends. The old cycle, waiting for them.

Room eight was on the left, at the end of the hall. The hall lights only half worked, but their eyes were beginning to adjust to the dimness. They had their coats open. Takamäki wondered if he should have his gun out. Once he did that, it might start to become a habit.

Joutsamo listened with her ear at the door for a moment, then shook her head. She didn't hear anything.

The door didn't look very sturdy—they could have

opened it with a good tug—but Suhonen held out the master key and glanced at the others. Takamäki nodded. Joutsamo's hand went to the butt of her pistol.

Suhonen shoved the key quickly into the lock, twisted it, and yanked the door open fast. Takamäki went in first.

"What the hell?" a man said in irritation, jumping out of his bed. It was Johan Svensson, in his underwear. His body was thin. You could see his ribs. His gray hair hung limp and tangled and his eyes seemed frozen in his head.

Joutsamo followed Takamäki in, pulling her Glock and holding it in front of her when she saw the knife in Svensson's hand.

"Filthy pigs," Svensson rasped, his eyes darting, looking for an exit. There was none. The best he could have done was the window behind him, but the plywood that covered the opening would have slowed him down considerably.

"Merry Christmas," Takamäki said calmly. "There's no need to panic. We just want to talk to you."

Svensson was confused. He tilted his head to one side, like a bewildered dog. But he still had the knife in his hand.

The room was almost perfectly square. The bed was on the left, a writing table and chair on the right. In the back corner there was an old tube television. On the wall were two anti-alcohol posters like the ones in the hallway.

"Why don't you sit down on the bed so we can chat?" Takamäki said.

"I . . . I . . . um . . ."

"Just sit down, Johan," Takamäki said, stepping forward to stand next to the desk. He turned the chair around and sat down on it. Joutsamo stood next to the door, aiming at the knife. Suhonen stood next to her.

Svensson sniffled, dropped the knife, and slumped onto

the bed. He buried his head in his hands. "I . . . I . . ."

Takamäki could see that Joutsamo was ready to rush in and handcuff the man, but he gestured for her to come inside and put away her gun. She and Suhonen remained standing next to the door.

Then Takamäki noticed the Xbox games on the floor. They were smashed, as if they'd been thrown against the wall. The discs had fallen out of the green boxes.

"Johan," Takamäki said, but Svensson didn't respond.

Joutsamo was still watching the red-handled knife on the floor. It was lying right at Svensson's feet. He could pick it up quickly and attack Takamäki with it. Joutsamo thought the lieutenant was taking a needless risk.

"Johan," Takamäki said again, in a calm tone. "Look at me."

The man slowly raised his eyes.

"Why?" Takamäki asked.

"I'm not confessing anything," the man said weakly. "I haven't done anything."

Takamäki peered momentarily at one of the computer games on the floor—a hockey game. "So that isn't what you were looking for."

Svensson shook his head. "No . . . no . . . it isn't."

Takamäki picked up another game—*Battlefield*. "Or this one?"

"No . . ." Svensson said, his eyes sharpening. "I, um, I'll tell you everything. If you do me one favor."

"What?" Takamäki asked. They didn't have much physical evidence from their preliminary investigation of the crime scene, so a confession would make it quite a bit easier to close the case. At this point there were only a few police, ambulance crew, and staff who were aware of how Max Karstu was killed. If Svensson knew the method used to kill him, it would link him to the crime, but the man had to say it in an official interrogation.

"I need *FGS*," Svensson said. "Then I'll tell you."

Takamäki looked confused. What the hell was *FGS*?

"*FGS*," Svensson repeated. "That's all. It's important."

"*Final Great Soldier*," Suhonen said from the doorway. "I managed to get one by ordering in advance. Lucked out."

The clock read 2:55 a.m. Takamäki sat in his car in front of an apartment house. He'd been waiting there for ten minutes, but he was in no hurry.

Snow had started to fall quietly. He wiped off the windshield.

The area around the building was completely deserted. No one to be seen. No one coming home drunk from the bar, no one taking their dog out to pee, no newspaper carrier, no one returning from the night shift. No one. Takamäki enjoyed the moment of quiet.

He saw the lights first, at the corner, and soon Suhonen was parking next to him. Suhonen got in the passenger seat and handed him the game. *Final Great Soldier* was the international hit of the season. Takamäki remembered his own son mentioning it now. It had been sold out everywhere for months.

Takamäki had blue wrapping paper and tape with him. It only took a moment to wrap the package. In the cramped car it didn't look exactly wonderful, but authentic. He taped the card to it. The text was short: *For Paul. Merry Christmas. I love you. Daddy Johan.*

Takamäki got out of the car and put the package safely under his coat. It would be a shame if the ink ran.

The two of them walked together toward the door of the

building. Svensson had told them the door code. The door to the fifth-floor apartment would read, *Lind.*

"Why did Pickax kill Karstu?" Suhonen asked, although he could almost guess the answer.

Svensson had been taken from his apartment to the station. Takamäki and Joutsamo had stayed to question him. The interrogation had been delayed for an hour waiting for the attorney to arrive, but that had given Suhonen time to pick up the game.

"When they were in jail, Max promised to pick up a copy of the game for Svensson, and Svensson promised it to his thirteen-year-old son for Christmas over the phone. He said it was a really, really big deal. So on Christmas Eve, right after Svensson got out of jail, Max had forgotten about the whole thing, which made Svensson fly into a rage. When he didn't find a copy of the game in the break-ins, he went to Karstu's apartment. Max just laughed at Pickax for getting so worked up about it, and things quickly got out of hand. Svensson didn't plan to do it. It just happened, in a fit of rage."

"Did he describe the method, how Max was killed?"

Takamäki nodded. "He's going back to prison."

The elevator carried them to the fifth floor. Suhonen opened the elevator door.

"What's so great about this game?" Takamäki asked, looking at the package in his hand.

Suhonen laughed. "I don't know. It's not your typical shoot-'em-up. There's a right side to be on and you feel like you're doing good. It's hard to explain. There's something compelling about the conflict."

Suhonen crouched down and silently opened the mail slot. Takamäki slid the package through the slot and it landed with a thud on the floor of the apartment.

"It's just addictive," Suhonen said.

They got back in the elevator and Takamäki pushed the button for the first floor. "Once in a while real life works like that too."

SNOWY SARCOPHAGUS

BY JUKKA PETÄJÄ

Meilahti

Translated by Jill G. Timbers

No one could have predicted the course of the next
several days. Everyone talked only of the heavily
gusting snow and the snowdrifts that were bury-
ing the city and forcing the fleet of plows into action in the
middle of the night. But more snow fell than could be plowed
from the streets. Traffic was badly muddled, as were the city
residents, particularly those driving cars. The Meilahti neighborhood on the western side of central Helsinki felt walled
off, though it was only some five kilometers from the center
of town. The snow rendered the distance great in a different
way, at least insofar as what was close was now just as far away
as the city's remotest corners—the many faceless annexed
areas that were more like human pens or snow dumps than
actual parts of Helsinki. All of a sudden Meilahti had become
a suburb forcibly separated from the city center, a suburb that
led its own sleepy life and could just as well have been situated
dozens of kilometers away on Helsinki's eastern or northern
border. Trudging home through the unbroken snow, the deaconess of the Meilahti parish church, the Church of the Good
Samaritan, was the first to notice the snowmen—as would
later become evident from the police report.

Two larger-than-life snowmen stood in the swirling snowstorm in the courtyard in front of the church's main doors. The deaconess, panting in her bulky coat, wondered how the children had managed to reach so high. Perhaps adults had been helping them. The thought of grown-ups and children building snowmen together warmed her heart. The world was not all evil. Hope remained, if faith sometimes wavered, and fortunately you could lean on God. He had atoned for the sins of mankind with His own blood, the minister had said as he removed his clerical collar. One of the snowmen had an empty beer can for a nose. For the other, a newspaper was rolled up for the purpose. Their eyes were bottle caps and the mouths were made from cigarette butts. Their smiles would surely have exposed nicotine-yellowed teeth, had the snowmen been possessed of chewing equipment.

The sky stretched heavily over the church like a blackout curtain. Heavy snowflakes wafted down like white balls against a black velvet background. The scene could have been straight from a pointillist painting. Georges Seurat at the North Pole. Frozen points. Heavenly Morse code. The deaconess stood gazing up at the heavens which did not seem to belong to the everyday world but rather to some more perfect reality. A reality you couldn't charge into wearing muddy boots. She felt as if she were in communion with something greater than herself, some mystical state of existence that could not be captured with words but produced a strong physical sensation. One's soul was filled with light and warmth even though outside it was dark and cold. She thought again of the children and on her face appeared a smile scarcely visible behind the raised collar of her quilted coat. A burst of warmth surged through her heart. She thought of the minister's languid eyes when he glanced at her in the vestry after the service. A lovely moist film sparkled from his eyes and his gaze was lingering, somehow penetrating, and she wanted to believe that the minister was slowly undressing her in his mind. The warmth traveled down her body. Snowflakes danced in her hair. She had forgotten her ski hat at home. She sank in over her knees in the deep snow, and her trip home to Pikku Huopalahti, a part of town which nearly merged into Meilahti, though it had only been built in the 1990s, did not go very quickly.

Where the different parts of town met, different time periods seemed to collide. Rent-controlled postwar Finland that had eked out a living under the war reparations stood side by side or, better, one behind the other with affluent postmodern Finland with its Nokia. Life, however, was such that the snow whirled evenly, democratically, through both neighborhoods.

The deaconess calculated that despite the weather she would probably make it home in fifteen minutes and could then open her well-earned bottle of red wine. She looked behind her one more time. The snow softened the outlines of the snowmen so that they didn't seem to begin or end at any certain spot and the vanishing outlines slid in gradations into the misty landscape. The snow around them was untouched, pristine, without a footprint, or else new snow had buried any footprints long ago. The thought crossed her mind that the snowmen had been conceived from nowhere as if from the Virgin Mary. At least, that's what she told the police at the questioning at the Pasila police station.

Hell broke loose four days later.

The temperature had climbed to nearly -4°F, the skies had cleared, and the snowstorm had subsided. Traffic had started to move again and the buses and streetcars were running almost on schedule. Life was returning to normal. The machine was working again. As if the collapsed grid had been erected anew. Only a few snowflakes drifted down. Two bare-handed boys were making icy snowballs in the churchyard; they'd tossed their wool mittens, heavy with crusted ice, into the snow. The boys had leaned a red plastic sled against the church's frost-covered yellow brick wall. They stood next to each other, legs braced, and aimed their snowballs at the snowmen that were now cloaked with a sparkling coat of ice which reflected the cold sunshine directly into their eyes. It was only on the fourth hit that a chunk broke off one snowman's side. When the piece crashed down and sent up a spray of white, the boys were still as mice for a second and then started to scream for all their worth. The snowman had a black arm that had frozen in a pleading position. It was the arm of a Nigerian woman— as later became apparent. There were two victims. Each had been buried in a snowy sarcophagus.

Two murdered Nigerian women in Meilahti. The frozen corpses had been transported to the Institute of Forensic Medicine located just a kilometer away from the crime scene—assuming that the young women had been murdered in the churchyard. What was behind this? Meilahti was not exactly a part of town where people were murdered. It was chilling how someone had made both of the bodies into snowmen. Was there some hidden message?

At the Pasila police station, Inspector Pekka Suokko of the Helsinki Criminal Investigation Department ran his hands through his increasingly thin hair, and his dry scalp snowed white on the keyboard. There were several grease spots on his shirt, and the cuffs had dirty edges, even though in his hurry he had thought he was choosing a clean shirt. That was meant to counter the chaos inside him. He did not want anyone peeking into his head. The crime scene inspectors were still working in the churchyard. He had no real expectations.

They would only end up with buckets of water, melted snow, to bring to the Institute. The autopsy would probably reveal more.

As he turned his cell phone to silent, Suokko glanced at the old wall clock. The second hand no longer worked. You could still tell time by it, anyway. Not much else at the police station worked either. The Meilahti church deaconess would be in the questioning room any minute now. It was she who had summoned the police. The patrolman said that the frightened woman had hurried into the yard when she heard the boys scream.

Whores. That's what the Nigerian women likely were. It would be the natural explanation. They'd hardly come to Helsinki to clean, Suokko thought as he rose with difficulty. His knees cracked under his weight; maybe they were protesting the pace he was keeping. Didn't matter. His life was on track. At most a bit skewed, like his kneecap. His wife was vacationing in Madeira with her lover. Suokko knew he could do nothing about it. Their marriage was going through a phase that did not exactly make him feel light-hearted—quite the opposite.

Still, he had stayed dry, even though he had not attended an AA meeting for two weeks. When it came down to it, he was satisfied with the decisions he had made. A little over two years ago he had finally understood the advantages of a slower career and had requested a transfer from the position of assistant police chief to criminal investigator because his motivation, belief, and strength were at an end. He was no longer in control of his personal life and was not getting any satisfaction from his ever more administrative job. It had all become just routine. He had chased away low spirits with unrestrained drinking. The diagnosis was right, the medicine, wrong. Not many people could change an organization to fit themselves; they themselves had to change to fit the organization. It was shit. Not good for anyone.

Suokko tucked his shirt into the tight waist of his pants and stepped into the dimly lit corridor that smelled of the same cheap disinfectant used in all the government offices. At that moment, he stopped. Damn. Same empty head summer and winter. He remembered what he'd forgotten and he went back to get the photographs of the murdered women. He had received them from the Institute of Forensic Medicine fifteen minutes earlier.

He had known that at some point a Nigerian sex-trafficking ring would have to turn up in Finland too. But he had not been expecting murders. The first inkling had come over a week ago when he had received an e-mail from Brussels asking him to check on the situation of Nigerian women who had entered Finland, legally or illegally. Behind this was a just-completed investigation by Nigerian officials according to which as many as 40,000 girls or women had been smuggled to the closest West African countries to become sex workers. Simon Egede, executive secretary of the National Agency for the Prohibition of Trafficking in Persons, reported that investigators had found slave camps in Mali, the Ivory Coast, Burkina Faso, Niger, Libya, Morocco, and Cape Verde, full of Nigerian women and girls. Nowadays, human trafficking was part of Finnish reality too. Nearly two hundred million homeless people were on the move in the world. Some of them were merchandise. Simon Egede had asked him to survey the situation in Finland and the other Nordic countries, because he suspected that there were many more Nigerian pimps and whores than the police thought. Egede wanted to expand his investigation from West Africa to also include the EU, so that

EU residents would at least become aware of the miserable reality of the Nigerian women who had fled poverty to become victims of human trafficking, and also of the indifference of Europe's national police forces and immigration offices.

The deaconess sat in the bleak room with her back straight, her hair in a tight bun, and her mouth a tight line. The woman could actually have been pretty if she had had even a touch of style. As he squeezed onto the narrow bench, Suokko cast a furtive glance at the woman's breasts, which would have made many a woman in civilian life proud. Not bad, not bad at all. He cleared his throat when he realized he was gawking, raked his straggly hair, raised his chin, and stared at the ceiling as if something extremely important had just occurred to him. But his head was empty. The fluorescent light on the ceiling was on its last gasp. He saw in it a metaphor for his own life. Got to pull himself together or this won't go anywhere. Suokko pulled his chair forward and sought a more natural position. He announced in a loud voice (keeping in mind the recording and the subsequent report he'd need to make) the topic of the questioning, his own name, his rank, those present, and the precise time at which questioning of the witness was beginning.

To the clearly terrified deaconess, he said as nicely as possible that she need not be scared of anything because she was there only as a witness, not a suspect. It did not help. The deaconess, white-faced, just looked more frightened. Her body crumpled like a balloon losing air. Suokko was sure that Lieutenant Kauko Mähönen, sitting behind the one-way mirror in the observation room, was snickering to himself. Fun for him. Suokko turned on the microphone and started the tape.

The deaconess, breathing heavily, was not able to answer even the simplest questions because she was not at all sure what she had seen and didn't remember when she had first noticed the snowmen in the churchyard. She spoke in such a confused and incoherent way that Suokko was unable to construct an exact timeline for what she had done on the night she spotted the snowmen as she left for home. The deaconess nervously toyed with a loose curl on her forehead, winding it around her index finger. She got badly off track talking about barely related things and then she began to blather about the minister's blue eyes that offered comfort in the midst of the deepest sorrow. Suokko tried to cover his irritation and requested as nicely as he could that the deaconess answer the questions posed. They were not here to talk about anything else. In the end he managed to extract a few morsels of valuable information from the woman. The deaconess had not seen any tracks in the snow, not even any snow-covered depressions suggesting that someone had walked to the yard to make the snowmen or left the spot after the job was done. The snow had been pristine, virginal—like the deaconess herself, thought Suokko.

Suokko spread the photographs on the table and asked the deaconess if she knew or had ever seen these Nigerian women. She shook her head firmly as she stared at the expressionless death masks, but she was too horrified to get a word out. Suokko believed her. He quickly removed the pictures because he did not want to cause any more anxiety for this woman who was clearly unused to violence and death. Strange, though. You would have thought she'd be accustomed to constant funerals and the continuous tolling of death bells. Didn't the whole Lutheran church base its salvation doctrine on the crucifixion of Jesus, on the death of God's son? Then he pulled himself up and resolved to banish heretical thoughts. The whole stupid session was just a waste

of recording tape. Bending closer to her, he asked the deaconess if she suspected anyone of the murders. She was alarmed.
She blanched white as snow.

"Lord the Father. The Devil."

Suokko tried not to laugh. He suspected the woman did
not mean that Lord the Father and the Devil were one and
the same. He told the deaconess the interview was over and
thanked her for her time. Once on her feet, she curtsied.

Suokko returned quickly to his office and only after sitting
down did he realize he had left the photos in the interview
room. The bitter cold could be felt inside too, insofar as the
air in the room was dryer than ever and full of static electricity
that made his thin hair stand on end.

Mähönen could drive him to Meilahti where he could do
some honest footwork, thought Suokko. He wanted to talk
with the minister and interview the residents of the nearby
buildings, in case they had noticed anything unusual over
these past days. An unexpected witness observation—he
could use that right about now. The temperature had dropped
and it was snowing again. He looked out the window, from
where, beyond the rows of three-story buildings, he could
make out Keskuspuisto, Helsinki's Central Park, that wooded
swath that ran through different parts of the city all the way to
the Töölönlahti Bay. He stood rooted in place, staring into the
distance. Dark window. Snow on a TV screen. White noise.

Seen from Mannerheimintie heading straight into downtown,
the bell tower of the Meilahti Church looked like a chimney
of some waste treatment plant. But no smoke came from it.
Suokko fingered the dashboard nervously. He glanced around
and waited impatiently for Mähönen to turn the car onto
Kuusitie. The clock ticked. The tires spun. The drifts had

been neatly plowed to the side of the road and several cars were buried in the snow. He knew that the bell that ended up in the bell tower had originally been meant for Vyborg's old cathedral, but it was never installed there because Finland had to relinquish Karelia to the Soviet Union in the last stretch of World War II. They finally managed to smuggle the bell into Finland, despite the war, and it was eventually donated to the Meilahti Church in the early 1950s when the church was being constructed. A bigger problem than the installation of Vyborg's old cathedral bell was the resettling of nearly a half million evacuees who had fled Karelia after the war. Displaced Karelians settled in Helsinki's densely populated areas as well as its annexed areas, but some also landed in the old apartment buildings alongside Mannerheimintie Street, where more room was made by adding floors. Since then, the area's ethnic balance had not changed. Instead, the socioeconomic map had been redrawn over the past decades. Studio apartments had been renovated into attic suites where interior decorators, designers, producers, and consultants lived. If this sort went dancing, they'd go to the city center or to Kallio and wouldn't hang around their own neighborhood in the evening. Meilahti was a safe harbor for the Finnish bourgeoisie, even though it had its share of international schools and day care centers. The students came in from other places. For that reason alone, the murder of the Nigerian women spawned fear and confusion among the residents. The last murder, actually manslaughter, had occurred in the early 1960s when a group of drunks had knifed a guy to death for stealing a buddy's bottle. In the past ten years the police had documented only two narcotics offences. With a deep sigh Suokko loosened his seat belt. Heartburn. Maybe he shouldn't have eaten bacon earlier that morning.

He felt shitty even though untangling the fate of the Nigerian women had pumped a good shot of adrenaline into his system. If he had seen a shooting star in the sky he would have wished for his wife to finally leave the other man. But only snowflakes danced in the sky. No hope, no good omens that would give him a pretext to imagine the situation would draw to a close. He couldn't even guzzle himself into a drunken stupor. That option was no longer open to him.

Snow-whipped Meilahti looked empty, deserted, as if people had been removed from the landscape because they did not fit into the elements of Finnish architecture. Most people were of course at work and others were inside because of the weather. Meilahti was not a sketchy part of the city—far from it. It didn't have a single lively night spot, just some coffee shops. People here went to bed at ten p.m. or drank behind drawn drapes. The car came to an intersection and the back went into a skid. Mähönen stepped on the gas.

"Left here."

"Gee, thanks. Wouldn't have thought of it."

"Enough."

"Shall I also brake when we reach the church?"

"Yes. If it's not too much trouble."

Suokko shook his head and was about to add some personal barb, but he controlled himself, albeit with difficulty, because there was no point wasting his powder on Mähönen, who could be a real ass at times. But this wasn't the time to niggle. Here they were. Mähönen engaged the parking brake and turned off the engine. The sound of flapping sails could be heard, but the sea was at least two kilometers away. The sound came from the wind crashing against the police tape that roped off the site of the crime to prevent outsiders from disturbing possible tracks and evidence. As he climbed laboriously out of the car, Suokko watched carefully where he set his feet so as not to slip. Just then his cell phone beeped. He was so busy concentrating on staying erect that he dropped the phone into the snow as he pulled it out. Shouldn't have put on the goddamn leather-soled shoes after all, he fumed as he glanced at the screen, wet with snow.

The message from Europol revealed that the Nigerian women had come to Madrid six years ago from Ikeja, outside of Lagos. According to the border officials they were cousins, one twenty-two years old, the other, two years older. Suokko humphed. It might be that the women were only cousins on the officials' papers, but it was absolutely certain that they were political refugees—the religious, political, and ethnic situation in Nigeria was that chaotic. Suokko was sure they'd already started whoring in Spain, though probably not completely voluntarily. And no doubt continued in Finland. This meant that either a pimp or competitor was behind the murders, or else a customer. But he could not imagine why they had been buried in the churchyard.

Was there some hidden message in that? Or had the murderer been forced to hurry? It was also possible that the murderer simply wanted to lead the police astray. Suokko did not believe it was a ritual murder, though the tabloid chatter was painting it that way. Maybe that was the best way to frighten the readers.

Right away came a second message. This was from the Institute of Forensic Medicine on Kytösuontie. The district forensic pathologist reported that preliminary examination showed that the women—or *girls*, as he referred to the corpses—had suffocated to death. Bits of plastic had been found in one girl's mouth and throat, while the other's neck had obvious signs of strangling that were strangely asymmetrical, as if the murderer had only partially used his right hand. The force had nonetheless been strong enough to crush her larynx.

He texted back asking the forensic pathologist to send the photographs of the wounds to him at his office. Nothing to do with any rituals or occult ceremonies, Suokko thought again, as he almost slipped on the slight incline. Luckily, Mähönen had stayed in the car and was not here to sneer. Damn. No question. This was clearly a sex murder. His socks were getting waterlogged. His shoes were wet from the snow. He raised his collar against the icy wind; he didn't think people were at their best deep-frozen.

Once inside he began to perspire immediately. The body was not cold-blooded either. The church had been completely renovated ten years earlier. The minister received him in the congregation's church hall with the Paavo Tynell light fixtures that called to mind Christ's crown of thorns. The lanky minister shook Suokko's hand and welcomed him. His voice was low, his eyes blue, his gaze somehow both feverish and penetrating. Suokko felt contrition at once. He wondered why the minister was wearing black gloves even though it was so warm inside. For a moment he imagined the deaconess in the room in just a bikini, but this image produced by his errant soul only heightened his burden of guilt. Damn, he thought to himself, and pulled himself erect. He cleared his throat and looked the minister right in the eyes. The minister returned his gaze. There was a strange feeling in Suokko's hand. The minister's grasp had been surprisingly limp, even timid, for such a tall man.

The questioning produced nothing, as Suokko had feared. The minister did not recognize the Nigerian women when Suokko showed him the now wrinkled pictures of the victims. He had never seen them at church events, where in fact he had only seen black visitors a few times. Twice, he had noticed a few black men on the second Sunday of Advent, when Christmas carols were sung at church. Otherwise it was only the congregation's regular members who came to church, familiar people who lived in Meilahti. Nor had he noticed anything unusual in the church's front yard at the time the deaconess had first noticed the snowmen. He himself had only heard about them the next day from her, because he had left the church through the low wing of the building instead of the main door. He recalled trying to dig out the ceramic relief by Armas Tirronen of the Good Samaritan from the snow plastered against the wall, but he had abandoned that effort after a few minutes of useless scraping. The snow had been packed hard against the wall. He also advised Suokko to take the deaconess's stories with a grain of salt because she was slightly unbalanced mentally and her relationship with reality was at times very thin, although she was an extremely conscientious worker. The minister suspected some sort of sexual repression. Then he apologized that he had a lot of work, excused himself, and hastened off to prepare for a baptism. Suokko remained standing a moment in the aisle leading to the altar. Lord the Father! Not a single eyewitness. Nothing. Even the church's own surveillance cameras were no help. The tapes just showed falling snow. White. As if the film were overexposed.

Suokko asked Mähönen to drive from Pihlajatie Street to Kuusitie Street. The names meant *rowan* and *spruce*; nearly all the streets around here were named for some stupid tree. He wanted to ring doorbells and question the people who lived in the apartment buildings in the area, though he didn't think much would come of it. But experience had taught him that sometimes a trivial or seemingly unimportant remark, doubt, feeling, or phrase could be exactly what triggered a break-through in a murder investigation. This was why no stone could be left unturned, no matter how tedious it was.

Mähönen was silent, he would have liked to return to the Pasila police station and was tired of sitting in the car wait-ing. Suokko thought to himself that it would do the old chap good to sit a few more hours in the car. He asked Mähönen to contact Lyly, who worked in Internet-monitoring and might be able to do a quick search for horny men in Meilahti.

The end result was four liters of weak coffee and a stomach-ache. Pictures still flickered past his eyes from the family al-bums some of the elderly women had been determined to show him. No one had seen anything, but quite a few of them knew for sure who was guilty. He'd been advised to investigate the activity of some Indians and Japanese who had moved to Kuusitie Street, because the daily routine of that whole group was very strange, not to mention their customs. He would find the guilty party in that crowd, he was assured. No one else in Meilahti would fool around with black women. Suokko knew very well that nearly 80 percent of all murders in Finland oc-curred within the family or former family or group of friends. Police very rarely found any clear motives for these acts. They were often committed by someone drunk, in the grip of jeal-ousy or rage. But he kept his mouth shut. One retired labor union activist suggested that Suokko should leave the Mei-lahti residents alone and head instead for Pikku Huopalahti to take it up with the folks there, where there were buildings full of Somalis.

It was cold in the car, even with the heater going full force. Mähönen was eating a greasy meat pie he'd picked up from a store around the corner. Suokko knew they had to find a cli-ent of the Nigerian women. He'd have to run through online sex ads and porn forums. Maybe he'd get some ground under his feet there, something solid. The windshield wipers cleared the snow from the car's front window. Only sparkling streaks of water remained on the windshield from the snowflakes and then they, too, vanished beneath the wipers. No trace. Effect without cause.

His wet shoes were drying on top of the reports on the desk. Suokko had stuffed them with crumpled newspaper to dry the soles. He curled his toes, frozen from tramping around in the snow. His wife had just phoned from Madeira. Her voice sounded happy, which did not improve Suokko's mood. The air in the room smelled like a wet dog was lurking in the corner. Even the window was fogged with moisture. Nor did it lighten his mood that he had bumped into Chief Raatikainen in the hallway just as he'd been opening the door to his office. On his way to meet with some trendy interest group, Raatikainen had expressed his hope that the case would be solved as quickly as possible so the evening tabloids and social media wouldn't get the chance to mock police incompetence and spread unnecessary terror. Suokko had told a number of reporters that day that the police could not release any information about the investigation at this point. It would be interesting to see how many lines they could construct from that information-free statement.

Pulling his chair closer to the desk, Suokko dug out from under his shoes the photos of the victims that the forensic pathologist had sent him and began to study the strangulation marks. The women's expressionless death masks made them look somehow inhuman, as if they were not flesh and blood but rather some sort of artifacts. Both had bloodshot eyes which brought to mind a coronal cloud on the sun. But nevertheless, there was no more life in them. Suokko imagined someone—if he only knew who—beginning rough sex games with the women, placing one woman's head in a plastic bag and forcing the other to watch. Perhaps the first woman was suffocated by mistake? The shithead would have murdered the other on purpose because he wanted no witnesses alive.

Suokko felt like he was beginning to piece together the chain of events. A pimp would not up and kill two prostitutes who brought him money. Nor did Suokko believe in turf battles between pimps from different countries—that simply did not happen in Finland. Maybe in Germany or Denmark, okay. The problem was that he still had no evidence to support his theory. He picked up a magnifying glass and studied the strangulation marks on the neck of Temitope Oyelami—this was evidently the name of the younger prostitute. These marks bothered him, but he could not come up with a reasonable explanation for why they were lopsided. Bruises made by the thumb and index finger of the right hand were clearly visible. Then there was a sort of clean area that ended in what was presumably the pressure mark from a little finger. For some reason the force had not been distributed evenly. Haste? Alarm? Just then the phone, the landline, rang. Suokko grabbed the receiver with one eye still on the magnifying glass.

"Suokko."

"Forgive me. Virtanen here."

"Evening."

"I really don't know if I should even have called."

"Well, tell me what's on your mind, since you did call," Suokko said, trying to hide his impatience.

It took a little while before Suokko realized it was the deaconess who was calling. Her slurred voice suggested she had uncorked a bottle of red wine some time ago. The deaconess, breathing heavily into the phone, was even more upset about the murders than she had been during the questioning. She could not comprehend how anyone could descend to such brutality. She lamented that she had been unable to help. She would have liked to help, with all her heart. After a few pointed comments from Suokko, the woman gradually caught on that he was in a hurry, and she let him continue his work. Suokko expressed his gratitude. The gesture was Jacob's, the motive, Esau's.

The snow had paused, the temperature dropped, and the pipes of the police station banged. Overhead, the sky spread out like a black shroud.

The motive? What was it? Bad question. Why had the bodies been left in the churchyard?

Suokko could not come up with any explanation for the murders other than self-defense and fear of being caught buying sex. That did not make the murders any less brutal. The right hand. He could not get that out of his mind. It wouldn't leave him in peace. His shoes smelled of sweat. There they sat right under his nose. The summary from Lyly of local online sex purchasers before and after the murders listed only three men, two of whom Suokko knew by name. They couldn't be murderers. Suokko signed into the police register to do further research. The third man also seemed very unlikely to be guilty, although someone had suggested chemical castration for him. Another dead end.

Suokko heaved a sigh and thought in frustration that the guilty party might not be caught for months or even years. That sometimes happened when no evidence was found right at the beginning of a criminal investigation. He kept turning it over in his mind. He was sure he had overlooked something important, something that could lead to a breakthrough, if he could only figure out what it was. He lifted his shoes from the desk, walked over to the radiator in his socks, and placed the shoes on it. They could dry there as long as necessary. He thought about Meilahti. It was a cocoon where murder had no place, because murder demanded feelings, anger at the very least, that clouded reason. He could not associate passion with Meilahti. In the northwest the big gray complex with the maternity hospital and children's clinic, along with the university's general hospital, cancer clinic, and medical research institutes, spread all the way to churning Humallahti Bay. In the middle of Meilahti was the church. The graveyard was cleverly situated the next neighborhood over. Meilahti was a closed, self-sufficient entity where people were born, lived, died, and were sent off on the final journey. He sought some metaphor but could not quite catch hold of it. But slowly it came to him. He thought of the sun. People who lived in Meilahti were like tourists clustered on a sunny beach. The sun did not burn them because they were careful to sit under beach umbrellas. No mark appeared on them, not even of life.

Something kept nagging at him. He went back to the police register and began skimming through it. He could not get comfortable on the chair, and after lifting and resettling his backside a few times, he realized what was wrong: he was sitting on the magnifying glass. On top of everything else. As if his ass weren't big enough already.

The night progressed but he stayed where he was. No need to hurry home to toss and turn in bed and jealously imagine what his wife and her lover were doing in Madeira. All of a sudden a familiar name caught his eye and he stopped aimlessly perusing the register. Just for the hell of it he decided to see what the register had about the minister of the Meilahti church. He had realized, when the minister left to prepare for the baptism, that he did not like the man. Though friendly enough, the minister seemed somehow artificial, as if he were playing a role and was not even present. On the other hand, wasn't being a minister purely a role anyway, Suokko thought, as he began checking the man's record, which was irritatingly unblemished. Damn. The man had his doctorate and had even done ecumenical work in Africa. A good man, even for a minister. He'd also done well in the army and attended reserve officers' training. Suokko swore. The minister had never wallowed in ditches, wasn't even an alcoholic like Suokko.

Rubbing his eyes, Suokko was about to stop reading when his gaze, growing heavier and heavier, was suddenly arrested. Fatigue vanished. He had it at last. He couldn't believe his eyes. An accident during shooting practice in the army had taken two fingers from the future church minister's right hand. Suokko recalled the man's limp and awkward handshake. Goddamn bastard.

He quickly ordered a patrol car for himself. It wasn't more than a ten-minute drive from Pasila to Meilahti, with no traffic on the road at this hour. The minister lived next to the church, on Jalavatie. Suokko almost forgot his shoes on the radiator as he rushed into the hall. The moon had risen. It illuminated the snow, now an ugly gray from sand, dirt, and traffic exhaust. Suokko thought of the alb, a minister's basic liturgical vestment, which no longer gleamed so white.

DEAD CINCH

BY TUOMAS LIUS

Central Train Station

Translated by Douglas Robinson

I

I hate Helsinki. I hate the piss-drenched cobblestone streets, and those fucking tweens that hawk their yellow gobs of spit on every disgusting inch of space around stores, bus stops, and train stations. I hate that shit-for-brains look-how-important-I-am rushing from place to place on buses, trams, and metro trains, and god how I hate those swaggering self-centered pricks who are always putting some fucking bar in Sörnäinen up on a pedestal, or going on and on about how only an asshole would ever say *Hesa* for Helsinki instead of *stadi*. These jerkoffs think they live in some kinda fucking metropolis even though you could throw a rock from here and hit one of the five *million* people who live in St. Petersburg, which is really what this half-chewed cough drop some truck driver spat on the map would so dearly love to be . . . Yeah, okay, fine," he added after a pause, "not everybody who lives here's a prick. The worst loudmouths are the ones who moved here from somewhere else and became born-again Helsinkians. Those dumbasses have the gall to shoot their mouths off about somebody else's dialect or whatever even though they were scraping cowshit off the soles of their rubber boots like a month ago."

His rant was followed by silence. Probably some of those who had been listening to it had dissenting opinions, but the speaker's views were not open for discussion or comment. None of those present were there to challenge other folks' opinions or views anyway. Each of them had his or her own pain, about which he or she was waiting to speak without challenge from others—with only the warmest support and open-minded acceptance.

Jari-Pekka Laukia took a deep breath and let his eyes rove over the faces in the group. "I have never felt so miserable. My wife claims that we live in a nice neighborhood, but the neighbors all treat each other like lepers. I'm not saying we should be hugging everybody we meet on the street, but wouldn't it be nice if every now and then a guy could feel welcomed by the assholes up in the VIP stands?"

Laukia stared off into the distance for a moment. "I know I shouldn't point fingers at others," he whispered, in a voice that broke with every word. "I know that I should just talk about my drinking, and not harangue you with the same problem every fucking week . . ."

The ponytailed guy sitting on Laukia's right touched him on the shoulder and nodded. "Let 'er rip," he said. "Whatever you need to say, man."

Laukia's face didn't change. His breathing rasped as if he had a piece of paper caught in his throat and the air blowing past was flapping it around. "I just can't get past the thought that it's all my old lady's fault," he whispered finally. As he heard the words coming out of his mouth, he gave a sad little laugh and glanced around at the others with an almost imperceptible look of apology in his eyes. "But no. I made that bed, I have to lie in it. You know what they say, there are no evil women, just spineless men." Laukia cleared his throat with a quick little harrumph and focused his gaze on the man who had given him the floor. "I'm J.P. and I'm an alcoholic."

"Hi, J.P." The response came in unison as from a chamber choir.

Laukia nodded and said the words that would end his testimony: "I haven't taken a drink in three weeks."

Although confession was an integral part of AA meeting discourse, the applause that followed sounded sincere and deserved. For whatever the words preceding the confession were, whatever they dealt with, every person present knew that they came from the heart.

Laukia walked back over and took his seat again, fished his pack of nicotine gum out of his pocket, and slipped two mint-flavored pillows into his mouth. Then his eyes landed on a guy sitting across the room, against the wall. The man didn't turn away when their eyes met; he smiled and gave an encouraging nod.

Laukia responded to this stranger's gesture with a touch of embarrassment. He was nearsighted, couldn't see the faces on the other side of the circle clearly, but he was certain he'd never met this man before. Laukia turned to watch the next speaker, but felt the stranger still staring at him. He leaned just a bit to his left, into his nearest neighbor's space. The man kept staring. He was wearing a flannel shirt and corduroys.

"Who's that guy over by the door?" Laukia whispered.

The man gave Laukia an amused look, as if about to remind him what the second A in AA stood for.

"I mean, have you seen him here before?" Laukia hissed, looking back across the room. The stranger was now intently focused on the group leader's speech—or at least pretending to be.

"No. Why?" the man whispered back.

"Just wondering," Laukia whispered one last time, and straightened his back.

The meeting ended at seven thirty. The drizzle that had started coming down earlier in the evening was now being whipped around by a stiff wind into a minor storm. Laukia walked up the stone steps from the apartment building's basement into the courtyard.

He raised the collar on his jacket and jammed his fists deep into his pockets. He hadn't sat behind the wheel of a car in a year and a half, ever since his wife had managed to get his license revoked. Laukia strode across the courtyard, stepped out into the intersection of Bulevardi and Annankatu, and checked his watch. The next local train to Kirkkonummi was leaving in seven minutes. Two decades and fifteen kilos ago he might have made it by a hair. In his current state, at age fifty-two, after two knee operations, he decided to wait for the one leaving in half an hour. And what hurry was he in to get home anyway? No more tonight than any other night.

Laukia cut through Ruttopuisto—Plague Park—toward Mannerheimintie, the main drag. The old church park made memories from twenty years ago spring into full-blooded life. Memories that were among the very few happy ones that Laukia had of Helsinki. The park had been the favorite place for him and his only daughter, Kaisa, to go when she was still preschool age. Jari-Pekka and Kaisa had had countless picnics there.

Even then he'd sensed the depths into which an unhappy marriage was dragging him, and those fleeting moments when he could just listen to his little daughter laughing were the pillars on which he built the crumbling ruins of his life.

The last time father and daughter had sat in Plague Park—

well, the last time so far—was when Kaisa graduated from high school. A few months after that day the Laukias got their first postcard from Berlin, where their daughter had moved.

The main Helsinki train station was less than a kilometer away. As he walked toward it, Laukia kept his eyes on the tips of his shoes. Whenever he lifted his gaze to the faces moving toward him, he imagined them judging him, criticizing him— as if his testimony had blared out over the streets of the city through loudspeakers. And so Laukia felt like even more of a loser tonight than he usually did when returning from an AA meeting. It was like he was a pariah, an outcast, someone who had betrayed his community and would be driven onto the rooftops by angry villagers with torches and pitchforks. It was no effort at all to see in his mind's eye the lynch mob led by his wife, or especially his father-in-law: *There goes the lousy bum!* To which some friend from the city would add: *The drunk's ducking for the station! Grab him!*

Laukia slouched into the train station building through the main entrance, the one guarded by the statues of the lantern bearers. The hall was only quiet at random times of the day, since alongside the main entrance there were not only ticket windows and doors out onto the platforms but the gateway down into the Station Square metro station.

Now, too, the hall was filled with sounds and smells the likes of which at rush hour would have tightened Laukia's spiritual screws to the breaking point, but for some strange reason he felt relieved to become part of this larger group of nameless strangers than his anonymous alcoholics. Here he didn't even have to talk. Here he could disappear for a moment, briefly be one nameless person among hundreds and hundreds of others.

Laukia set a course through the crowds toward Eliel, the station restaurant, where outside of rush hour it was hardly ever a problem to find a seat.

He snagged a tray and loaded it with a slice of chocolate cake, a coffee, and a glass of water. There was no line to the cashier. Laukia slid his hand into his inside coat pocket, but to his surprise didn't feel the fake leather surface of his wallet on the tips of his fingers. In dismay he stepped back from the counter and scanned the floor back the way he'd come. Had his wallet dropped out while he was taking a tray? The situation unnerved him to the point where he paid no attention to the man standing behind him, patiently waiting his turn in line. Laukia was studying the floor in front of the glass case when he noticed the person in line behind him putting something on his tray. A wallet. Astonished, he turned his eyes up to the man standing there, a short, plumpish, balding sort who despite the sadness in his eyes was smiling with his whole round face. The fiftyish man looked remarkably like an American actor whom Laukia had seen in countless films: like Paul Giamatti, most famous for his role in *Sideways*.

"Guess this must be yours," the man said.

Laukia nodded and instinctively checked it for his money.

"Don't worry, it's all there," the man laughed, and raised his palm in a gesture of innocence.

Laukia realized that, instead of being grateful to this man, he had insulted him by automatically suspecting him of dishonesty. He stuffed the wallet back into his pocket with a little embarrassed smile on his lips.

"Thanks."

"Don't mention it. Always good to help a fellow sufferer."

Laukia wrinkled his brow, and now realized that this was the same man he had been wondering about at the AA meeting.

"You ain't seen me . . . right?" the man said in English, imitating a sketch from the popular British comedy series *The Fast Show*.

The pop culture allusion went right over Laukia's head, but he tried to cover his confusion with a forced smile. "Can I buy you a coffee as thanks?"

"Come on," the man said, waving his hand and moving to turn away, "it's no big deal."

"No, I mean it," Laukia pressed, and put another cup on his tray. "With or without milk?"

"Well, with milk, if you insist, but there's really no need."

Laukia nodded. "But you didn't need to help me either."

"After that round condemnation of Helsinki of yours, I thought maybe you'd appreciate a gesture of friendship from a local," the man laughed.

Laukia smiled. "I do appreciate it. What'll you have with the coffee?"

"Thanks, just the feeling of having done a good deed," the man replied, giving himself a smack to his bulging belly. "A corner table okay with you?"

"Yep," Laukia said, and followed the man to the back of the restaurant.

"You left the meeting like a bat out of hell," the man said, dabbing at his high forehead with a hankie. Despite the chill outside air, it was glistening with sweat. "It took all I had to keep up with you."

The men sat down at a table and studied each other. Both seemed to be thinking the same thing: *This is the moment when a normal guy introduces himself.*

"Uh," Laukia began, sticking his hand across the table, "J.P." His voice had an uncertain note in it, as if wanting to ask whether a handle consisting entirely of initials was okay outside of AA.

The man shook Laukia's hand. "Tapsa."

"Thanks again. My wife would have thrown a hissy fit if I'd lost my money."

"I have to ask," Tapsa began, then sipped his coffee. "If you hate Helsinki so passionately, why do you live here?"

"Short answer: my wife's from here."

"I understand," Tapsa nodded.

"I can't stress the shortness of that answer enough," Laukia added, rolling his eyes at his coffee companion.

"My sympathies," Tapsa laughed. "How long have you two been married?"

"Twenty-five years."

"Kids?"

"A daughter."

Tapsa heaved a deep sigh and shook his head. "And the situation is really that bad?"

"It really is," Laukia said with a weary smile. "Every single fight goes unresolved because my wife doesn't give a shit about any attempt I make to make up, or to talk about the problems in our relationship, let alone my feelings. She has never once admitted she was wrong, or that she'd harmed anyone else with her actions. It's always someone else's fault—usually mine."

Tapsa wiped the corners of his mouth with a paper napkin and leaned back in his chair.

"Finally, she broke my spirit and I started drinking," Laukia said, washing the last crumbs of cake down his throat. "You can imagine what kinda torque a wife can get out of a weakness like that."

"A patient suffering from narcissistic personality disorder

does not feel he is sick, and the best treatment for a narcissist's victim is to leave the narcissist."

Tapsa's words surprised Laukia. He had thought the conversation was over; instead, he noticed that the expression
on the man's face had deepened, as if he had actually started
to reflect on his anonymous acquaintance's marital problems.

"No hope of a divorce, either," Laukia lamented, and
dropped his spoon ⟶ the edge of the ceramic plate.

"Why not? No prenup?"

"Every cent I've ever earned in my life has come through
her family's business," Laukia replied. "You'd understand if I
told you the family's name. So if I give her the boot, they'll
give me the boot, and haul me out with the trash. I'll be paying court costs for the rest of my life."

Tapsa wrinkled his brow. In every possible way he looked
like someone who listens to people's troubles for a living: a
psychologist, a therapist, something like that. Among AA
members one could find top doctors whom the bottle had en-
slaved just as effectively as it had some temp who'd gone years
between jobs. Whatever he was, the man who'd introduced
himself as Tapsa was someone Laukia felt comfortable talking to.

"I'm too old to make a new start, especially since I never
made it past the ninth grade. I've basically let my whole life
get played on a single card, so if I pull the plug on my marriage, I pull the plug on my whole life."

Tapsa sat there for a moment digesting Laukia's words,
his elbows resting on the edge of the table. "Why doesn't she
want a divorce?"

"She . . ." Laukia began, managing to make even that first
word drip with scorn, "is not a nice person. She enjoys the
power she has over me."

"Interesting."

Yep, Laukia thought, *this guy is definitely a shrink on the skids.* "But also," he added, "her family is right-wing and fanatically religious. Divorce isn't in their vocabulary. It's till-death-do-us-part, the whole bit."

"At least you have your child," Tapsa said comfortingly. "I hate to say it, but it seems that in way too many marriages the younger generation is the only thing holding them together."

"That's what she was for us too," Laukia nodded with a wistful smile. "Kaisa isn't at all like her mother."

Tapsa sipped his coffee and waited patiently for Laukia to continue.

"But she's grown up now. Thirty, living abroad. I hardly ever see her. And I certainly can't blame her for never coming home. She isn't on the best terms with her mother, which is completely understandable."

"I'm sorry to hear that," Tapsa smirked.

"So what's *your* story?" Laukia laughed sarcastically.

"Let's not go into that now," Tapsa said, shaking his head with a sad look in his eyes.

"Come on, spill. It can't be a wife at least."

Something flashed in Tapsa's eyes. "Why not?"

"I don't see a ring."

"Very observant," Tapsa laughed. "I've been married fourteen years." He pulled the collar of his sweater down and revealed the pendant hanging on top of his undershirt. It was a gold ring strung onto a thin silver chain. "Here's my wedding ring. I've never been one for jewelry."

"After fourteen years you call it jewelry instead of a shackle," Laukia chuckled heartily. "That's a good sign."

"Well, yes . . . My nightmare has nothing to do with family." He opened his wallet and showed Laukia a photo in a plastic pocket.

"Good-looking kids," Laukia said, and shifted his gaze from the kids to the blond woman standing behind them. "Good-looking wife."

"Thanks," Tapsa said, nodding and taking another look at the photo himself. The smile that warmed his face as he did so spoke volumes.

"So, fourteen years," Laukia sighed, shaking his head.

"Yep," Tapsa nodded. "I can honestly say that I've worked my ass off to keep them, uh, happy."

"Sounds nice."

"And mostly it is." A tender smile flickered on Tapsa's lips. The man looked like the guy next door. For the life of him, Laukia could not make out what might have driven him to alcoholism.

Laukia glanced at his watch and realized that he was going to have to split. "Damn," he grunted, jumping up, "train's in two minutes."

"Nice chatting," Tapsa said, looking Laukia straight in the eyes.

"Ditto."

"Can I ask one more thing?"

"Do it fast."

"Tonight at the meeting, why'd you ask the guy sitting next to you who I was?"

Laukia stopped to gaze back at him.

"I didn't get my nose out of joint or anything," Tapsa rushed to explain.

"My wife," Laukia laughed, pulling his jacket on.

Tapsa looked understandably confused.

"A couple of times she's sent her friends to follow me, to make sure I am actually going to a meeting," Laukia explained.

"Sick."

"What're you gonna do?" Laukia shrugged his shoulders. "But as the program teaches us, *one day at a time* and *this too will pass.*"

Tapsa snorted at the familiar platitudes. "You know . . . if you want to talk about this stuff again, I'd be happy to listen. Anonymously, of course."

"That wouldn't be such a terrible idea."

"Next week, same time, same place?"

"Why not?"

"Don't forget your wallet."

Laukia laughed. *Yep, that sealed it: my new friend's a shrink.*

II

The next week Tapsa met Laukia in the station restaurant, at the same table where they had launched their anonymous acquaintance. Laukia had two empty beer steins in front of him, and after a few swigs they were joined by a third.

Tapsa held a mug of tea when he sat down across from his backsliding friend. It wasn't long before Laukia was venting about an argument with his wife that had lasted days, and in which his in-laws had participated. Tapsa said he'd heard about marriages in which the wife indulged knowingly in emotional violence, taking great pleasure in the results of her actions, but that the Laukias' case sounded like something else altogether, completely unique.

"Have you considered the possibility that middle age has blown things completely out of proportion?" Tapsa began in a conciliatory tone, sipping on his tea. "Maybe this will pass?"

"I've been waiting for it to pass for twenty-five years. I can't wait any longer. I don't have the strength for it." Laukia folded his hands and looked the man across from him in the

186 // Helsinki Noir

eyes. "The truth is that I'm trapped with a mean-spirited shrew of a wife."

Tapsa scratched at the stubble on his cheek and knitted his brow. "Listen, J.P.," he sighed, "I have an idea, and I'm just going to blurt it out."

"Go for it."

"Once you've heard it you may want to storm out of here, or maybe have another beer. Hell, you may want to deck me. Do you still want to hear what I have to say?"

"How could I refuse after that introduction?"

Tapsa pushed his tea aside and leaned toward a confused-looking Laukia. "In my work I've had to travel a great deal, both here in Finland and out there in the world. I've gotten to know people that a dad from Eiranranta wouldn't necessarily get to know." He paused, as if to see what kind of reaction he had awakened in his listener so far. Laukia was curious, that was for sure. "I've seen many kinds of couples and witnessed how a few doomed marriages were saved by extramarital— projects . . ."

Laukia rubbed his forehead and motioned for Tapsa to continue. The latter laid a business card in the middle of the table, text side down, and left his finger on it until he'd said his bit. "There's a phone number on this card. It belongs to a certain person who is extremely capable at what she does, and very discreet. She might be willing to meet you, if you so choose."

Laukia swallowed and cleared his throat. "Is she a . . . whore?"

"No, of course not," Tapsa laughed with affectionate sarcasm, "she's a Sunday school teacher."

Laukia smirked and glanced over at the table next to them. The young couple sitting there were obviously doing

Europe on an InterRail pass. They did not represent a significant risk of getting caught.

"I would recommend, however," Tapsa added, giving Laukia a long look from under his brows, "that you not use that particular job title in her presence."

Laukia slid the card toward himself and turned it over. "Madame Kismet," he sneered. "My my . . . peel off your outer layer and what do we find but a closet perv—"

"I've never cheated on my wife," Tapsa interrupted with a calm look. "Nor, needless to say, am I pressuring you to do anything you don't want to do. But if you feel that a little adventure might loosen a knot or two in your relationship, reset the counter to zero . . ." He could see in Laukia's eyes that he had made up his mind. "She has a room in the Vaakuna Hotel." Tapsa nodded in the direction of the hotel in question, which stood maybe a hundred paces from where they were sitting.

Laukia slipped the card into his shirt pocket, wiped the corners of his mouth, and stood up.

"Not going to finish that beer?"

"I don't seem to be thirsty anymore," Laukia said with a sly smile.

"In that case," Tapsa laughed, "I seem to have helped you more than AA."

"I'll tell you how much it helped next week." Laukia smiled and tapped himself on the chest.

"Spare me the details."

Laukia winked at Tapsa and clapped him on the shoulder. "Thanks."

"Don't mention it," Tapsa replied. "The pleasure is all mine."

III

Rarely had a week passed so quickly in Jari-Pekka Laukia's life. He had arranged to meet Madame Kismet the night of the next AA meeting, and as he moved through his week he noticed himself feeling sensations in his body that he'd thought had been numbed years before. The last time Laukia had been so keyed up was back when he was a teenager, when his easily excited imagination had aroused him at the most inappropriate times.

During those seven days nothing affected Laukia but the thought of his approaching date, which began to swell in his overheated thoughts beyond all proportion. Laukia began to believe that this would be no sordid quickie with some anonymous sex worker but a kind of catharsis that would burst his invisible but oppressive shackles.

Laukia had been galvanized—and he owed it all to Tapsa. *Now there's an alcoholic who has truly earned his whiskey bottle.*

The only thought that troubled Laukia was how close he had come to not experiencing any of this: if he hadn't lost his wallet, this would never have happened.

Laukia stepped a bit unsteadily out through the Vaakuna's main entrance onto Postikatu. He stopped to look at the traffic at the Station Square while his breathing calmed. Whenever he left an AA meeting he was always sure that people could see right through him, see his weakness. Now he was sure that he reeked of sex, and that he would find his debauchery in a dark hotel room projected onto billboards throughout the city center. Laukia knew he was grinning like an idiot, but felt he had a right. At last he felt like a man, in the sexual-identity sense, and if that feeling bubbled up over the rim a little, so what? *Now it's my turn.*

* * *

Tapsa sat at the men's regular table at the back of the almost empty restaurant.

"Hey there!" Laukia called out cockily, as if he owned the world.

"Hello," Tapsa said in his polite, restrained style. "How are things?"

"Right now things are unusually good," Laukia smirked.

"So," Tapsa said, a smile tugging at the corners of his mouth. He took his glasses off, folded them neatly, and laid them carefully on top of the book he'd been reading. "What happens next?"

The strange question stumped Laukia. "In what sense?"

"Did your meeting with Madame Kismet produce the desired result?"

"One of them, at least," Laukia said.

Tapsa allowed this crude allusion a joyless laugh. "I didn't mean that, exactly."

"Nothing else matters a good goddamn," Laukia said, stretching his arms luxuriously.

"But of course it does," Tapsa said sternly, folding his hands on the table.

Laukia wrinkled his brow. *What the hell's going on here?*

"Are you planning to give your marriage another chance?" Tapsa enunciated his words with exaggerated care.

"How the hell would I know?" Laukia burst out. "Not fifteen minutes ago I had the goddamn wildest orgasm of my life. I want to recover from it in peace, not rain on that particularly wonderful parade by thinking about my marriage."

"But that was precisely why you did it," Tapsa noted. "In order to decide whether you want to continue with your current life."

"What the hell is wrong with you?" Laukia snapped with

such intensity that Tapsa fell back in surprise. "What bug crawled up your ass? And what fucking business is it of yours what happens to my marriage?"

The man who called himself Tapsa scratched his nose, let his gaze fall to the book on the table, and took a deep breath. "Have you ever heard of the study," he asked with a toneless, almost whispering voice, "that found that 3 or 4 percent of men and 1 percent of women are born killers?"

"Can't say I have," Laukia responded irritably.

"They write of individuals who can take another person's life without the tiniest shred of remorse," Tapsa said, raising his eyes to meet Laukia's.

"Fascinating. Has all this trivia driven you back to drink?"

"Consider," Tapsa continued as if Laukia had not sneered, "three or four men in a hundred can kill without remorse, but of those, one in a thousand is even more exclusive: he isn't just capable of it, he's addicted to it."

Laukia and Tapsa glared at each other. They were like two schoolboys in a staring contest.

"Do you mean to say . . ." Laukia wheezed, his pure disbelief withering his voice down to nothing, "that you . . ."

Tapsa said nothing.

"This is bullshit," Laukia hissed.

The empathetic look in Tapsa's sad eyes had grown cold. "Thirty-seven," he said slowly, easily. "Or thirty-eight if you count the woman who choked on her own vomit while I was cutting her husband's head off with a bread knife." Tapsa scratched an ear.

Laukia sat there silent, listening. Even though he didn't believe a word this guy was saying, he began to feel an uncomfortable rumbling in the pit of his stomach.

"I have succeeded in restricting my appetite to a single

victim per year. That way I can keep everything under control, and I'm able to promise myself to let my will manage my desire and not the other way around."

Tapsa had not taken his hollow gaze off Laukia's eyes throughout this little speech. Sheer astonishment had let Laukia's mouth fall open. He could only sit and stare at the stranger across the table from him.

"Jesus F. Christ," Laukia sighed at last. "Are you insane?"

"That's certainly one diagnosis," Tapsa nodded, raising his eyebrows.

Laukia burst out laughing. This had to be a big joke—a sick one, to be sure, black humor of the rarest sort, perfectly executed. "Okay, you got me! Why the hell would you confess something like that to me if it was true?"

Tapsa watched Laukia as he writhed helplessly in the throes of anxious giggles. "You asked me to tell you about my own problem."

"Yeah, but my problem was that I'm sick of my marriage," Laukia said with sudden heat, spit flying from his mouth. "Walk around the train station tapping men on the shoulder and you'll find a hundred of them that will confess the exact same problem without the tiniest hesitation. But you—you reveal that you're a serial killer! What's gonna stop me from calling the cops right this instant?"

"Good luck proving it," Tapsa replied calmly, without raising his voice.

"But the tiniest hint of a thing like that would be enough to ruin your reputation, your life," Laukia insisted. He wanted to see where Tapsa's sick mind game was leading them.

"If you want to talk about ruining someone's life, what if I were to feel obliged to bring up your sick behavior in the Vaakuna Hotel?"

Laukia felt a lump rising to his throat and sticking there. "*What?*"

"The webcam video is a bit grainy, but it's clear enough to make out who's doing what to whom. I was especially taken with that intriguing moment when you were choking your partner, then rammed into her ass and shouted a man's name. Am I wrong in surmising that to be your father-in-law's name?" As he spoke, Tapsa tipped his head to one side, like a scientist studying a rat in a cage.

Laukia was breathing hard. His heart seemed to be pounding in his head, harder and harder with every beat. "You little shit," he hissed through clenched teeth. "What, are you blackmailing me?"

"Of course not!" Tapsa laughed. "I mean you no harm. You can consider the knowledge that such a recording even exists a safety net."

"A safety net?"

Tapsa nodded. "I've learned the hard way that when friendship reaches a certain level of trust, certain individuals seem to feel a temptation to abuse that trust."

Laukia buried his face in his hands and leaned forward on the table. "What the hell do you want?"

"The way I see things, we can help each other."

"Oh yeah?"

"You have something blocking your path in life, and to start over you need to clear it out of the way. And I—" Tapsa broke off for a moment. "Well, there is a gigantic pit in the path of my life, and I have to keep on filling it in order to proceed."

Laukia looked Tapsa straight in the eye, hoping against hope that this would be the moment at which he would stop the charade, reveal that he was just kidding. In his heart, however, Laukia knew that this was not going to happen. "Monster," he huffed.

"Don't try to tell me you never toyed with the idea yourself."

"What?" Laukia whispered with a quiver in his voice. "The idea of killing my wife?"

"I hope you'll see this as the only window that will ever open up in the stone wall of your suffering," Tapsa said. "You do understand, don't you, the unique nature of this offer? The only thing left for you to do is make sure you have an airtight alibi."

Laukia could feel himself freezing inside. "Did . . . did you really cut off a man's head with a bread knife?"

"A person has seven neck vertebrae," Tapsa said, bending his head and pointing to his neck, "the thinnest of which are up here at the top. Severing them with a bread knife is not an easy task, and quite distasteful. It's mostly hard work, sawing away for a very, very long time. Well, I was young then, and impatient."

Laukia gulped. His heart was beating almost intolerably hard.

"You'd be surprised at how much junk there is in a neck. Muscles, and especially the ligaments that tie the vertebrae together, plus a bunch of other stuff that requires a lot of energy to cut through quickly. You have to insert the knife at the intervertebral disc. It simply won't go through the bone. To cut or crush that you need something a lot more powerful. In fact, your ordinary household knife is in every possible way a bad choice if you're trying to cut off a man's head. You're much better off with a broadaxe for that job."

Laukia closed his eyes. He could feel the cold sweat popping out on his temples. *This cannot be happening.*

"Nor should we forget the bleeding," Tapsa continued with

a dry laugh and a snap of his fingers. "Just how much blood you get depends on the target's physical attributes, of course, but let me tell you right now that when you start chopping through the arteries and other blood vessels in the neck, the mess is incredible."

Laukia rubbed his face. He felt nauseous. He pressed his palm to his mouth and forced the rising vomit back down his throat.

Tapsa ordered two glasses of water and two coffee liqueurs. For ten minutes the two men just sat there in silence. Laukia stared at the table and Tapsa went back to reading his book. He was in no hurry, and he knew that Laukia would pick up the thread of the conversation again once he had gotten over his quite understandable initial shock and horror.

"It would never work," Laukia finally whispered. "Not in a million years. The cops would be all over me."

"You don't know me, " Tapsa said, without bothering to raise his eyes from the pages of his book. "You don't know my name, you haven't offered me any money or services in return, nothing. You didn't hire me to kill your wife. As far as you know, you just spilled your guts at the AA meeting—a group whose whole reason for being is that you can talk about anything you like with people you don't know. You've talked about your fears, your nightmares, your anxieties, precisely as you've been encouraged to do. You can't be held responsible for what your listeners do with what you tell them. Maybe one of them followed you, and acted on his own sick fantasies."

"That *is* how this looks," Laukia growled.

"As we've agreed, each of us has his own demons," Tapsa shrugged. "Don't you want to be rid of your own?"

Laukia sighed deeply. He could not believe he was having this conversation.

"You've told me that you never truly loved your wife. That there are no feelings between the two of you—"

"That's not the problem!" Laukia snapped, trying to keep his agitated voice down to a whisper. "I hate her, and promise you that the feeling is mutual—but we're talking about murder!"

"You've criticized your wife's family for their religious fanaticism." Tapsa gazed across at Laukia over the top of his glasses. "You've called it empty moralism. Aren't you doing the same now?"

"We aren't talking about throwing Jesus at gay marriage. This is a crime, and a fucking serious one!"

"Sure, from one point of view," Tapsa smiled. "And yet at the same time, somewhere in this modern world of ours a Muslim dad kills his daughter because she's seeing the wrong guy. In some Iranian village a woman is stoned, or burned, because she got raped, or because she is seen as shaming her husband's family. In those cases murder is seen as the only option. As merciful and justified, as a liberation for everyone involved."

"What a pity we didn't meet in Iran," Laukia laughed contemptuously.

"Isn't it true, though, that laws and religions are all human inventions? They were created to serve a worldly purpose, and the number of purposes the world has to offer is surprisingly large. Civilization is a sleight-of-hand. If human beings truly were superior beings solemnly charged by God to dominate all other creatures, this primitive desire wouldn't drive me."

Laukia shook his head. "I couldn't do it to my daughter. How could I live with myself afterward?"

Tapsa sipped his tea and gave Laukia a moment to gather his thoughts. "Time heals all wounds," he finally said with an understanding smile. "Your shared grief would bring the two of you closer."

Laukia stuffed a piece of nicotine gum in his mouth, then hid his violently trembling hands in his lap. "What if I say no?"

"Then you say no."

Laukia gulped. He couldn't look Tapsa in the eye. "Would you kill me?"

"No. I'd just disappear from your life. Even if you changed your mind, and later wanted to take me up on my offer, that option would never be on the table again."

Laukia sighed with relief and nodded his head. "Maybe it's not . . . such a terrible thing."

"Well," Tapsa said with a fleeting smile, closing his book, "you know the answer to that better than I."

Laukia was afraid he was about to burst into tears. His mind simply could not grasp the enormity with which it had been burdened. It had all been staged, all of it, from the very beginning. His wallet hadn't dropped out of his pocket: Tapsa had lifted it, knowing at a very early stage what Laukia had to offer him. And what did Tapsa have to offer Laukia? A ghastly service that would become a secret that would haunt Laukia for the rest of his life. But for that price, that unbelievably heavy price, he would *gain* the rest of his life. He would be free. Not unconditionally free, certainly, but freer than he'd been for a quarter of a century. And after hearing this offer, could he return to living in a cage? Could he look himself in the mirror and meet the eyes not only of an alcoholic who had thrown his life away, but a coward?

Laukia's wife had been murdering her husband for twenty-five years.

Now it was Laukia's turn.

"Okay."

"Okay what?"

"Let's do it."

"Really?" Tapsa smiled.

"Yeah," Laukia nodded. "What do I do?"

"Nothing. As I said, all you have to do is make sure you've got an alibi. I've done this lots of times. I don't make mistakes."

Laukia's head was trembling with uncertainty, but he forced it to nod.

"The less you know about what I'm going to do, the better it will be for you."

"I believe you."

"It'll happen one week from today, while you're at the AA meeting. Will your wife definitely be home alone?"

"She will."

"Speak up at the meeting. After that, go out to eat some-where. Talk to people, be visible. Don't overact, but play it so that you're seen, so you have eyewitnesses."

"Got it."

"It won't be an easy week for you," Tapsa said, giving Laukia's arm a squeeze, "but I promise that after it's over things will take a marked turn for the better."

"I don't know why I even want to say this, but . . ." Laukia found himself swallowing a sob. "Promise that you won't hurt her too much."

"Too much?"

"Jesus Christ!" Laukia snapped. "Promise you'll do it quickly."

"I'll do it however I feel like doing it in the moment," the man replied carelessly. "You have to understand that after this conversation is over we have a binding agreement, and if you try to break it, the consequences for you will be horrific. What you are doing in this conversation is handing her over to me. She is my property now, and I'll do to her whatever I have to do."

Laukia cleared his throat and dabbed at the sweat coursing down his face.

"Are we crystal-clear on that?" Tapsa insisted.

Laukia nodded in agreement. "Do you want to see her photo?"

"No," Tapsa said sharply. "I want to see her face for the first time at the same instant she sees mine."

"Goddamn," Laukia muttered, turning his face away and pressing his palms against his eyes so hard that his knuckles glowed white.

"Do you have a security system in your house that I should know about?"

"No. And the nearest neighbors are a hundred meters away."

"Then we have nothing to worry about," Tapsa said with a sweet smile.

Laukia rested his face on his palms, breathing heavily through his mouth. Tapsa got up out of his chair and came to stand briefly next to him.

"If this all seems way too easy, believe me, it'll get tougher," the pleasant bureaucrat lookalike killer said, and laid a hand on Laukia's shoulder. "But no matter how tough it gets, remember that you won't get caught. It can be a bitch, at first, living with the guilt, but weigh that against what you're gaining."

Laukia looked up at Tapsa and saw on his face the same warm smile he was wearing the first time they met.

"Thanks," Tapsa said, and stuck out his hand for Laukia to shake. Laukia noticed now for the first time how muscular it was, how inappropriate it seemed at the end of that body. He hesitated for a moment before taking the hand that would end his wife's life.

"Thank *you*," Laukia said, an exhausted smile playing at the corners of his mouth.

The anonymous alcoholic picked up his bag and his umbrella and headed through the restaurant toward the door. Then he disappeared into the faceless and nameless current of humanity coursing through the station, and Laukia never saw him again.

IV

If the week before his meeting with Madame Kismet had zipped by as if on fast forward, the seven days before the next AA meeting crawled by at a snail's pace. Laukia didn't sleep at all that week. Every night he lay in bed awake and stared at the unsuspecting person lying beside him. The wee hours of the morning were the worst. Then his subconscious came alive, tormenting him with the most lurid storms of guilt.

Could I be the one after all? What if our marital problems are my fault? Could we start over? Maybe flee together? What if he found us?

Night after night that last thought threatened to fibrillate Laukia's heart. He saw Tapsa standing over in the corner of their darkened bedroom with a bread knife in his hand, his black eyeballs gleaming with death—and after that vision it was pointless to hope for sleep.

Laukia had "forgotten" his phone, left it lying on the bedroom floor in front of the wardrobe, when he headed out for the AA meeting a little early—deviating only slightly from his usual routine.

When he left, his wife was down in the basement drying the autumn potato harvest.

What if she hears Tapsa breaking into the house, manages to close the fire door, and call the cops? What if Tapsa is still in the house when I come home?

Laukia realized that he was facing an evening that would mercilessly try his mental stability. *How on earth am I going to act normal?* Tapsa had even asked him to go out for dinner after, to a restaurant! *No way is that going to work! Everyone will see the guilt shining on my face like a neon sign.*

On the train ride from Kirkkonummi into downtown Helsinki, Laukia managed to calm himself just enough so that he was no longer trembling or sweating. A couple of stiff drinks would have worked wonders, but tonight of all nights it was important not to backslide and give the cops the slightest cause for suspicion.

The AA meeting seemed to last forever. Laukia could remember having spoken up every week before, but had absolutely no memory of what he'd been saying today. As the other members took their turns, said their bit, all he could think of was his house, and his wife in the basement.

How would Tapsa get in? Boldly ring the doorbell? What would he do to his victim first? Stun her and tie her up, or kill her quickly and cleanly? Would his wife realize before dying that her husband was behind the whole thing?

Will the last breath she takes be spent screaming my name?

Laukia was torn out of his thoughts when the leader adjourned the meeting and wished everybody present strength and a blessed week ahead.

Laukia headed down Bulevardi toward Stockmann's, where he managed to kill almost half an hour. He wandered through the departments, stopped to chat with a few salesladies, and hoped they would remember him as a polite and good-natured person—someone who wasn't acting strangely.

To his great fortune he ran into a couple who used to live near him, caught up on the news with them, and managed to get his wife into the conversation: "She's doing fine, thanks, I'll pass along your greetings! And please come see us around Christmas!"

Laukia began to feel relief setting in as he exited the department store.

Maybe the deed is already done. Maybe Tapsa has filled his annual quota and disappeared from my life. So has my wife. Permanently.

Laukia stopped one more time, to down a couple of non-alcoholic drinks at Casa Largo, before heading home. At the bar he chatted for a while with a Swedish businessman, offering him tips on Helsinki restaurants. The bartender put his oar in on the subject as well, and Laukia felt that he had found himself two more witnesses who would confirm his alibi.

As he left the bar, Laukia was filled with the kind of warm feeling he imagined a convict would feel upon being released from life in prison.

Remember that you won't get caught, Tapsa had said. Now, for the first time, Laukia began to let himself believe it.

V

It wasn't a long walk from the Kirkkonummi train station to the Laukias' home. Would the cops be there already? Laukia considered this, then shook his head. No: who would have called them?

He now realized that it was his job to find the body.

What if Tapsa used a bread knife again? Laukia felt a stab of fear pierce him. Nausea roiled up in his stomach. *Let's just hope he broke a window. I can call the cops if a window's been broken. They would tell me to stay outside in the yard, in case the intruder is still in the house. And since I left my phone at home, I'd have to go to the neighbors, and they would see too how scared I am.*

The thought nearly brought a smile to Laukia's lips, but he managed to keep a poker face. Even now a random dog-walker could ruin everything: *Yeah, I saw Laukia walking home from the train station. He was smiling like he'd won the lottery!*

He turned into the cul-de-sac that led to his house, and saw the blue lights flashing against the dark late-evening sky. He took a few running steps, and the house's silhouette emerged from behind the thick firs. Then he stopped as if hitting a wall: their front yard was full of vehicles—an ambulance, police squad cars, and crime-scene investigators' cars. The cops had cordoned off the yard, but a few neighbors had already shown up.

Laukia gulped and ran a hand through his hair. *Did Tapsa blow it?* Panic swept over his mind like a tidal wave. *Should I turn and run?*

Maybe Tapsa had killed Laukia's wife in the yard, and someone had seen the body? That must be it.

He forced his legs to propel him forward. He slogged toward the emergency vehicles. His eyes fell on the ambulance, its rear doors gaping open. A uniform cop and two EMTs stood there talking to the figure lying on the gurney.

Laukia felt his legs growing heavier with every step. His heart was pounding like a sledgehammer. His ears were filled with a loud rushing sound.

The uniform cop turned toward the street, saw Laukia, and shouted something. Laukia didn't hear a word.

The EMTs stepped away from the gurney, and at that instant Laukia's eyes met his wife's. He felt the blood drain from his head, and his consciousness crash. His legs buckled underneath him, and he dropped to the wet asphalt on his back.

Running footfalls echoed somewhere out on the peripheries of his consciousness. The EMTs kneeled beside him, bent over him. Only with great effort could he keep his eyes open.

"My wife," Laukia whispered. "What happened?"

"Someone broke into your house," the uniform cop said, as one of the EMTs supported Laukia's head. "Your wife is alive, but . . ."

"But?" Laukia felt the tears running hot down his cheeks. He raised his head and saw his wife on the ambulance gurney. Her face was distorted with an unfathomable agony, and she was screaming at the top of her lungs.

An older cop bent down nearer to Laukia and looked him in the eye. "Your daughter was found murdered in the house."

Laukia stared back at the cop in horror, his eyes like saucers. "That's not possible," he whispered, an invisible fist tightening its grip on his windpipe. "Kaisa . . . lives in Berlin . . ."

"Your wife wasn't home when it happened. Your daughter had come in with her own key. Preliminary investigations suggest that the perpetrator was already inside the house, waiting . . ." The police officer's voice faded out to nothing.

"A killer like this," one of the EMTs said to his colleagues, "always gets caught."

"This one *won't* get caught!" Laukia's sharp retort startled the EMTs and older police officer.

The man sitting there on the asphalt stared into his wife's eyes, a strange, disturbed smile spreading slowly across his ash-gray face. "This was a dead cinch."

PART III

Winds of Violence

GOOD INTENTIONS

BY JESSE ITKONEN

Itäkeskus

The girl wore white. A sleek summer dress that grasped her hips like a lover. She had jet-black hair that hugged her milky-white shoulders. She sat opposite Koskinen on the metro for the long ride from the city center back home and he found himself staring. She caught his eye and they both looked away awkwardly. When the train rumbled into the Itäkeskus stop, they were the last two in the car. A tall man stood at the platform, waiting. She ran into his arms as Koskinen quietly sidestepped them and ascended the escalators.

He crossed the bridge over Turuntie and the girl and her man followed. He heard her crooning and him responding in monosyllables. The cracked boulevard led them toward a hive of cheap apartment buildings. The man and the girl ducked into an underpass and disappeared from view. Koskinen played with the thought of one day escorting a girl like that home, then dismissed it as fast as it occurred to him.

Behind him, he heard a sharp scream cut short. He knew the sound all too well. No matter the source, it always rang the same. The panicked yelp and sudden comprehension of things turning sour. He'd heard it from women at the bar, when their men had too much to drink and even more to prove. He'd heard it from his mother, when she wasn't quick enough to evade his father of the week. He turned on his heels and looked back at an empty street. He thought of the girl with milky-white shoulders and black hair and found himself walking toward the underpass.

Koskinen wasn't a big man. He wasn't short, but in that massive pit of *average* that infuriated him so. In the seventh grade, he had shaved his head to fit in and the habit stuck. There was no ideology behind it, he told himself, and often believed it as well. When you fought someone, it didn't matter what the color of his skin was. Everyone bruised the same.

The girl was pressed against the wall of the underpass, her man's hand around her chin. "Where'd you put it?" the guy was saying over and over. "Where'd you put it, you bitch?!" Again and again she whispered something frantic and each time he repeated himself louder and louder. Koskinen saw as the tall guy's hand rose from her mouth and, just as she was about to respond, returned back with force. The slap knocked her head backward. Koskinen didn't waste time with pleasantries. He dove at the guy and both of them toppled to the ground. The guy squirmed and Koskinen sat on his chest. He pressed his knees on the guy's hands and applied pressure. The girl yelped in panic and skirted out of the way.

"What the fuck?" The tall guy's eyes focused on Koskinen, who answered the stare. "I'll fucking kill you, asshole!" he squealed, and Koskinen slammed him in the face. "Fucker!" Another hit.

He kept punching until the responses stopped coming and a soft, helpless whimper took their place.

Koskinen picked himself up and wiped his hand on the guy's shirt. His knuckles were bleeding and already swollen. He turned to the girl and suddenly felt guilty about something. She pushed him aside and tended to the tall guy who whimpered her name and cried. She shushed him and said they'd be home soon. She took Koskinen aside and told him to leave, her boyfriend meant no harm.

He watched from one end of the underpass as she helped the tall guy up and carried his weight while they stumbled out the other end and out of view. He wasn't sure who he was more angry at.

That night Koskinen spent his time drinking and counting the lines on the ceiling. The apartment above his echoed and he listened. Finnish sounded like machine-gun fire when people spoke angrily. A blitzkrieg of rolling r's and emphasized v's. At one point, the police had responded to domestic disturbances quite quickly in the area, but now it was easier to get a taxi on a weekend than it was to find a police car.

He thought of the people living up there. The woman was a redhead, he knew that much. The man he'd seen once or twice and didn't much like him. They'd lived there for about six months and had maybe exchanged three words in the hall-way. *You could pack us like sardines in a can,* he thought to himself, *and we'd still do our best to avoid communication.* Koskinen didn't have a girlfriend to call his own—not if he was honest with himself—but he was certain that if he did, he'd never be mean to her.

The next morning he saw the redhead. She was taking the trash out as Koskinen leaned over the thin railing of his French balcony and practiced blowing smoke rings. Her chin touched her neck and every step she took was deliberate and careful, like she was dancing in a minefield. When she turned back toward the apartments, she glanced up, her eyes focusing in the sunlight. Koskinen gave her a wave; she didn't respond.

When he got to work that night, Koskinen wasn't feeling like himself. Most nights he could navigate the bar like he was wearing blinders; today he felt raw and exposed like a nerve.

"What you need," said Nalle, as they were bringing up crates from the basement, "is a woman." He waggled his eyebrows and grinned. He looked to Koskinen like a pug dog that had collided with a wall at top speed. Koskinen assured him that he was fine, which Nalle took to mean that he was looking for a guy and replied that Koskinen should forget it as he was already spoken for.

At home again, he listened to the neighbors shout. Someone threw dishes. They shattered on the floor directly above him and the house fell silent. As the sun came up, he thought he heard sobbing echo in the pipework. After breakfast, he sat smoking on the benches near the trash shelter. After three smokes, the redhead came down with trash bags that jingled with empty bottles.

"Morning," Koskinen offered. She responded quietly. Her bangs were brushed over her right eye and her face was heavy with makeup. "I live downstairs," Koskinen said, more bluntly than he had intended.

She threw the trash into the bin. "I'm sorry," she responded.

"It's not me you need to apologize to."

She shrugged. "Force of habit. Can I bum one?"

Koskinen lit a smoke and handed it to her. He offered her a seat; she remained standing.

"You okay?" he asked.

She blew smoke. "You lived here long?"

Koskinen nodded.

"Then do you really need to ask?"

They continued to smoke in silence for a bit. She took long drags and held the smoke in longer. Koskinen sipped at his smoke, not in a hurry to go anywhere. He stole looks at her and thought of something to say. She did it for him.

"How long did it take you to gather up your courage to come and talk?"

Koskinen coughed, the smoke going down the wrong pipe.

She grinned and he felt a rush go through his stomach like he was on a roller coaster. "My guess is a week."

He had no answer.

She dropped the rest of her smoke, now down to the filter, and stepped on it, then held out her hand. "Kati."

Koskinen shook her hand. "Jari."

She smiled and he returned it. "I'll be fine, Jari, he doesn't mean it." She turned and walked back into the apartments, leaving Koskinen to wonder if someone could be both turned on and angry at the same time.

Weekends were a time to vent. The bar would fill up with people and you had no time for thoughts of your own. Koskinen worked the downstairs—where the people could escape the dance floor located above—alone. As the lights flickered for last call, Nalle wobbled down the stairs and came behind the bar. "You're off early tonight, get outta here."

"Something wrong?" Koskinen asked, and handed a beer to a young guy who could barely stand.

Nalle placed his hand on Koskinen's shoulder. "You, sir, have a date."

He pushed the hand off. "No, I don't."

Nalle shook his head and pointed at the stairs. "Yes, you do."

Koskinen looked and Nalle grinned. By the stairs lounged a petite blond girl who was wearing something Koskinen didn't think qualified as a whole piece of clothing.

Nalle pushed him away from the tap. "No need to thank me."

"No thanks."

Nalle frowned. "What do you mean?"

"I don't know her, who the fuck is she? Besides, I've got things to do."

Nalle sighed, annoyed. "Her name is Elise, she works in the city, likes lots of things including—most importantly— you!"

Koskinen gave him a suspicious look. "Why?"

"*Why*? If you need an answer for that, you've got bigger problems than a girl, man." Nalle wiped at his eyes. "She said you look like Bruce Willis, so maybe that's why, but who gives a shit?"

Koskinen frowned. "I look nothing like Bruce Willis."

"You're bald," Nalle said, and Koskinen nodded in the affirmative. "Close enough." Nalle waved at Elise and gestured for her to come over. She sauntered in a deliberate, practiced manner that screamed lustful and filthy carnage with every sway of the hip. "Elise, this is my friend I was telling you about."

She smiled with a row of blinding pearly whites and held out her hand. Her skin was smooth as silk and Koskinen couldn't help but smile. "Nalle says you're having an after-party," she cooed.

Koskinen glanced at Nalle, who whispered in his ear, "I left a few bottles in your bag, you crazy kids have fun."

They took a taxi home and Koskinen tried clumsily to make conversation. She smiled coyly and answered with a word or two, her hands brushing at his shoulders and playing with his ear. By the time they got to his apartment, her tongue had found its way into his mouth.

"Do you want a drink?" he asked as he came up for air.

She shook her head and her hair danced on her shoulders. "I'm good," she purred as she advanced, her fingers gliding over the buttons of his shirt. She opened the top one and the rest parted like Moses had met the Red Sea. Koskinen sighed sharply and took another step back. She looked him in the eye. "Is this your first time?"

"No," Koskinen replied. "It's just . . . how did you say you knew Nalle?"

She studied his face. "You know," she said, half-smiling, and kissed his chest.

Koskinen considered this. "Know what?"

Her shoulders slumped and for the first time she looked annoyed. She peered up at him from under her brow. He stared back at her, confused. Her features softened and for a second the huntress took a break. She raised her head and gave him the look that people give when everyone else is in on the joke except for you. "*You know*," she repeated, pressing the words.

Her cab arrived in ten minutes, which felt like an eternity. Koskinen escorted her to the door. He apologized for wasting her time and she shook her head and touched his cheek and assured him that she had already been paid.

The building was silent. He lay down on his bed and didn't sleep until the sun crept up the following morning.

Nalle demanded details at work, none of which Koskinen provided. They worked on separate floors again and Koskinen left without talking to anyone.

Smoking in the yard soon became a habit. After a while, Kati started taking the trash out at the same time he was out, even if there wasn't much to bring. Sometimes she smoked, other times she didn't. She wore more makeup on the days that she did. Sometimes they talked a lot, other days they barely exchanged words. Every so often he asked her if she was happy and every time she responded by smiling and changing the topic.

"You need to find yourself a girl, you know," she said one day. "Nice guy like you."

He shifted uncomfortably in his seat and looked away. "I dunno."

She grinned. "A guy then?" He flipped her the bird and she cackled. "Would be better for you, women are crazy."

In his dream they shared a house outside of Itäkeskus. Somewhere where you couldn't hear the road. He saw a forest and fields. Anything but roads. No beggars by the metro. No metro at all. In the dream she wore no makeup and smiled from ear to ear.

A sound of crashing dishes broke into his dream and he woke with a start. He leaned up and checked the time on his phone. Three in the morning. He pulled on pants, opened the door to the balcony, and went out for a smoke. There was a faint echo of sobbing running through the pipes.

Weekend came and he disappeared into his work. He took the road through the underpass home. Nobody walked on the road and most of the lights in the houses were off. He counted his steps and walked by muscle memory and didn't see the parked van until he almost ran into it. An ambulance with its back doors open. The door had been propped open into the stairwell of his building. Koskinen could feel his stomach cramp up and something heavy sink to the pit of it. Two paramedics came down the stairs, carrying someone on a stretcher. Koskinen gave them room and craned his neck to see who. He didn't need to; he already knew the moment he saw the ambulance.

Kati was lying on the stretcher with her eyes closed and a

part of her head wrapped with gauze. The white towel under her head was soaked on one side with blood. Koskinen pushed his way closer. "What happened?"

A flustered voice spoke over the paramedics: "She slipped."

Koskinen turned toward the door. A man with messy hair, drunken eyes, and insecurities pouring out of his ears—whom Koskinen recognized as Kati's boyfriend Jarno—stood by the door. He was covered in hipster clothing, some of which Koskinen was sure was meant for women. His eyes kept darting between the paramedics and Koskinen, trying to see who bought the story. He came up with nil. Koskinen glanced at the paramedics, a younger and an older man.

The older man shrugged as if to say, *Look, we just do the driving.* "She'll be okay in a day or two. We're going to take her to the hospital for the night." They gave Jarno the name of the hospital and drove off.

Koskinen pushed past Jarno, who jumped back like a frightened dog. "She's just so clumsy, you know?" he simpered. Koskinen stopped and turned. Jarno shrugged. "Just doesn't look where she's going."

Koskinen stepped closer. "She do this often?"

"Oh yeah, man, well, you've seen her." Jarno gestured at him like it meant something.

"Have I?"

"You know, talking to her and stuff; she's a klutz."

Koskinen smiled. "Funny." He chuckled and Jarno tried joining in. "She never seemed like that around me." They stopped laughing. Koskinen turned away. "Must be the company she keeps." He ascended the stairs and left Jarno at the door.

* * *

He told Nalle about Kati the following night. Nalle, in turn, told some of the regulars. It was quiet and they'd decided to keep the upstairs closed. It was soon decided that men who hit women are not men at all. The regulars—former factory workers, others permanently unemployed—talked, each relaying stories of what they'd seen or heard. The women told of old flames who had hurt them and the men swore up and down that they would never do such a thing. The women cooed and cackled. "Now that's a man!"

Had anyone asked him a few days earlier, Koskinen might have joined in as well. He would have waxed lyrical about what to do with men like that, how beating them in return seemed too kind, and someone would have laughed and he would have felt sated, his dreams filling the hole in his heart because he knew that talking wasn't enough. Not tonight though. Tonight all Koskinen thought of was slick plastic polymer and the chiseled pistol grip that he could still feel pressed into his hand. He cleared glasses from tables and joked with the regulars, but he might as well have been doing it over a phone.

The clock struck two and the last stragglers wandered out. Koskinen closed shop and picked up his bag from the back room. He felt its bottom and something hard brushed against his fingertips. That very morning he had bought a gun from people who asked no questions and barely spoke the same language, and it had taken him most of the day to realize just how much it actually weighed.

Before the gun and that night, Koskinen would probably never have considered ever handling a weapon again. He'd done his mandatory military service, and knew which way to point a gun. Everything else was stuff he didn't care about. And if he didn't care about something, it may as well have never existed. The redhead, Kati, she existed, and someone had to do something.

When he got home he pulled his chair next to the front door and waited. He listened to the footsteps in the corridor and counted the floors as the elevator hummed up and down. The door downstairs clanged shut and someone entered the lift. It droned past Koskinen's floor and stopped at the one above. He slipped the door ajar and listened. Keys jingled as they scraped at the lock on a door. Quietly, Koskinen slid out of the apartment, walked up to the landing between floors, and waited. Jarno pulled the door open and Koskinen was upon him.

He pressed the gun into the back of Jarno's head and shoved him inside. The door slammed shut behind them and the room fell dark. Koskinen fumbled at the light switch and Jarno bolted into the other room screaming, "What the fuck, what the fuck, what the fuck?!"

Koskinen flicked the switch on in the living room. Jarno turned and all color drained from his cheeks. He stared at Koskinen, at the gun in his hand and the void in his eyes. A stain ran down his trouser leg and his body turned to Jell-O. The acidic smell of piss mixed with the reek of stale alcohol.

The French balcony behind him opened to a view of the front yard, high enough so that people couldn't see in. "Open the door," Koskinen ordered, his voice menacing. Jarno did as he was told. He avoided eye contact and mumbled something that got stuck in his throat.

"You know what it's like with some people?" Koskinen asked. Jarno whimpered. Koskinen exhaled sharply. "They're really clumsy."

Jarno weighed very little. Koskinen could feel his ribs as he shoved him over the railing. The guy didn't struggle. He sobbed, but didn't struggle. His upper body flopped over the thin metal railing. His legs flipped over and into the emptiness. There was a short scream and a sudden stop. Koskinen didn't look over. He backed up and left the room as it was, the balcony door an empty frame where Jarno had just been.

As he closed the door to his own apartment, Koskinen stood and listened. The building was silent. He didn't hear screaming or ambulances until morning.

Kati returned from the hospital three days later. Her eyes were as red as her hair and she didn't look up as she got out of the taxi. She slumped and dragged her feet. She rode the elevator in silence and disappeared into her apartment where, moments later, she broke into hysterical and inconsolable sobbing. Koskinen listened and practiced what to say. It pained him to hear her.

He knocked on her door and the wailing stopped. He heard her tiny footsteps approach and stop. The door didn't open. He peered through the peephole and saw her standing motionless by the door. She wiped her eyes and reached for the lock. The door opened with the security chain still attached.

Koskinen felt a stab of pain in his chest. He stammered, "I c-came to see if you were okay."

She sniffed. "No."

He shifted his weight. "Can I help?"

She shook her head and didn't meet his eye. "No."

His face fell and he took a step back. "I'm sorry to bother you," he said and turned toward the stairs. She looked up and watched as he gently raised his hand to gesture goodbye. Kati closed the door and Koskinen could hear the lock jingle and fall. She reopened the door, fully this time.

They sat on opposite sides of the living room. She didn't offer anything to drink and he didn't ask for anything. They did this for what seemed like a long time. Koskinen stared at her and realized that she had shrunk. Her figure was tiny and her shoulders were hunched. Her hair looked unwashed and her cheeks were gaunt.

"Why are you so sad?" he asked. It escaped his mouth the moment he thought it and echoed in the room like a deafening explosion.

She finally whispered, "What?"

He leaned forward. "You're free now. Why are you sad?"

She screwed up her face, fighting hard not to cry. "Fucking asshole."

He nodded. "He *was* a fucking asshole, he—"

"I'M TALKING ABOUT YOU!" she screamed, and it made his ears ring worse than anything ever had in his life. He felt his cheeks grow hot and his posture collapse. He looked confused, which enraged her further.

"He. Loved. Me," she hissed.

He shook his head, not believing what he was hearing.

She nodded and tears fell more freely. "He loved me. He didn't mean to do anything. He just had a temper. And I told him—he came to see me in the hospital—I told him he could just go to hell. Die for all I care. I told him that and he jumped off a balcony." She was sobbing loudly again. Koskinen wondered if he could just hold her; she'd see then that things were all right. She sniffed and sobbed and hiccuped. "Why would he do that?"

"He was drunk," Koskinen said, finally. "He was drunk and stupid and didn't deserve you."

Kati bolted up. "Get out," she spat. "Get out right the fuck now."

Koskinen stood up; this was one of the few times he towered over someone. "I was—" he began, then stopped. "I'm just trying to help."

She pointed at the door. "I never asked for your fucking *help*. Who do you think you are? Get the fuck out of my house."

Koskinen moved toward the door. "I don't get it," he muttered. She cocked her head. "I just don't get you women. You get together with these spineless shits and you take the punches day in, day out, and you put on more makeup and pretend like nobody notices. Then when someone does and tries to do something about it, all you do is mope and whine after the shit who did this to you." He felt himself burning from the inside out. "You like being where you are, is that it? You like this? You like being scared? I can make you scared. It's easy. The easiest thing in the world. You know what's hard? Love. Love is fucking hard." He was breathing fire and his fists were clenched. He stopped speaking and inhaled deeply. His eyes darted to his hand and a shiver of guilt coursed through him.

She had moved away. Her back touched the glass between the apartment and the balcony. She stood where Jarno had stood and looked just as scared as he had. She cried, "What are you?"

Koskinen contemplated this. "I'm just a nice guy."

He disappeared into the hall and closed the door after him as Kati slumped on the floor and howled as quietly as she could into the palm of her hand.

He sat in his chair and smoked for what seemed like hours. He stared at the walls and shifted in his seat. His legs were numb, but he didn't bother to get up. Kati had been scared of him. *Of him.* And for what? Helping her.

There was shuffling upstairs. More sobbing. Then voices. He listened. One voice, Kati's. She was on the phone. He stood up and his legs twisted and screamed pain. He balanced himself on the chair and cocked his ear upward. She was sobbing to someone. He couldn't make out what, but she was frantic. Then he heard the words, clear as anything else: "Help me." He could hear the balcony door creak open and her heavy breathing carried down with the wind.

Koskinen sat down again and stretched his legs. Whoever she was calling would show up. Sooner or later. Probably would take longer than ordering a cab. Nah, he thought, if she doesn't see it, others will. They can come here, he said to himself, and they can talk. They can say whatever they like and point any fingers they want—but they'll know. Deep down, they'll know and they'll think, *He did right by her*. In the end, who knows, maybe she will too. She'll wake up one day and not be scared. She'll look around and realize she didn't have to put on more makeup or tiptoe around her own life anymore. She'll realize it.

All he wanted to do was help.

This story was originally written in English.

THE BROKER

BY KARO HÄMÄLÄINEN

Fabianinkatu

Translated by Jill G. Timbers

The man is standing in the rain. He lets the raindrops hammer his head and soak his hair and his numbingly expensive suit.

He could wait for a taxi under the shelter or indoors, where the wind, whipped into a storm gale, wouldn't slash at his chin, cheeks, and nose, but he does not want to turn anywhere for help. He doesn't want help, nor shelter. He has to cope on his own. He has to be alone.

He's lost several million, but in truth he's lost more than that.

Gains and losses are part of stock trading—the gains should just be greater than the losses. This loss has been more money than any earlier gain, but he can handle that. Being taken is the hard part for him to swallow. He's the one who's used to outwitting the others, not the one who has to pay the bill.

He has lost everything, and he wants to get wet. He wants to walk home on the asphalt strewn with yellow leaves. He wants to be blinded by the xenon lights of cars that appear from nowhere in the rain, to let the wetness soak into his clothes and glue his hair to his skull. For he wants to think about what there is when there is nothing.

I

He stood in front of the granite wall of the Helsinki Stock Exchange building and felt old. Yesterday, or twenty-five years ago, he had strode briskly through the glass doors, leaving the others behind both with his steps up the staircase and with his decisions in the trading hall on the second floor.

He exerted himself to keep his posture erect and he had learned to raise his chin, because small things like a gaze fastened on the ground spoke louder than words in shaping the image of a person's vigor.

He could do nothing about the fact that his face resembled sand after a downpour. When they'd taken pictures of him for his seventieth-birthday interview in the *Helsingin Sanomat*, the newspaper's photographer had arranged the lights so that the furrows cast deep shadows on his face. In the pictures he looked like old Samuel Beckett, just as the photographer had wanted. He looked like what Ernest Hemingway would have liked to look like.

After that he had refused to be photographed, even at family celebrations. Not because he was ashamed of his wrinkles, but because a less skilled photographer would not be able to take such rugged shots. The series of photos, to which he had bought the rights, showed a man who had weathered wind and hail.

Harsh conditions had made him tough, and even though the harshness of the conditions was not in his case the result of natural forces but rather of the capriciousness of market forces, his background gave him a strength you can only obtain through living.

The man wore a refined everyday suit, dark gray with pale gray pinstripes. It was the work of one of the city's rare

224 // HELSINKI NOIR

tailors who through the years had always adjusted measure-
ments by eye—added a few millimeters to the waist and back
seam, tucked a bit somewhere else. He had noticed it when
he sometimes tried on the old suits that still hung in his closet
like skeletons of times past: the suit he had worn to receive an
honorary doctorate from the school of economics, the suit in
which he had celebrated the ten million marks he'd made off
the Metsä-Serla warrant.

Blue he had never liked, even though it was favored by the
patriotic. His fatherland was money, which knows no color.

When he stared at himself in the window of the clothing store on the ground floor of the hundred-year-old granite
building, he saw a man who looked like him: someone pleased
with himself, dignified, respected, someone who enjoyed company and could still captivate a small group, but who drew
back the moment people appeared whom he did not know.

He looked, in fact, too thriving, considering that someone
had tried to kill him earlier that morning.

He was Ransu Grundström; Rafael, in official documents.
The nickname was unusual for one his age and brought to
mind the children's TV puppet dog—everywhere in Finland
except this neighborhood. At the Helsinki Stock Exchange,
Ransu meant nothing but Grundström, the legendary securities dealer who founded the brokerage that ruled the Finnish
stock exchange business in the 1980s and early 1990s.

R. Grundström Brokerage was famous for its bold ma-
neuvers, both on behalf of its clients and for its own benefit.
Some years Grundström brokered more trades than even the
securities trading units of the traditional commercial banks
Kansallis-Osake-Pankki and Suomen Yhdyspankki. This
lead position meant that Ransu had all the information that
moved within Helsinki. No one dared enter the game without

first asking his view or without informing him. Anyone who overlooked the rule discovered he had lost money, because R. Grundström Brokerage would attack the markets aggressively and force their opponent to operate the way they wanted. That is what Ransu did if he felt that someone intended to move on his own, or against Ransu's interests.

He had conducted bruising battles and driven his smaller competitors into bankruptcy. He had recruited the sharpest brokers to his firm, and no one had ever declined. Along with success, he offered merit-based pay, which was very unusual in a Finland accustomed to fixed monthly wages and as close to the Soviet Union as a country that called itself "Western" could be.

"Good morning, Ransu!"

Mr. Lauri Rosendahl, CEO of the Helsinki Stock Exchange, waited, holding the door open. Grundström stepped inside and the CEO hastened to open the second door.

They briefly discussed the situation with the US housing markets, and the previous night's PMI that had caused US markets to drop. The fall had continued in Asia, the CEO reported, as he checked the real-time Nikkei score on his iPhone. The anticipated index futures indicated that Helsinki would open to a fall as well when the first trades were made after ten a.m.

When Ransu Grundström had stepped through the outer door of this same building every day thirty years ago, brokers had not talked about index futures but about companies whose shares they sold to each other and bought from each other at two-person desks in the great trading hall on the second floor, rather than sending bulk orders electronically to a data center somewhere in Sweden based on what had happened in US and Asian markets.

Nowadays the stock exchange building was a hollow place. Trading had gone electronic by the early 1990s. The company running the stock exchange had first ended up under Swedish ownership and most recently been sold to the world's largest exchange operator, NASDAQ, known best as the quotation market for hot IT and biotech companies. Ownership of the pale gray granite fortress designed by Lars Sonck had been parked at a foundation.

NASDAQ's Finnish office did not need many employees or square feet. The old stock exchange hall that had once doubled as a meeting room for the city council now served occasionally as a seminar space, and the rooms on the Fabianinkatu side had been turned into offices.

Grundström had leased one of these for himself. Not because he needed office space—he was retired and traded only occasionally, for the sheer love of it. On the upper level of his two-story home in Kaivopuisto Park he had a fully equipped office with a broad view of the sea. Here, on the other side of narrow Fabianinkatu Street, there was a ramp to the Nordea building's parking garage, and that ramp, along with one side of the building, formed the main view out the window. Nonetheless, Grundström had made his offer the moment he heard that space was being freed up from stock exchange use, and he had agreed to renovations at his own expense, without trying to negotiate a lower rent.

The location was practical, between Esplanade and Aleksanterinkatu, a block from the main market square and a short walk from his home. Most important, there was an indoor stairway he could use to get from the office to the Bourse Club where Grundström made a habit of lunching. The lordly, conservative atmosphere of the exclusive club felt cozy to him. He might laugh at some details, but at the same time he took pleasure in the fact that modernization had not yet reached quite everywhere.

Here he could live amid the days of his own greatness. For it could not be denied: his greatness was history, visible as affluence, independence, and prestige, but it had been at least ten years since he had been a feared market force. Nor was there need to deny it. Disregarding facts was one sure way to lower your chances on the markets.

The massive walls of the granite fortress sheltered Grundström from the winds of change that whipped wildly past and caused the stock markets to plunge and soar with abandon. The once radical daredevil had become a conservative whose thoughts frequently escaped to the intense trading of shares of now-forgotten and repeatedly merged companies.

Ransu Grundström shut himself into his office, which had no nameplate on the door. He spread the *Financial Times* on the dark-stained conference table from the building's original furnishings and skimmed the pages without paying much attention, looking at the headlines and pictures. There was so much information that you couldn't gather, analyze, and manage it all. The present time operated with different logic than the 1980s, when information was limited and you could make money simply by concentrating.

After reading the paper he went to freshen up in the bathroom, which sported unnecessarily modern furnishings. A family-owned investment firm that had made its fortune in faucets controlled the office next door, and its CEO was one of Grundström's regular lunch companions. The man had managed to convince somebody that a soft stream of water and the latest design in faucets were essential for the hundred-year-old building.

Grundström looked at himself in the mirror. He tugged

the left sleeve of his suit jacket. He brushed some black polish onto his pant leg. He used a little soap to scrub the polish off his hands, enough but not too much.

At eleven thirty there was a knock on his office door.

Grundström did not have any employees. What would he do with them? He was a stockbroker and he was used to taking care of his own mundane tasks. He accepted advice and help, but he was perfectly capable of carrying his own newspaper and opening the door if someone knocked on it. He picked up coffee from the club or the Aschan Café on the next block.

On the balcony corridor that circled the inner courtyard stood a tall man. He was at the ideal age, career-wise—about thirty-five—an age when one has enough experience behind him but still hungers for success, unlike fifty-year-olds who are beginning to secure their positions and don't dare take risks. Grundström had not met this man before, though he had heard much about him.

Grundström had wanted to meet the man in person. But he did not invite him in.

II

Jarkko Aalto was among the most talented of his generation when it came to making money on the stock and derivatives markets. He had downed many liters of flavored mineral water in head hunters' conference rooms, listening to the offers their clients would make him. Then with great indifference he would say, at the end of the discussions, that he was content with his current job in the markets unit of the largest bank in the Nordic countries. The merit pay was good, advancement opportunities were available, and he had enough money at his disposal.

But when an invitation arrived from Ransu Grundström,

Aalto cleared space on his calendar by moving a breakfast meeting earlier and rescheduling a lunch. And thus it was that on each side of the threshold stood the toughest gambler of the Helsinki finance world, then and now.

"Have you eaten?" Grundström asked. Without waiting for a reply, he stepped out the door and started toward the staircase. Aalto strode beside him.

They climbed up two floors to the Bourse Club. Aalto always left his top shirt button open, but on the stairs he pulled from the breast pocket of his suit a shiny salmon-pink tie and fixed it loosely around his neck. Several loaner ties in different patterns hung from a hook in the men's room of the club where ties were required, but turning to one of those would have signaled poor preparation. One factor in Aalto's success was that he always thought through upcoming situations in advance: It was likely that they would lunch at the club, just as it was likely that the German investor who had bought UPM-Kymmene shares the day before would buy more today. With each, he'd place his bets accordingly.

They sat down at a table which Aalto guessed was Grundström's regular spot. Food selection was not difficult. They were both men who knew what they wanted, and they knew that the purpose of the lunch was not the food. They would barely notice the dishes that appeared before them.

"Do you know," Ransu Grundström said, once the waiter had filled their glasses with sparkling mineral water, "someone tried to kill me this morning."

The language of financial centers was generally filled with dramatic metaphors. Life and death were small words, used the way teenage girls discuss their infatuations. But Aalto quickly realized that Grundström was not speaking metaphorically.

"A man, just one man, grabbed me under the arms from behind as I left home. On Laivasillankatu, on the park side of the street."

Aalto knew that Grundström lived in one of Helsinki's finest areas, near the house, now a museum, of Field Marshal Carl Gustaf Emil Mannerheim, who had led the Finnish armed forces in World War II. Aalto would sometimes take international customers to that museum. Residences there cost more than in Manhattan.

"From behind some bushes, in the shadows, out of nowhere," Grundström recalled. "The streetlight is out right there." He explained that he had consistently supported a so-called night-watchman state. "All sorts of useless income transfers—cost-free university education, government pensions, lavish social security, free school lunches. Nowadays I could even accept some of that, if society would only take care of security. There should be a night watchman."

"You got away without injury."

"The bum wanted money. I tossed some bills as far as I could. He ran after them. I escaped down the hill."

Aalto listened to the former stock exchange czar's tale with fork and knife frozen and wondered if he was expected to show empathy. "It's good to have money with you," he said.

"It makes life-and-death choices easier," Grundström replied. "I saw the flash of a knife blade. He held it against my throat. It was *this* close." He showed a tiny space between his thumb and forefinger.

This sentence was followed by a considerably longer pause, which emphasized Grundström's shock; Aalto did not want to interrupt the moment, even though arrogance and flagrant disregard for convention were among the characteristics he cultivated. His indifference to propriety often annoyed his superiors, but they never said anything. One does not let go of a money machine nor even irritate it. He annoyed his superiors most of all by earning more than them.

There was a reason for Aalto's unusually respectful comportment. This man who bowed to no one admired only one person other than himself in the world of investments: Ransu Grundström.

Some ten years earlier a guest lecturer at the school of economics had gotten carried away telling stories of the wild stock exchange of the 1980s—not yet restrained by the Securities Market Act—in which the custom of the land was like that of doping in endurance sports. These stories often included the name Ransu Grundström. Aalto had known immediately that he wanted to hear more about that legendary stockbroker. He maneuvered himself to chat with the guest speaker after the lecture and was able to hear more about this broker who operated with a smuggler's morals—the secretive czar of the stock exchange.

He got hold of books on the history of the stock exchange and commercial banks, where he found Grundström in the indexes. With a disciple's dedication he drank up Grundström's intellectual world. He was not interested in Omaha ukulele players, old softies worshipped by the whole investment world. He was interested in the scruples-free stockbroker who had made his own fortune by sufficiently honest means.

Grundström said that he certainly did not want to bore a busy young man with chitchat about such a commonplace matter as death—people died all the time. He wanted to talk about these markets that were so different than they used to be.

"The computer screen is full of data and more keeps pouring in faster than you can see. Index decimals flash past.

How do you make money anymore?" Grundström asked.

The clever quips Aalto used to entertain his well-to-do guests on the streets beside Nice's beaches and in the bistros on the slopes of Alpine ski resorts would not cut it now. He had asked some older colleagues who knew Grundström about the man's personality and was told that he had no interest in empty talk. The only topic that really spoke to him was money.

"The market hasn't changed. It just looks different."

"Everything happens at lightning speed."

"It's wrong to think that speed is the decisive factor," Aalto said. "Whoever is fastest is fastest, but the stock exchange is not a hundred-yard dash. What interests me is who makes the most money."

Grundström laughed and declared that he had no reason to feel otherwise.

"You can make a little money, quickly. If you make a little money, you need to do it often. You have to hammer out trades all the time, with big capital. If you're lucky, in a day you'll make the operational expenses and a little more. If you're not lucky, you lose a lot."

"Probably quite a lot."

"A goddamn lot. No point trying for tiny profits with a million shares. Only with tens or hundreds of millions does it start to be felt. And if something goes wrong then, it's *really* felt. You have 90 percent leverage and the company posts a profit warning . . . No. Fast trading is a game of chance, and the odds are with the casino. It's a bit like the retail trade: big turnover, lots of capital, low coverage, small margins. Differentiation factors, scarce. Who would want to be the Tesco or the Walmart of the brokerage business? Who wants to fight with robots?"

Aalto noted with satisfaction that his words were sinking in. He spoke only the truth, but deliberately painted an incorrect picture. He was not lying, just adapting what he said to suit the listener.

Grundström listened to him carefully, seemingly ready to buy his story.

"I'm old-fashioned," the young man continued. "On the markets you can make a little money or a lot of money. I'm interested in the latter."

"How do you do it?"

"By buying stock that's going up before others do, or selling whatever's about to drop." So as not to sound unintentionally flippant, he hastened to add that he had his ways of sniffing out which would go up and down, and that, with the right information, you could improve the ratios. "The market's still the same in that way too. Information is power that turns to money."

"Back in the good old days when Wärtsilä was getting orders," said Grundström, "the directors swaggered about on cruises or dining at the Savoy. To make money you just needed to know the right people and use a little power of deduction. Nowadays they send out stock bulletins from every store and new office. Information has become worthless. Everyone has it."

"Information has become a *scarce* commodity. That's why it's even more valuable than before," Aalto declared.

"Is it enough for making money?"

"No. It's not enough. Fortunately, you don't need information," Jarkko Aalto explained, watching Grundström's pupils. "I don't look for truth but for market movement. Communists shout that the markets are headless. Indeed they are! I completely agree! Fundaments are reflected in prices slowly. That may be enough for a holder who wants to become prosperous. But if you want to get rich—if you don't want to make just one fortune but rather multiple fortunes—that pace is far too leisurely.

"Truth-seeking is Greek philosophy. Fine. Lovely!" he went on. "In recent years we've seen that the Greek tradition is perhaps not the most optimal in terms of managing financial matters. That's why I'm with the pragmatists: truth pays! More essential than a company's true value is its price movement. I'm not interested in how a company's doing. I'm not even interested in *what* the company's doing. I am only interested in how I can make money with the company's stock."

Inferring from his nods that Grundström was still listening with interest, Aalto continued the presentation which he had practiced in front of a mirror to get just the right facial expressions and emphasis to bolster his message.

"Okay. Some ways are easier and some are harder. The easiest are index changes. Derivatives are constructed on indexes. Index funds invest according to the indexes. They have to buy a company due to rise on the index and sell off slips being kicked off the index. Simple: buy the companies rising on the index before the index changes."

"Twice a year, at most four times a year. The rest of the time, just twiddle your thumbs?" said Grundström.

Aalto cleared his throat. "Of course, more advanced ways also exist."

"Such as?"

"I slaughter the algorithms that are based on technical analysis," Aalto said. "I watch what they do and once I've learned, I do the same thing before them."

He took as an example the moving average—even an old man would understand that. Users of technical analysis peered at stock trends. When a stock came up from below to break the running average curve calculated from the previous thirty days' quotes, the technical analysis set raced to buy it. Of course, the thirty-day average did not work anymore. You needed more complex methods to make money, methods that Aalto could illuminate a little, should Grundström express interest.

"I look at appropriate stocks that are close to the curve and I buy them. And one can always help break the curve a bit, if necessary."

Grundström gave a laugh. "Pump and dump. If that still works, the market really is the same as it was."

"That's forbidden," Aalto said. He allowed his cheeks to twitch.

Pump and dump was the classic method for manipulating rates. The stockbroker would begin buying lots of one specific stock and its rate would rise under the buying pressure. He would pump up the rate by buying more and more, skillfully timing his purchases. Bit by bit the other investors would become interested in the rising stock and start buying. Once the rate rose high enough, the original pumper switched from buyer to seller. He dumped his shares and raked in the profits.

Aalto knew that Grundström had used this method with great success. The giant of the 1970s and '80s stock exchange had benefited from his reputation. When people in the Helsinki Stock Exchange trading hall noticed that R. Grundström Brokerage was buying stock, those at the desks of other banks and brokerage firms believed that Ransu knew something they didn't. Sometimes this was true: yield data had reached Grundström or he had heard of some factory fire and was reacting to it.

Sometimes there was no reason for the purchases. But the

others did not dare *not* to follow Ransu's moves. Grundström was able to make money with and without information.

Aalto moved his glass and placed his phone between the plates. He opened an app and the screen filled immediately with an impressive number of price graphs, which he showed Grundström.

"Here are a few attractive objects on the Helsinki exchange right now," he said, explaining to the former stock exchange czar the meaning of the abbreviations along the edge of the screen.

"Dull ones," Grundström remarked. "Doesn't it work for Fintec?"

"You like Fintec."

"Fintec is one of the companies I've made the most on. It was always a good security. It was traded a lot but not too much. It was easy to bring others along with that one."

Aalto typed in the Fintec ticker symbol and brought up the company's price curve. He had forgotten how little Fintec shares cost these days and how little they were traded. It had been a hot item in the IT bubble at the start of the millennium, its market value ten times its current value. One month Aalto had doubled his student loan payment thanks to Fintec's high rate in the fall of 1999.

The program did not show Fintec shares as particularly strong. Moreover, the share trading was so low that Fintec in no way belonged among the stocks he traded. A professional game required sufficient liquidity, market depth.

But if the old man wanted him to demonstrate his skills on precisely that ticket, the security dear to his heart, Aalto could do so.

"The traditional method won't work here, but that's no problem," Aalto said. "Actually, technically speaking, Fintec shares can turn into extremely desirable objects in a moment. If it just breaks this curve heading down from above, the others will start selling, and then . . ."

Grundström waited. "Does that work?" he finally asked.

"You doubt it?"

"I always doubt."

"Would you like me to actually do it?"

The waiter set down steaming dishes before them. Meat loaf and mashed potatoes, with brown gravy and colorful vegetables.

"Yes. In fact, I would," Grundström said. He bent toward Aalto. "As you see, I am already an old man."

And then Grundström said exactly what Aalto had wanted to hear.

III

The fierce October wind whistled from the north, from the university area, and bit his ankles through his thin socks. Wind collected in the narrow Fabianinkatu passage, whipping candy wrappers, receipts, and leaves into the air.

Jarkko Aalto pushed his hands into the front pockets of his coat. Gloves did not suit his style.

He was about to make the trade of his life. On the sacrifice side, he would cause the rates for Fintec stock to drop, and along the way earn several grand. The reward would be becoming the chief shareholder of R. Grundström Brokerage.

Moreover, under astoundingly good terms.

He almost felt as if he were swindling the old man, who must still be a little disoriented. Evidently the morning mugging had shaken Grundström and caused him to think about life's impermanence, and that was probably why the man wanted a successor for his company, fast. Without bothering about the terms.

It was a situation where the seller wanted to sell. An exceptionally good time to buy.

Aalto had learned not to feel empathy. He did his job and nothing more: maximized his investments' yield. If he had to choose, first came personal benefit, then employer's and clients' benefit. He had no need to think about anyone else's benefit. He did not need to care what happened to the others or how they felt. He represented his bosses. Other interest groups had their own representatives. It was important to choose good advocates if one wanted to survive in this game.

It was not his responsibility to think about secondary things like human suffering. He was not even *allowed* to do that, if he wanted to fulfill his social obligation. If he started to get sentimental, the markets wouldn't work efficiently and wouldn't price the future right; instead, vague human considerations would distort the prices. He was a pureblood, straightforward market fundamentalist who did not care what others thought of him.

No. Actually, he did care what others thought of him. Jarkko Aalto wanted everyone to think he was the market tough, the Ransu Grundström and Gordon Gekko of today.

He had more than enough money. He thirsted for fame. He salivated for immaterial symbolic values.

He had suspected the reason for Grundström's invitation to meet. Insight derived from intuition based on careful research was his most important capital. Even so, the directness of their conversation had startled him. He had expected the first meeting to involve probing, testing, getting a feel for one another, but Grundström had surprised him by saying that he hoped Aalto would rise to continue his work at R. Grundström Brokerage.

Grundström was selling, he was buying, and both ought to feign reluctance in order to obtain the most propitious terms. But Grundström had not even tried. Once he demonstrated to Grundström that he could carry the market, they'd conclude the deal: he would buy Ransu Grundström's stake at a remarkably low price and agree not to sell the company or change its name for the next ten years.

It's true that you have to be realistic: R. Grundström Brokerage no longer gleamed quite as brightly. Nevertheless, it still performed and scattered money to its shareholders. Some of the ownership had moved to the directors whom Grundström had taken on as partners, though he had kept a clear controlling interest for himself. R. Grundström Brokerage was one of the desirable merge partners when the small agencies and property management companies clustered in the blocks around Aleksanterinkatu Street planned for the sector's future. There was no doubt that Grundström had received lucrative offers.

But Grundström had chosen him as his successor. Aalto had never in all his career received more flattering praise. Merit awards of a couple million paled in comparison.

Ignoring the icy wind, he dug out his phone and pulled up the Fintec data page. The company's market value barely exceeded a billion euros. Big investors hadn't turned on their machines to trade for something so small. He would easily get the rate moving with a small number of shares, and once the market movement was seen, enough investors would join in. He could manipulate small investors into selling by using a few of his aliases and dropping negative hints on the Kauppalehti chat page about Fintec's big service contract with the Swedish government.

As he walked from Fabianinkatu toward Esplanade, Aalto

put some Fintec shares up for sale from his own portfolio. He didn't have any Fintec, but that wasn't a problem. Never had been. He would just buy them back at a lower price before the closing bell.

Brokers were of course absolutely forbidden to short-sell their own portfolios. He should have notified the compliance officer of his sale, and he should not have closed his position before three months at the very least.

Those rules were for losers. He had managed his own investments the whole time through a controlling interest company he'd registered in Luxembourg. He had neglected to report it to the internal regulators, and no journalist had the means to untangle the company's background. It wasn't wrong. The Luxembourg investment firm merely put him in the same position Ransu Grundström and his colleagues had occupied in the 1980s.

His phone jingled that his e-mail program synchronization was complete. The sale confirmation mails had arrived.

Aalto strode across the street to Esplanade Park and sat down on a bench. There were some empty ones: Helsinki at freezing point and spitting rain did not entice people to linger outdoors. He opened his e-mails. The highest purchase bid was surprisingly strong. He had only gotten it to move three cents with his sales.

Well, the first set of sales had been an unusually small one. He had just used it to test the market traction.

Fintec was a tricky stock in that he could only operate on the Helsinki Stock Exchange. The ticket did not really trade on other markets. Usually, with the bigger companies, Aalto took advantage of simultaneous quotations on the virtual exchanges. Finnish companies' markets were noticeably thinner on the virtual exchanges than on the Helsinki Stock

Exchange, which meant that getting the rates to move there took a lot less capital.

Aalto sold a second batch, twice the size of the first, at the highest bid. The technical sell signal was thirteen cents away, which meant a price shift of over 8 percent for the stock, but he didn't need to reach that. Just as long as the others joined in. That would be enough to show Ransu Grundström that he was able to steer the market just as Grundström had done thirty years ago.

Fintec's price still moved only a cent. He checked the completed sales: he was the only seller; Nordea, Evli, and Nordnet were the buyers.

Usually with a stock like this, the sale of several hundred thousand shares would spur more movement. Aalto was puzzled, but maybe old orders had piled up, since Fintec's rate had stayed unusually stable. Moreover, 1.5 euros was a comfortably exact sum per order. That's why there was more demand than was in any way warranted.

His phone had buzzed a meeting reminder ten minutes ago, but he had muted it. He could go late and enter without apology. That was his custom.

He wanted to concentrate on Fintec, because after this, the rules of his old job would matter little.

Aalto put the next batch up for sale. By now the cold had started to numb his fingers and the strength of the stock price caused some unease, but he brushed away both the physical and psychological discomforts.

IV

The umbrella was totally useless. The wind whipped the water at a forty-five-degree angle and would have inverted the umbrella in an instant, so I strode across Tehtaankatu with the closed umbrella in my hand and got wetter with each step. I was wet from the water pouring from the skies, and wet from the splash of a car plowing over a puddle on the uneven cobblestones. Water streamed from my dark all-season coat even before I had walked the short distance from the Kaivo-puisto streetcar stop to Itäinen Puistotie. Water sloshed in my shoes.

The late-October rain had continued unbroken for three days now. It would stop on the weekend, if the predicted cold front reached Fennoscandia and changed the stuff falling from the sky from water to snow. A five-month November would commence, in which the slush from efforts to salt away the snow would be interrupted only by a few bright days of frost, which in turn would transform the streets into bad skating rinks.

I couldn't do anything about the weather. My forefathers had selected this peninsula for their home. I could have moved somewhere and supported myself as a freelancer, but I was trapped by the language. In other countries they spoke noticeably poorer Finnish than in Helsinki, even though Helsinki's current speech patterns, with the eternal contractions and mangled vowels, were not a pretty thing, either.

And then there was the fact that the people I knew lived here. Among them Ransu Grundström, who had invited me for a visit. I always accepted his invitations with pleasure, because Ransu was a sharp old guy, and even though his unbeatable contact network had thinned and drifted away from the burning issues of the day, he often knew things that were useful to me in my work as a journalist.

Helsinki's bank circles had been buzzing all that rainy day about the stockbroker considered the most talented—in other words, the greediest—of his generation, Jarkko Aalto, and his surprising resignation. I expected to learn more about it from Ransu.

I asked the servant who opened the door to take my outer clothes to the bathroom to dry. He kindly handed me a soft plush towel, traditional Reino slippers, and dry socks, which I exchanged for my soaking wet ones. My feet got warm right away and I began to feel a little better.

Ransu Grundström was waiting in the living room, where seamark lights sliced at intervals through the grayness outside the full-wall window. A birch fire in the hearth cast a warmth that made the flue hum softly and steadily.

Ransu was clearly in splendid spirits. He asked his servant to bring us both glasses of cognac for a start, "from the bottle that looks like an aftershave bottle."

I asked if we had something special to celebrate.

Ransu smiled. "Fintec is treating us to these drinks."

"You were involved in that too?"

IT company Fintec's share price had soared two days earlier when an American competitor had made an extravagant offer to buy out the company's shares. The premium had increased almost 70 percent from the previous day's closing quote.

"It's good to be part of something like that," Ransu said, and there was no doubt he had known of the plans before they were made public.

The unspoken agreement between us was that whatever Ransu told me directly—or at least, directly enough—about his own activities would never become public through me. On the other hand, if he hid something from me and I found out some other way, I did not hesitate to hit him full force on the front page. After I had exposed Ransu's fuzzy Nokia trades, which led to a police investigation, he had not kept secrets

244 // HELSINKI NOIR

from me, he had just been mysterious. I had demonstrated my
toughness and he, his.

"I happened to obtain a large number of them a few hours
before the buyout offer was announced," Ransu said.

"Poor seller."

"He suffered from his own greed."

"Do you know who was selling? Did you make a block
trade?" I probed.

"Perfectly ordinary trading. I submitted purchase instructions through three brokers and let the slips fall into my lap.
Someone had a sudden strong urge to sell."

"You're not telling the whole story."

"Correct. I can't tell the whole thing because if I did it
would make someone look ridiculous. That's not what I want.
I don't embarrass. I don't humiliate."

"You take the money."

"True. That's my handicap."

We ate prime rib sandwiches with mineral water and had
another round of cognac. We chatted about this and that, pol-
itics, finance, music—Ransu had an opening-night ticket to
the National Opera where they'd just started performances of
Verdi's *La forza del destino*. When I thought it was appropriate,
I asked if he knew anything about Jarkko Aalto's unexpected
resignation.

"If there's no new job waiting, it's a firing dressed up as
voluntary," said Ransu.

I told him I had talked with Aalto by phone a few hours
earlier. Aalto said the non-compete clause prevented him
from disclosing his plans.

"Not the best time for a gardening holiday," Ransu
snorted.

It was true that in the banking sector people usually resigned in March or April, after the previous year's bonuses were paid, if the departure was of their own volition.

"You evidently don't like Aalto."

"I do, I do! I've actually met him only once, but I am grateful to him for a great deal. He's a man of the present."

I asked Ransu to elaborate.

"Nowadays profits come fast and losses even faster," he stated.

More than that I could not extract from Ransu, but he had expressed his opinion with such conviction that there had to be information behind it. This was how I had learned to work with him. Once I had spoken with him, it was always easier to find out more from other sources. I'd make a few calls the next day and be able to write my own scoop about Jarkko Aalto's firing.

When I left, the servant asked if I wanted a taxi. I declined—it was only a short walk to the streetcar stop, and the rain wasn't coming down as hard as when I arrived.

I pointed out that Ransu still walked from here to the city center to work.

"This is a good place for walking. The city does an admirable job taking care of the area. It's always safe to move about here," he said.

I waited, because even though I had one foot out the door, it was clear that Ransu wanted to say something.

"Yes?"

THE SCRIPT

BY ANTTI TUOMAINEN

Lintulahti

Translated by Lola Rogers

J uhana Lauste knew that he was being watched. That in itself wasn't a surprise. He had come into the bar to be recognized. Or rather, not just to be recognized. That was merely the first step. A pleasant electricity shot through him, from the soles of his feet through his whole body.

Lauste tried to find the best stance. He lifted his foot onto the ankle-high steel footrest and lowered his right elbow onto the bar, checking first to make sure that the spot in front of him was dry, not wet and sticky like it would be later in the evening. The so-called music, a generic drumbeat mixed with sighing meant to be sensual, wasn't yet loud enough to be annoying. The open door to Uudenmaankatu provided ample ventilation. Later, when the door was closed, the smells of sweat, piss, and a thousand people exhaling would torment the senses like a public toilet. Which the place was, of course, even if it pretended otherwise with its chandeliers and black leather couches.

Juhana Lauste was dressed casually in soft tan leather shoes, two-hundred-euro, distressed designer jeans, and a thin white button-up shirt with wild patterns reminiscent of flowers or stars woven into the front in multicolored thread.

Lauste had only been wearing the shirt for the past couple

of hours. He'd done something he often did—gone to a clothing store, flirted with an anorexic, garishly made-up saleswoman toddling about on high stiletto heels, and shoved the shirt he was wearing into the trash bin (Diesel, a hundred and sixty-nine euros, one he unfortunately still liked and had only had for a few weeks, but sometimes you just had to show people who was who). Then he'd put on the new shirt, careful to let the empty, desperate eyes of the thirty-something clerk, with her fringes of false eyelashes, linger as long as possible on his tanned, muscular torso. While he did this he chatted familiarly, his voice pleasantly soft and friendly, and behaved as if he could be anyone at all, although of course he couldn't. He was Juhana Lauste, producer, the king of Finnish film and television.

It was his weekend. His wife, who was his second wife (or did Malla count too? In that case, Tiina was his third), had taken the children with her to visit her parents up north in Oulu. Lauste hated his in-laws. He didn't really like his wife and children, either, but that was different. His wife and children were sort of required, part of the package. They were something to be had, just as in the spring you would purchase the most expensive riding mower with the biggest Briggs & Stratton engine possible. They were all part of the same presentation that showed people that he always got what he wanted. Which was everything. The worst thing about visits to Oulu was of course that he wasn't recognized up there. Or if he was, his name didn't impress anyone. They could have their Lapland, and fuck their reindeer.

It was different here in Helsinki, and in south Helsinki in particular.

More and more often Lauste felt like the city ought to be divided from the rest of the country by a wall. On the other side of the wall would be the woods that stretched from Helsinki's farthest suburbs almost to the Arctic Sea; a nearly uninhabited wasteland with a surface area the size of Central Europe where bugs and ugly people sucked the life out of anyone the slightest bit interesting who happened to turn up there.

South Helsinki suited him: stone buildings, expensive apartments, boutiques, award-winning restaurants, trendy bars, stylish customers. Here people recognized him, flattered him, sucked up to him, awaited his next creation.

His television shows were what are called mass-audience programs. In other words, they were made cheaply, sold out their ad spots, and cultivated a kind of humor ("I'm soooo drunk." "Me too. Except I'm so drunker." *Studio audience laughs.*) anyone can understand, even if they're senile, retarded, sedated, drunk, or so numbed from stuffing themselves with sausage that they have to get around on all fours like some cross between a sheep and frog, which was how Lauste described the target audience for his shows.

He had the good fortune not to have to spend his Saturday evenings in front of the television. This was a thousand times better: a pulsing nightclub filled with the scent of women, the sweet expectation of sex. He rarely made the first move, and only when he had a particular reason. Women approached him—young women. He himself was already nearly fifty (he'd celebrated three forty-sixth birthdays, and had resolved to do the same with his forty-seventh, if it ever happened to sneak up on him), which meant two things: he had to go to the gym every day, and his bed partners were younger than his oldest son, Timo, a Subutex user whom he hadn't seen in six years. Lauste had also started taking large amounts of Viagra and Cialis. *Just in case*, he would tell himself as he sat in the front seat of his SUV and swallowed the little blue pills.

It took a minute for Lauste to locate his observer. The woman was sitting alone at a table near the door. And what a woman. About thirty, shapely, with short bangs and thick, straight black hair. A modern Cleopatra. Lauste felt her brown eyes hot on his cheeks, forehead, and lips. The distance between them was about fifteen meters. The intervening space was filled with groups in lively conversation, men and women talking over each other, their eyes constantly straying to nearby tables.

Lauste's right hand went instinctively toward his pants pocket. Only one year ago he wouldn't have been able to tell you why the right front pockets of jeans have a smaller pocket sewn into them. Now he knew. That was where he carried a handy dose of liquid Rohypnol. He'd first heard of the drug from a foreign acquaintance who was also a film producer. His movies were euphemistically called adult entertainment, though they didn't waste time with needless aesthetic considerations and explored something other than interpersonal relationships. This fellow producer's stories of the drug's effects had piqued Lauste's interest. He asked if his colleague could get some of it for him too. Well, not exactly for *him*, of course, but for his use.

Lauste performed his first test of the drug on his wife. Tiina had just put the children to bed and they were drinking wine in front of the fire downstairs. The glass doors to the terrace were open, the water of Jollaksenlahti was gleaming in the moonlight, the night perfectly windless. They touched glasses and drank. Tiina was saying something about the children and Lauste was doing what he always did—pretending to listen, behaving as if he were interested, lying in his replies. When Tiina got up to go to the bathroom, Lauste poured some of the drug into her glass. She returned to sit beside

250 // Helsinki Noir

him on the sofa and took a drink. Lauste waited. After several minutes, she looked at him as if she were trying to remember something. Something crucially important. Then an expression of confusion came over her face, and then it went lax. For the sake of practice, Lauste took off her clothes, had a long session with her, and carried her to bed. In the morning, she remembered nothing of the evening at all, she simply wondered at the strange salty taste in her mouth, the tenderness in her rear end, and the heaviness in her extremities. Lauste had patted her on the aforementioned rear end and said it was no doubt due to the hot lovemaking of a summer night and the wine she'd imbibed.

After that there was no going back.

It was hard to say what he liked best about drugging women. It wasn't that he suffered from any shortage of females, or their naked bodies. But something about that moment—the moment when a woman realized she'd been deceived, that fleeting fraction of a second when she realized that something had gone terribly wrong, realized that the evening, and that particular moment between them, was not at all what she had imagined it to be—was endlessly fascinating to Lauste, made him tingle, before and afterward, made him finally feel something. And the certainty that the moment belonged only to him, would remain only in his memory, made it completely unique, utterly incomparable.

Lauste picked up his glass—a fresh, sparkling gin and tonic—and turned his back to the bar. He looked at the dark-haired woman on the other side of the room. And as it happened, the woman smiled. Lauste fixed his attention on the redness of her lips. Then she stretched out her wrist slightly and pointed at the chair in front of her. Lauste hummed with contentment. Once again, he hadn't had to make the first move.

Up close, the woman was even more beautiful than he'd thought. Her black hair gleamed, falling over her shoulders like a raven's feathers, and her eyes were dark and elegantly moist. Her shoulders were strong yet graceful, the fullness in her breasts really was truly just full breasts, not part of a heavy build. Even seated, she gave the impression of being the proverbial ten, physically, and Lauste liked to collect those.

Then came the scintillating moment: introducing himself. What made the moment scintillating was its utter redundancy. Lauste knew she knew who he was.

He stretched out his hand and said his name. The woman's smile was just what he'd expected. There was no surprise in that smile. She said her own name.

"Minna."

Her voice was slightly low, and ever so slightly husky. Lauste sat down across from her. Just as he was leaning his elbows on the table, before he had a chance to say something that one says in such situations, like, *I couldn't help but notice you,* or, *How nice that the most beautiful woman in the city just happens to be sitting here alone,* the woman said, "You're the film producer."

Lauste had hardly anticipated that he would have even less work to do this evening than usual. But then the woman did something. The woman, this woman named Minna, leaned to one side and took a leather bag, a woman's dark-brown purse, from the chair next to her and opened it. Lauste could see in a second what was happening. He'd been led into a trap, he knew it instantly. Under normal circumstances he would have walked away. But the woman was so beautiful, so incredibly desirable, that he didn't want to, wasn't able to.

She pulled out a stack of papers, laid them on the table, and looked him in the eye. He could feel the powerful gaze of her brown eyes in the pit of his stomach, and lower, bolting through him like a flash of lightning, leaving him stripped and shaken, but in a pleasant way. Her eyes contained such animal promise that they conquered the revulsion he felt for the stack of white paper she'd just put on the table.

He hated these piles of paper more than anything—with the exception of the people who created them. He knew what the paper on the table was. A script. He didn't have many rules in his life, but there was one he followed absolutely faithfully. He never read scripts.

Then the woman, this woman named Minna, said: "I have a script here that I'd like you to look at."

Lauste felt a mixture of lust and loathing. The lust was directed at the woman's body, the loathing at her script. Scripts were a dull, stupid waste of time. They were full of childish, utterly incomprehensible ideas that writers thought were important. Lauste left it to his underlings to read the scripts and talk to those walking bedsores, the burdensome scribblers who wrote them.

He made his decisions based on how a thing *sounded*.

If someone suggested, for instance, a talk show with two of the hottest young actresses of the moment scantily clad and interviewing some idiot, he might look into the matter. If somebody suggested a multilayered, subtly tragic story of survival that the author describes as "written from the heart," he wanted to murder the receptionist who let such a piece of human trash into his conference room. And of course he said no. But never directly. Because you never know, one of those thousands of clowns might strike gold with that dull pickax of his one day, and you had to be ready to make use of it if he did.

And now he was in a situation where he ought to . . . he ought to play his cards right.

"What's it about?" he managed to say.

The woman leaned forward. Lauste could smell the fruity scent of her perfume. The smell carried with it other sensations: a dark night, the sweat on a woman's skin, a g-string buried in the groove of her ass.

"You should read it yourself," the woman said in her husky voice, pushing the sheaf of paper across the table toward him. Lauste felt the same feeling he'd had a moment before—a mixture of urgent sexual pressure and repellent loathing.

"Tell me about it," he said.

She stared intensely into his eyes. "I don't know how I would describe it. I wrote it from the heart. Said everything I wanted to say."

Lauste was able to contain the burst of laughter before it reached his face. He knew in an instant that here was something he could take hold of.

"That's the most important thing," he said, nodding. "In all writing, that's what matters the most. Honesty, integrity, vision." How easy it was to talk like this. He'd learned them all—asinine phrases to use with writers if you were forced into contact with them. He went on: "There are so many writers who just try to please, who write what they think a producer wants. But the most important thing to me has always been exactly that—a creator with a strong point of view of her own."

This, of course, couldn't have been further from the truth. There was only one point of view that Lauste respected or even considered: his own.

"That's just what I've done," the woman said, laying her left hand on top of the stack of paper. "I haven't considered in the slightest what you or anyone else might want, only what I myself want."

Lauste's gaze followed her hand down to the paper. Her hand was slim and delicate, her fingernails long and red. The hand covered the text in the middle of the first page—doubtless the name of the story and the author. Those hardly mattered.

"It sounds good," Lauste said. "A writer should be honest with herself. She shouldn't think about commercial considerations at all."

At that moment, lying felt even more pleasant than usual. Perhaps it was because of her brown eyes, her thrusting breasts, her tongue licking a drop of red wine from her lips.

"It's really nice to hear you say that," she said, her voice rough and soft. "And a little surprising."

She took a sip of her wine. Lauste reminded himself that he would be wise to call this woman Minna. Women were often offended if you didn't remember their names.

"Unfortunately, Minna, many people have the wrong idea about me. So many envy my success. But my success has always come from the fact that everything I've done has been first-rate, of the highest quality."

That last statement was perhaps the biggest lie of all. But it sounded so good that Lauste would gladly believe it himself. He couldn't tell from the woman's—or rather Minna's —face what she was thinking. He decided to make use of an approach that had been tested in real-life situations and proved valuable.

"Between you and me," he continued, leaning slowly forward and gently touching, caressing, the manuscript, "and this is strictly confidential—I never agree to requests like this. But in your case I could make an exception. I have the feeling there might be something in it. Something very promising."

And then Minna smiled, smiled in a way he understood,

there was only one thing a smile like that could mean—he'd broken down her wall of hesitation.

"You don't know how good it is for me to hear that," Minna said, her husky voice like a sigh. "I've done such a terrible . . . such a terrible lot of work to get here. And now here you sit, praising my manuscript, even though you haven't—"

Lauste raised his hand. They were sitting with their faces so close together that he could have almost reached his tongue out to her lips, between her lips.

"Keep in mind how long I've been doing this. I only need to read a few lines to see if it's got the goods."

He was so close to her brown eyes now that he could have torn them out with his teeth. There was something in those eyes that kept drawing him deeper, to some unknown destination. Then he heard her say: "Should we go someplace quieter and continue this conversation?"

A hot summer Saturday night in Helsinki, a city on overdrive. The sun wouldn't set for a couple more hours, and the parks, streets, and bars buzzed with life, swarmed with revelers. There were two different Helsinkis, two different Finlands: the summer and the winter. Summer could be seen in people's faces—not just their suntans, but their looks of credulity, of relief, of surrender, even. Winter's cold, miserable damp, its unrelenting chill and endless slush, didn't just turn skin pale. It sucked everything into its all-pervading darkness. But on a summer night everyone was awake and restless and insatiable. Lauste loved these nights.

He knew he was over the blood-alcohol limit, but he drove anyway. He'd never been caught before, and he wouldn't be caught now. And Minna had murmured to him as they were leaving the bar, asking him not to call a taxi. That suited him. His Porsche Cayenne was parked practically around the corner on Tehtaankatu. He let Minna move in front of him to the other side of the car, and he had a chance to appreciate her shapely ass. An erection appeared of its own accord, like a warm greeting from an old friend. Lauste's right hand flicked to check that he still had the drug in his pocket. And, of course, he did. His erection hardened, swelled tight against the front of his jeans. He had an urge to touch himself, but the time for that would come later.

Minna was sitting next to him in the SUV. Lauste wasn't worried about her seeing his car, feeling the warmth of the leather seat under her firm ass, or that she would hear his favorite music, melodic Swedish pop. None of it mattered. Lauste knew Minna wouldn't remember anything about the evening, and this drive was no exception. That was the effect the drug had. It wiped away everything as it went, even stealing some of the hours that preceded it. Lauste's producer colleague had described his own experience with the drug, said there was nothing like it—once he'd taken it he lost all capacity to make a record of the things he saw and experienced in his memory. He was conscious of what was happening, and conscious even that he couldn't commit anything to memory. He still knew that in the morning. But the events themselves were impossible to remember.

If Lauste was honest with himself (he was always honest with himself!), he had to admit that the fear of getting caught—however unlikely that might be—added to the excitement of the thing.

They drove along the shore at Pohjoisranta. On their left the proud, decorative façades of the Jugendstil apartment houses marched by, on the right the open sea. The water was black and reflected the city lights like a rippling carpet. Lauste glanced at the seat beside him. Minna looked calm.

"My place is in Lintulahdenkatu, between Sörnäinen and the waterfront," she said.

"Nice neighborhood," Lauste lied. Druggies, drunks, stuffy studio apartments, and stairwells that smelled like shit and piss, he thought.

He steered the SUV onto the bridge that connected Kruununhaka to Hakaniemi and Merihaka. Lauste often thought that crossing the bridges between south and north Helsinki was very much like traveling from Beverly Hills to the Soviet Union without border inspections. On one side people smiled with white teeth, on the other side people had no teeth, or if they did, their teeth would be browned by tobacco and poverty. And it had always been thus: gentlemen in the south, the unwashed in the north.

The traffic lights twinkled yellow on the Sörnäinen shore road and he picked up speed. He felt better than he had in a long time. Thank God Minna wasn't talking. A quick glance assured him that her breasts were still there where he could reach them. The seat belt passed between the pert mounds like it had its work cut out for it struggling to keep the two bouncing tits separated.

"Take the next left," Minna said. "There's a parking spot. Let's leave the car here. I live up there."

Lauste glanced in the direction she was pointing. Highrises climbed up the hillside and their inner courtyard was itself a steep slope.

The night was hot as midday and Lauste was bathed in sweat by the time they crossed the courtyard and reached the building entrance. Minna's scent was stronger than ever, perfume mixed with a woman's smell, a woman's moisture—he was sure of that. Her high heels clicked over the floor and he had an urge to lift her skirt. Soon, he told himself, soon.

They took the elevator to the twelfth floor. On the ride up she asked, "Will you take a look at my script now?"

Lauste stared into her eyes and thought how exciting her proud face would look with one eye blackened and the upper lip swollen and dripping blood. "Of course," he lied.

"Wonderful," she sighed.

They stepped out of the elevator. Minna turned right and took her keys out of her pocket. She opened the dead bolt, then the door lock. Lauste followed her inside and pulled the door shut behind him. As soon as the door was closed, she turned around and nuzzled against him, pressing her lips to his. He tasted lipstick and red wine and the salty flavor of a woman. Then she pulled away as suddenly as she had grabbed him. She took him by the hand and guided him to the living room. There she pulled the script out of her bag and laid it on the glass-topped table.

"I'll get us something to drink. It'll be nicer to read that way," she said, and went into the kitchen, which opened off to the left. "Why don't you sit down?"

Lauste neither sat nor even glanced at the script on the table. He walked to the tall living room windows and was surprised at the view. He hadn't realized how high up they were. You could almost see the entire city center and much of the outskirts. The night was bright and cloudless and lights seemed to twinkle all the way from Lauttasaari. He glanced around. It wasn't like an ordinary single woman's home. It wasn't like a woman's home at all. It was like a hotel room: sterile, neutral, without a single object that looked like it belonged to someone. I see, he thought, Minna has a rich man, a businessman, who supports her while she dreams of a career as a screenwriter. It wouldn't be the first time that happened. He heard her heels behind him on the parquet floor and turned around.

"White wine," she said, handing him a glass.

They drank. And as soon as Lauste had swallowed his wine, Minna pressed against him again, and they kissed. This kiss was long, wet, and hot. He even closed his eyes for a moment. He imagined she closed hers too. They sat down on the sofa. They kissed again. They drank wine and looked into each other's eyes. Lauste's thirst seemed endless, he had sweat through a whole hot summer day and night and his throat was as parched as if it had been blow-dried.

"You know what?" Minna said. "I should use the bathroom. It will give you some time to read."

They kissed once more, for a long time. Then Minna stood up, got another bottle from the kitchen, brought it to the table, and went into the bathroom. Lauste looked at the wine. He smiled. He waited to hear the water running in the bathroom, then reached into his pocket. He took out the tiny bottle and opened it. He was about to pour its contents into Minna's glass when he noticed that it was empty. He looked at it. Felt his pocket. Had it leaked? No. His pants were perfectly dry.

Lauste heard the bathroom door open. At the same moment, he started to feel heavy. And he realized what had happened. Somehow, she had—the first kiss!—slipped the bottle out of his pocket, emptied its contents into his glass—in the kitchen—and put it back in his pocket—the longer, wetter kiss! He tried to get up from the sofa, but it was no longer possible. He heard Minna's high heels on the floor. They were coming nearer. He meant to turn his head, but he wasn't able to. Minna appeared, sliding down in front of him. He started to say something, but it was better to keep his mouth shut, because it didn't want to open. His body felt like it was pressing down onto the sofa with a thousand kilos of weight. The feeling was actually very pleasant. It remained pleasant until he saw the pair of surgical scissors in Minna's hand.

From that moment everything happened in fragments, each one simultaneously unforgettable and immediately forgotten. Minna unzips his trousers. Minna pulls his trousers off. Minna cuts his underwear away from his body. Minna grabs his cock like it's a broomstick, stretches the organ to its limit, and cuts it off at the root. Blood gushes as if a valve has failed. Some of the blood spills on Minna as well, but she doesn't even seem to notice. Minna shows him the shaft of his cock. Then she roughly shoves it in his mouth. Minna grabs his testicles. The same thing happens: a long stretch, cut at the root, display, mouth filled. His cheeks and jaw are about to burst and break. He bleeds like a fire hydrant that's been cracked open. It's hard to breathe. He feels as if he's sitting in a barrel, in a warm and thick bath of blood. Minna sits down across from him and looks at him with curiosity, even fascination, her graceful latex-gloved hands covered in dark blood. Minna pulls the gloves off, peels the black hair off her head, and shoves her wig into her bag. Minna takes out her colored contact lenses. Removes her makeup, her high-heeled shoes. Changes her clothes and puts on sneakers. She looks so ordinary. And then Lauste hears her voice, which isn't husky anymore, but bright and clear, like someone playing a xylophone: skillfully, thoughtfully.

"Laura sends her greetings. You picked her up this time last summer. Laura's my sister."

She watched him as he bled out. His breath was quick and heavy at first, then labored and panting, and finally wheezing. Then it stopped altogether. Minna—which wasn't her real name, of course—sat a little while longer across from the dead body, in this strange apartment, rented for this very purpose. She looked at the man who had raped her sister and may have been the cause of the vicious cycle that had turned Laura—a bright, charming screenwriting and film theory student—into a permanent patient of the mental hospital, a wreck of a person, her life slipping away. The man who'd paid with his blood.

She stood up, then remembered the script on the table. Although it wasn't really a script. It was just a stack of A4 paper, blank white pages. Unlike Laura, she didn't care much for writing. The life she lived and the world around her were much more interesting than any book, any script. Those were just, for lack of a better description, words on paper.

STOLEN LIVES

BY JOHANNA HOLMSTRÖM

Vuosaari

Translated from Swedish by Lone Thygesen Blecher

I

It's three days before the burial, and Carin writes in her blog, *Everything from IKEA, possibly with the exception of potted plants, is completely "out."*

Celestine shuts her laptop with a snap and looks around her living room which could have come straight out of an IKEA catalog. Everything is matching in earthy tones of brown and beige, gray and white, harmonized from the same product lines, carefully planned so nothing stands out, clashes, or disrupts—and all the same it is lifeless, and now also, according to Carin, outdated.

Of course, Celestine thinks. *Carin would never make a mistake like this. Carin who shops in Missoni Home and orders her bedding from Bed Bath & Beyond. Obviously she's right. Because Carin has everything under control. Everything! Except her baby.*

Carin's baby takes his daytime naps outdoors just like all the other children, even if it is winter.

And that's the reason Finnish babies are so strong and healthy, Carin writes in her blog.

Unattended, Gabriel snoozes in his Emmaljunga stroller of black-and-white leather by the white plastered walls of the row house apartments, right beneath the window where the shades facing the street are drawn. Pedestrians pass by his stroller, and children with breaths of white clouds play in the nearby snow mounds with bright-colored plastic shovels.

The baby lies in the safety of his Emmaljunga bubble, behind a white cloth with a pattern of starfish and other sea life while Carin, with her shades drawn, is advising clueless mothers on how to best take care of their offspring. And Celestine is standing on her balcony right across the street, four floors above in the city rental housing, looking at the stroller by the row house wall. She wets her winter-chapped lips and breathes in the smell of melting snow through her nose.

The rental complex on Lilla Ullholmvägen is jokingly nicknamed the Castle. It is one of the only places in the area where subsidized housing is offered, and most of the inhabitants are on welfare or alcoholics. Large Somalian families stomp up and down the stairs to their apartments, filling the stairwells with the echoes of their laughter. Celestine is one of only a few with a Swedish last name. Everyone else is Finnish, Somalian, Arab, Kurdish, Vietnamese . . . She has tried figuring out how many nationalities are gathered underneath the same roof. There must be at least nine.

When you move up in the world, you move down, down to the row house apartments. If you do even better, you move to the villas with panoramic windows down by the innermost inlet. That's where you find the small boat harbor, the yachts, the private tennis courts, and the running tracks. And the closer you get to the waterfront, the whiter the skin color.

Carin and Anders live in the row houses, and their cars are parked by the curb in front of the Castle. They park for free right in front of the less fortunate. Celestine despises cars. She doesn't even have a driver's license. She takes the metro back and forth to the university and a bus in between. Just like most people in her building.

It's Carin who drives their town jeep. A Subaru Forester. It is not exactly luxurious. She jokingly calls it her little shopping box. They also have a Benz. That's the one Anders uses.

Celestine scratches the Subaru with her keys as she passes and Carin complains at length online. Celestine reads. She reads everything Carin writes. Her eyes glide greedily along the lines and she steals the pictures Carin posts. They are pictures of the new couch in brown antique leather. The soft, cream-colored shaggy rug. Pictures of the coffee maker that you feed with small single-serve plastic cartridges. And pictures from their frequent trips to European metropolises— trips that continued in spite of the family addition. The flow of pictures is punctuated with recipes for lemon meringue pie, homemade ice cream with real vanilla, and the perfect roast beef. And while she's writing, the boy is sleeping in his carriage beneath the window.

His name is Gabriel. The angel Gabriel. Celestine looks into his amazed blue eyes and smiles at him almost in real time when Carin posts a picture of something which is, most certainly, no longer just passing gas but a real smile. He doesn't look at all like Otto, Celestine's Otto, but there's something about him that makes her run her finger down the round baby cheek on the screen, very slowly, and when she closes her eyes she sees him.

She was six years old when he was born. Celestine's mother Harriet had already disposed of her first husband, Tomas, and was busy with the next one, Markku. She and Celestine had moved away from the single-family house in the town by the river where the church burned down when some young vandals threw a Mo-

lotov cocktail up onto the roof. Markku lived and worked in the capital and Harriet couldn't afford the long trips. It was a practical arrangement.

It was called a suburb, but it felt more like a bedroom community. The streets had names like Starry Eye Alley, Blue Bird, Air Castle Street, Winding Honey Alley, Mossy Path. It was a fairytale town by a sandy beach where you could see freighters like red and white spots far out at sea at all times of the year. The harbor was tucked away behind a promontory and you could hear the ships bellow at each other at night. The sound made her shudder. It filled the hollows of her body and seemed to reverberate inside her until she stood in front of the open window, shaking.

In her new school they made fun of her name. Celestine, out of all the names in the world. It was worth at least a snort and a giggle. The name belonged to a time when Mom still had dreams. Not just a bag to pack when it was time to dump Tomas, Celestine's dad. Not some deadbeat, but a musician just like Mom was back when she still gave kids names like Celestine. But with Markku, who worked in construction and had a regular income and a pension, all they could come up with was Otto.

The name is a palindrome. It has no beginning and no ending. It repeats itself forever, on and on, in a perfect symmetry of circles and the two crosses in between.

From the very beginning he belonged to Celestine and no one else. Their mom Harriet was no Carin. She didn't know any recipes for lemon meringue pie. She just played her music in bars so smokey that you could hardly open your eyes. She'd come back home long past midnight. Markku loved her, he said, and so he let her have her way.

—The girl can take care of the boy, Markku said.

He himself sat with a glass of beer at the bar where Harriet played and never took his eyes off her even when it got to be late

and they were both cross-eyed as they started toward home. For a
man like Markku it was no problem having to get up for work the
next day. For a man like Markku the alcohol is never a problem.
The only thing Markku had a problem with was his jealousy, and
when Harriet and Markku started breaking apart their love as well
as the furniture inside Air Castle Street number 4B, Celestine and
Otto had to escape out into the snow flurries.

II

Two days before the burial, she straightens up her things and
cleans the apartment as though cleaning up a crime scene. A
sock gathering dust on the floor goes into the laundry basket.
Papers that have slipped out of the printer are swept up and
land in a drawer by the computer. She wipes every surface
with a damp rag, polishes the mirror and door handles with
window cleaner, waters the basil, oregano, lettuce, thyme,
sage, and mint by the kitchen window. While she's cleaning
she drifts to another time, another place, and the images that
pass before her mind's eye are so strong and clear that she
loses herself in them.

Her tongue licks the snot from under her nose. The snot is
always running, tickling her upper lip, during those wet months. To
crawl across the frozen, icy snow in slippery rain pants or winter
overalls. The thumping sensation of the plastic shovel blade hitting
the snowbank. The constant sliding. The pointless, monotonous
digging. The woolen cap soaking up moisture, itching the skin. And
the eyes adjusting to the darkness that came creeping in from be-
tween the walls of the surrounding buildings.

The other children, everywhere, all around her, hinged together
by the common effort of conquering the snow mound and carving
it into a cavern of tunnels that one could crawl through in a slight
state of panic. A feeling of having narrowly escaped the death of

suffocation every time one reached safety on the other side. In the dark evenings the parents would light candles and place them in the tunnels, lighting the caverns from within. It was horrific. Beautiful. Like the sacrificial altar of some kind of death cult. A cranium lit up and burning all through the long winter night.

Celestine runs hot water over the dishes and pulls on a pair of green rubber gloves. The steam hits her face and it gathers in droplets on the down of her upper lip. The taste is salty.

She used to watch him through the window when he crawled around on the snow mound with the other children. The tip of his tongue licking the upper lip beneath his nose. The pom-pom on his cap bobbed up and down as he dug. When she was done with her house work she used to pull on her cap, jacket, and winter pants, the heavy boots, and then run down to join them. Halfway to the tunnel she would realize she had forgotten her mittens.

Her hands are still cold. She dug in the snow until her nails were bleeding. It burned like fire when they thawed. Then she screamed. Screamed and cried. But her hands never warmed up again.

III

The day before the burial she wakes up with a start and a violent gasp. Her mouth is dry and she sits up in bed. Her head is heavy with sleep, her thoughts at a standstill. She looks at her hands. *Blood.* Her breathing is fast, she's trembling, and she lifts up the blanket, the pink one with green and red flowers. The yellow sheet is stained. For a moment the sight drowns her in thick, hot darkness. The sun-filled bedroom disappears, but she is not thrown back into the snow-filled nighttime landscape of her dream where the candles that the parents had placed in the caverns of the snow mound had fallen over

and gone out. Instead, she is caught inside the limbo of esca-
lating panic. Suddenly, in a flash of clarity, she regains control
of her own body. Time and space returns.

Of course!

She's still clasping the blanket in her fist and staring at
the sheet. Then she parts her legs. Her thighs are covered
with sticky, dark-brown blood and her panties are soaked. She
breathes more calmly.

Typical . . . this would never happen to Carin.

Carin has a menstruation chart. Her ovulation is never
off. It's never irregular nor a few weeks late the way Celestine's can be. Carin would never have any shocking surprises.

At least not yet, Celestine thinks, when she gets out of bed
and walks to the bathroom to shower.

That afternoon she decides to call her mother. The thoughts
that have circled around Otto for the last few weeks drive
her to the cell phone, which she usually puts away on a shelf
as soon as she gets home from business college and hardly
touches again. She picks up the phone and opens the cover. A
missed call. From her mom.

She wets her lips, quickly pushes the buttons. Her mother
only calls when something is seriously wrong. Usually most
things are wrong, but not so terribly seriously that it warrants
a phone conversation.

Come on, come on, Celestine has time to whisper while
the call goes through. A scratchy pause and then Harriet's
squeaky, disoriented voice:

—Hallo? Through a cloud of psychopharmacology.

—Mom? It's me! Celestine!

—Celestine? Is it you?

—Yes!

—Why are you calling? Has something happened?

Harriet is slurring her words. Celestine can picture her. She's lying on the couch dressed in her dark-green winter coat, orange-knitted scarf, a felt hat, the henna-dyed curly hair in a tangle over the couch pillows, the hem of her skirt dragging on the floor, and still with her knee-high, dark-brown boots on her feet. She has collapsed in that condition onto the couch and then sailed through the night, more unconscious than sleeping, high on pills, low on alcohol, empty of joy. But whatever she is, Celestine understands her. For, in spite of everything, it was unforgivable. Celestine's betrayal.

It was your job to watch over him!

The cry rings through her head so suddenly that she thinks it's Harriet who's saying the words. She flinches, swallows, and pulls herself together.

—I should be asking *you* that! It was you who called me, says Celestine.

—I did? That's funny, I could have sworn my phone started beeping and then I answered it, and it was you. How strange . . .

—No, not just now. I called you because you called me earlier, says Celestine.

The receiver grows silent. Celestine checks the screen to see if the connection has been broken, but then she hears Harriet clear her throat.

—Yes, oh, right . . . now I remember. I called you . . . It's the anniversary of the funeral tomorrow.

He would have turned eighteen a week ago.

Celestine pinches her trembling lips together. Her eyes are stinging. Harriet's voice sounds like an old woman's. Brittle, sharp, and lonely. Celestine presses her thumb and forefinger against her eyelids but can't prevent the tears from coming.

She sniffles and tries to make her voice as light and cheerful as she can.

—Yes, Mom, that's right, she says, but can't get out any more.

—Celestine. I want you to know that I never blamed you. Whatever I said back then.

—I know.

—Celestine . . .

—I have to go now. Anders is calling. He's cooked up the most wonderful brunch with whole grain bread. He's saying that my macchiato is getting cold. You really should come and visit us. Gabriel would be so happy. He was just a newborn in the pictures I sent you.

—Wait, don't go . . . Harriet pleads.

—I have to check on Gabriel. He's sleeping in his carriage outside. I think he's crying. Oy, now I really have to run. Bye, Mom. Take care of yourself.

Bit by bit, Celestine has stolen Carin's life. Little by little, she has recreated it in her conversations with Harriet, in the e-mails to her girlfriends, Tuula and Hanna, who have both moved abroad to study. When she sometimes gets together with them, she's careful to meet them only in the center of town. In a café somewhere. And then she dresses just like she knows Carin would dress for a quick latte with a girlfriend. In a sensible, knee-length, dark-blue Fjällräven parka-deluxe with a faux-fur hood that matches her bleached-blond hair perfectly, beige velvet leggings and ankle-high dark-brown leather boots with low rubber-soled heals. She's left the baby with Anders, she tells them, and then chatters on about baby swimming and exercise classes, diaper rash and car seats. But it's not enough. Soon both Tuula and Hanna are going to want to see Gabriel. So far she's been able to make excuses because he's so little. But now he's already six months old. She shows them the photos on her phone and they say *ooh* and *aah*, but they both hint in asides and looks that it's about time she shows them the real thing, the real, live, bouncing baby. The tips of her fingers are sweating and her skin is tingling when she slips the cell phone into her pocket. The jacket was way too expensive. She'll have to take it back. She's made sure to hide the price tag underneath the carefully tied brown scarf, which doesn't really match the leather bag she got at the flea market in Lovisa where her mom sometimes even manages to find real Prada.

That night she sees his face as she lies in bed twisting and turning with insomnia. She blinks, and his face flickers before her.

It's March. She blows on his forehead and he closes his eyes. Throws his head back and laughs with sharp white baby teeth. His mouth, tongue, throat, everything is so clean. His breath has no smell. It just is.

The living room is lit by spring sunshine. Slowly the world is melting around them, running down the dirty window panes. She's thinking of spring cleaning, washing the windows, and looks at the piles of clothes on the floor. He's always complaining that he can't play with his Legos when there's so much stuff everywhere. Empty boxes. Pieces of paper. Beer bottles. So she picks up and cleans, but it never ends. His skin is pale with tiny blue veins, downy and completely smooth.

He opens his eyes and looks straight into hers. The glittering of his baby-boy blues fills her chest and she draws one last deep breath, as if she were diving into a still summer bay, before she falls asleep.

IV

Just what do you know about loss? she asks Carin's back in an army-green, long down jacket. It's the morning of the burial and she's standing on her balcony with a steaming cup of coffee in her hand.

The closest you ever get to a really dramatic situation is in the war zone of the supermarket when you grab the last of the discounted coffee boxes right from under the nose of some poor retiree. You have never looked into eyes which just hours before were laughing, and realized they will never laugh again.

Celestine gets increasingly agitated as she watches Carin's blond hair, pulled back in a thin ponytail. She is skinny in just the right way. Her pants are saggy in the back because they are empty. She's an exclamation point against the snowdrifts by the car, and now she walks back inside again, leaving the trunk open, and Anders shuts it. He laughs and shakes his head. Carin comes back out with two overfilled bags in her hands and laughs toward Anders. They stand by the closed trunk, babbling and laughing at each other before he reopens the trunk and Carin throws in the bags.

Celestine wonders where they are going. She feels uneasy. Carin has not mentioned any trip on her blog, but it's Thursday. Thursdays occasionally mean long weekend visits at Carin's parents. Sometimes they'll have been preceded by a few glasses of wine behind drawn shades the night before. And Carin sitting alone, sulking by the kitchen table gesturing angrily toward the living room. Then the brake lights when Anders drives off into nowhere late at night. The next day the car is packed with overnight bags, a foldable cot, and baby Gabriel. But Celestine has not seen any quarrel. Not sensed any new developments on Carin's blog.

Carin and Anders kiss each other lightly on the mouth and exchange a meaningful look. Celestine glances away quickly. When she looks back up again, Carin is waving her hand and climbing in behind the wheel. Gabriel is already strapped into the baby seat. Anders stays by the driveway as Carin pulls the car out. He raises his hand in a belated wave. Then he turns around and stares straight at Celestine where she stands on her balcony.

She quickly pulls back. Her heart is beating wildly and her eyes are wandering. She shakes her head. *No, how would he know?*

But why today and not any of the hundreds of times she's stood watching him in his gray jogging pants washing his car, or flipping burgers on the little round garden barbeque, or raking the leaves on the small patch of grass in front of the building? He's never seen her. Never so much as given her a single glance. But what if he's been watching her too? Completely unnoticed? Her chest is pinching and tingling and her hands are shaking when she sees him cross the street with decisive steps.

By the time he rings her bell, and in the exact time needed to climb forty-six steps to her front door, Celestine has undergone a total transformation. She's smoothed down her hair and her eyes are no longer flickering. Her hands are dry and fingers still. The front of her blouse is uncreased and spotless and she gives him a smile that makes it all the way to her eyes. She crinkles her brow quizzically and shakes her head.

—Hi? Is there anything I can do for you? she says in Finnish.

He quickly checks the name on her door and then fires off a smile toward her. She blinks, startled. He reaches out his hand and says:

—I assume you speak Swedish?

His hand is warm and firm, precisely as she has always thought it would be. She swiftly nods and shows her teeth when she smiles. His eyes twinkle.

—Of course.

—Very good. I'm Anders Johansson.

—Stine, she says.

She learned a long time ago that it's better not to be too conspicuous. For someone like her, it's better not to draw too much attention to yourself. It's already enough with the last name.

—Vårvik, he says.

—Yes, she answers.

—It's a lovely and unusual name.

She stands with her hand on the door and a questioning smile; he's losing his thread. Is just staring at her. She turns her face away and wipes her hands against the back of her pants.

—I'm sorry. I'm standing here staring like a fool. Perhaps you know us. Carin, my wife, is often out with my son Gabriel, we live right across . . .

He babbles on and she feels it coming over her, that thing that always comes over her when someone gets too close, when someone touches the purulent surface that will never heal. Something shuts down inside of her. A gear changes. She's running on empty and switches to autopilot. The feeling engulfs her whole body while she nods and laughs and plays along. Her psychologist has a fancy name for it. "Detachment." According to him, Celestine suffers from post-traumatic stress disorder. Just like a war victim. Like a child soldier.

He's gotten to the end of his speech and now he's serving up the final line.

—But actually, the reason I'm here is that I'm running for

office in the local elections and I wanted to tell you a little bit about my election program. A bit of . . . *propaganda*, you might say, he says, and laughs nervously.

She feels her upper lip tightening against her teeth when she laughs. With decisive steps, he has made the necessary leap across to the other side in order to fish for a few random votes in unexpected places. Perhaps he could mobilize some of the couch potatoes who usually don't bother going to the voting booths. He's chosen to live a little dangerously, and as a reward he gets to have her for a little while. He thinks she's nice. She can tell from his look. The smooth, even skin, the round, large breasts under the soft, rose-colored blouse. He's sweating. She wants to shut the door in his face but is forced to invite him inside to sit down, and later she has to make coffee and nod silently while he talks on about county borders and tax burdens and playgrounds full of heroin syringes, while she thinks that he's not the one she wants to get at. Not him. It's Carin.

In another life she could have been Carin.

Celestine sits in the darkening room by the balcony and waits for the Subaru. Waits for it to turn into the yard.

In another life she could have been Carin, if people like Carin had not messed it all up for her. Those terrific mothers. The all-seeing, all-hearing, powerful neighbors in their orthopedic shoes and their ears pressed against doors and walls.

She hears a car coming from the right.

The people who infected everything with their looks, who picked at every spot with their yellowing fingernails. Those people who would sometimes knock on their door with a well-meaning smile and concerned wrinkled brow, sniffing the air with a crinkled nose.

—Is your mother home, dear?

And she would stand silently, staring, always upward, at the downturned faces where the skin had started to sag, hardening their features when they peered down at her.

Carin's Subaru turns into the driveway.

They called social services. Again and again. And the social workers walked into their lives with blue plastic bags covering their shoes so they wouldn't mess up the floors, floors which Celestine wiped with wet rags and flower-fragranced scouring powder three times a week. But she suspected they wore the plastic bags to prevent her family's life from soiling the soles of their shoes, not the other way around. That's precisely how much they were worth to them. Not even the dirt under their feet. The social workers didn't see the shiny clean stove with never a spot. The well-polished tabletop. The rugs in straight rows on the floor with rubber mats underneath so they wouldn't slide about. They just saw the holes in the walls that Celestine had tried to cover up with awkwardly placed boy band posters, the cracks in the floor, the lack of ceiling trim, and the beer bottles in the refrigerator. That was enough. Their pant legs flapped as they marched from one room to the next. And the fact that it was Celestine they had to talk to when they came didn't make things better. Celestine. A ten-year-old in a too-large apron with rubber gloves on her hands.

—How do you manage all this? And homework too?

They asked, but they didn't think she could manage all that as well as homework, though she answered in a shaky voice.

—Yes, I do manage it. At least well enough.

Enough, they said. Children should not be taking care of children, and certainly not taking care of grown-ups. But the day they came to get them, they were no longer there.

Carin gets out of her car. She reaches in the backseat and lifts out Gabriel. Celestine gets up and walks to her computer. Fifteen minutes later Carin writes:

*Phew! Gabbe is asleep. Went to bring clothes to the flea
market and Emmi said they were great quality. I should
think so! Baby Gap and Benetton! From Daddy's parents, of course. It pays to recycle! Gabbe has almost only
shopped secondhand and you all know how good he looks,
tee-hee! Anders is at a meeting. He'll be back late. I'm
going to take a lovely, long bath. Have a nice evening,
everyone!*

Celestine gets up. She's got to work fast if she's going to
do it all. Carin in the bath, Anders gone. She hurries to the
closet.

A few minutes later she walks along the driveway up to
the baby carriage, dressed in her Carin clothes and with the
hood turned up. The bangs she's had cut the day before fall
down and itch her forehead in a way she's not used to.

It's snowing lightly. Her bare knuckles are red when she
grips the handle of the baby carriage.

*Late in March they came to get her and Otto. She was blinded
by the sun as she ran as fast as she could with her brother's hand in
hers. He stumbled in his big winter boots and she had to stop several times to drag him back up onto his feet. That evening she had
listened to Harriet and Markku and had known that it was time.
The sound of Harriet's resigned sobbing and Markku's attempt to
comfort her. But Celestine knew that it was her responsibility. She
and Otto would have to stay away just long enough for it all to
pass. She got to the woods and slowed down to a walk. They were
surrounded by trees. Protected from all eyes.*

She pushes the carriage in front of her. Leaves the row
house area behind her. Her hood is still up, and a neighbor
nods and smiles in recognition and she nods back. To the per-

son passing by, she is just a familiar mother taking her baby for a walk.

When they reached the top of the old garbage dump which had been made into a recreation area with a view of the whole town, Otto cried inconsolably. She had half carried, half dragged him up the kilometer-long hill, and he collapsed onto one of the massive stone piles and refused to move. Tears ran down his cheeks. He wanted to go home. She tried making her voice light when she pointed to the freighters and containers in various colors like big Lego blocks.

If only we could sneak onboard one of those boats and sail far away. To Namibia, Celestine thought, and blew on her hands to keep them warm.

She closed her eyes for a moment and imagined the darkness of the inside of a container. They would hide at first, but when the ship had left harbor they would sneak out. What could they do to them? Throw them overboard? Hardly!

She looked at Otto as he blubbered on the rocks. After a while he stopped. Then he just sat sucking on the worn blue collar of his snowsuit, and stared at his boots. She pointed out across town and took a deep breath of melting-snow air through her nose.

—You see that, Otto? That's the cathedral. And there's the onion-shaped dome. And the radio tower in Böle.

He stood up next to her. Searching for her hand.

—There's the water tower. And the Hertonäs' jumping hill.

And far out there, the open sea.

Gabriel is not crying. He's sleeping. He's warm. Celestine puts a finger inside his collar. His neck is sweaty. She aims for the Coffee Quarter. Luxury apartments with ocean views reflect into the oily water. Rich Russians buy up the apartments as soon as they are built. On the other side of the sparse spruce forest, just a stone's throw away, the houses are a few decades older and more worn down. The population, too, is scrambled together from various places around the world. Windblown. Hapless.

When Celestine and Otto got back home a few hours later the social worker lady was still there. She was talking with Harriet who nodded exaggeratedly and mumbled, "Yes," and, "Sure." Otto had started to freeze. And cry. There was nothing else to do but go home. Harriet met them by the door.

—Take the boy and stay away! she cried. You have already caused enough problems!

She did as she was told and brought Otto to the snowdrift which was so big that year that it reached up above the roof of the parking lot. There the kids, including herself, had dug tunnels like crazy all winter long. She took one of the shovels tossed on the ground and started working the snow but couldn't drive away the anxiety that crept into her body. Harriet and social workers. It was never a good combination. God only knew what Mom might think up to say to them. She would just run her mouth, making up one glib lie after another that only made things worse. They had already seen everything. There was no point in making promises and lying anymore. She took a quick look at Otto. He was sitting deep inside the snow tunnel sucking on a piece of ice. For a moment she hesitated. Then she said:

—Otto. Wait here for a bit.

And she walked off.

Inside the kitchen she had to sit on a chair and answer questions. She had been given a glass of juice. She had nodded and looked up into the social worker lady's face with big eyes. Then Harriet had sent her away again. Celestine's steps were lighter when she returned. It was all going to be okay, they had said. And she called loudly for Otto.

No answer. She hurried up. Ran a little. Saw from a distance *the car that had driven into the snow mound, and her legs started moving on their own. The man who had been driving was vaguely familiar. He lived in one of the small, charming, wooden villas a little ways from there and used to take the short cut through their area, by way of the bar. He stumbled out of the car and fell on his face, cursing, too drunk to stay on his feet. Celestine got there and was on top of the snowdrift in one leap. The system of tunnels and caves had collapsed. Where Otto had been sitting a few minutes before was now a solid wall of icy snow. The fender of the car had ploughed deeply into the hole where he was hiding. She plunged her fingers deep into the frozen snow and started digging.*

The hole she is digging in the snow mound that the small, yellow snowplows have been piling up for weeks is getting deeper.

People like Carin doesn't deserve to have children, Celestine thinks while she digs. *People who see their children as an accessory. Who exhibit them in their egocentric blogs, completely unprepared for the unexpected. So cluelessly lost in their almighty safety that they leave their doors wide open for anyone to walk uninvited into their cozy, warm lives. It's just a question of time before something happens. Carin should be glad that what happened was just me.*

She's sniffling. He'll be fine for a long time in the snow. Until it's time to go back and get him. After the worst excitement has passed. She's going to lay low for a few weeks somewhere else and then take him to Harriet's in Lovisa. She's going to say that they have to hide. That Anders has been violent for quite a long time. That she worries for the safety of the child. Harriet will understand. She won't question it. And then everything will be just like it was before.

—Just look at you, Celestine says when she lifts Gabriel out of the carriage. Carin is supposed to be the perfect mother. But here you are.

He whimpers in his sleep. His mouth is moving and the pacifier begins to bounce up and down with a smacking sound. He is waving his hands, dressed in thick blue mittens, in front of him. She carefully lowers the sleeping child into the hole and covers him up with snow.

When she leaves the spot, gripping the handle of the carriage firmly, large snowflakes are already falling, covering up her tracks. She pushes the carriage into a thick spruce bower and walks home.

That whole evening blue lights are blinking in the area. They knock on every door, including hers. She becomes one of them, the good and splendid ones. The ones who see and hear everything. Blond and fine with rosy cheeks and cold fingertips, she pulls her shawl tighter around her shoulders and furrows her brow. Moans and groans. But no, she has seen nothing suspicious. Heard nothing at all. The policeman hardly looks at her. It's just routine. She's not among the suspects. They contact the border patrols, the coast guards. The harbor with its departing freighters is under especially careful observation. Celestine remembers how Carin fell on the staircase and howled. The sound floated above the row house area like a foghorn and Celestine shuddered. She hugged herself. It didn't feel the way she had expected. Carin crawling down the driveway and then stopping on her knees where the carriage had been. It was like a scene in a dream. Not even the tracks from the wheels were left. Anders was gray in the face and pulled Carin by the arm but she pushed him away and he fell in the snow. Then he just sat there, panting. It was so raw. Much too primitive. Celestine wished she could shout out to them that they didn't need to worry. That Gabriel was fine. That he was warm and safe and almost certainly still sleeping.

But she just swallowed hard and, confused, pulled away from the window to an armchair to wait out the night.

The next day she reads about it in the papers. It's a big spread, takes up several pages. *Baby Found in a Snowdrift.* He'd been there for four hours. They had found him in the nick of time. The press speculates about who, where, how, and why. "When," they pretty much knew. Carin insisted she had checked on the baby just ten minutes earlier.

Sadly enough for Carin, Fredriksson's Anita had seen her disappear down along Lilla Ullholmsvägen with Gabriel in the carriage right about then. They had even said hello to each other. Anders could say nothing; he had not been at home. The state-appointed psychologist who came to talk to him a few hours after his wife had been picked up—no handcuffs necessary, she didn't resist—said that this kind of thing was more common than you would think. Carin had been pretty depressed right after the birth. She had generously shared all about that on her blog. No one could know when that sort of thing might get worse.

Three days later Anders brings Gabriel back from the hospital. He's wrapped in a blanket. It's exactly like the day when he came back from the birth clinic, but Anders is more fragile now and Carin is missing. His back is bent and his steps are slow. Celestine stands by her window looking at him.

He's going to need all the help he can get, she thinks.

During the three days that have passed since the burial, she's jumped at every little sound, convinced the police would come knocking at her door. But as the hours have multiplied, her anxiety has subsided. She has been able to follow all the main turns of events in the story of Baby Gabriel in the media.

The press has not published any photos nor mentioned any names, in consideration of the family. Celestine is relieved. For a moment she feels a sting of conscience when she thinks of Carin, but it quickly passes. Celestine has always been the kind of person to put her foot into a door left ajar. So she dresses in her best push-up bra and leaves the top button of her blouse open, as she walks across the street toward the row houses to extend her most sincere sympathy to Anders Johansson.

ABOUT THE CONTRIBUTORS

Toni Härkönen

RIIKKA ALA-HARJA, born in 1967, is an author of novels, short stories, children's books, and comic books. She has published six novels to date; *Hole* is her first collection of short stories. She lives in Helsinki.

Timo Abola

TAPANI BAGGE has published over ninety books. He received the Clue Award from the Finnish Whodunnit Society in 2007 for his novel *Musta taivas* (*Black Sky*). In his seven Hämeenlinna Noir crime novels so far, Bagge depicts the cops and cons of his hometown. He has also written four historical crime novels featuring Detective Sergeant Mujunen.

Mimi Ilocwaisky

LONE THYGESEN BLECHER (translator) is a prize-winning translator from Swedish and Danish into English. Her work includes translations of novels, plays, poems, children's literature, and short fiction. She lives in New York State where she is also focusing on a career in painting and pottery.

Harri Hinkka/WSOY

KARO HÄMÄLÄINEN, born in 1976, has two passions: literature and the stock market. He works as a financial journalist and author and has combined his passions in his recent financial thrillers, including the short story "The Broker" in this anthology. Hämäläinen has studied both the humanities and economics. Following stints in Munich, Berlin, and Tampere, he now lives in Helsinki. In his spare time, Hämäläinen likes running; his record marathon time is 3:04:04.

Pertti Nisonen/WSOY

PEKKA HILTUNEN published his debut thriller, *Cold Courage,* in 2011; it won three prizes in Finland, including the Clue Award for Best Crime Novel, and was nominated for the Scandinavian Glass Key Award. He is an award-winning journalist, and his novels have been translated into seven languages.

JOHANNA HOLMSTRÖM is a Helsinki-based author who was born and raised in Sipoo, on the partly Swedish-speaking southern coast of Finland. At the age of twenty-two, she made her literary debut with the story collection *Inlåst och andra noveller*, which was short-listed for the 2004 Swedish Radio Short Story Award. Her third story collection, *Camera Obscura*, was awarded the 2009 Svenska Dagbladet Literature Prize. Her second novel, *Asfaltsänglar*, has been translated into several languages.

JESSE ITKONEN is a writer and filmmaker from Helsinki. He has worked as a columnist, film critic, director, and screenwriter. He lives with his wife and two cats, and is currently working on his first novel.

TEEMU KASKINEN, born in 1976, has written novels, plays, and screenplays. He hates cops and other writers.

LEENA LEHTOLAINEN, born in 1964, is the most successful female crime author in Finland, with her titles consistently topping the country's best-seller lists. More than two million copies of her books have been sold worldwide, and her works have been translated into twenty-nine languages. In addition to her career as an author, Lehtolainen has worked as a literary researcher, columnist, and critic. Her best-known character is the tough, down-to-earth, and emotionally intelligent police officer Maria Kallio.

TUOMAS LIUS got his first break in crime writing as a nine-year-old when a provincial newspaper began to publish his detective stories in a weekly series. His trilogy—*Haka, Laittomat,* and *Härkäjuoksu*—has received both critical and commercial success with its unique blend of suspense, action, and pitch-black humor. He is living in rural North Karelia where he schemes new and exciting crimes and capers on an almost daily basis.

Juha Nieminen

KRISTIAN LONDON (translator) has translated several novels and over a dozen plays from Finnish into English. His translation of *Nights of Awe* by Harri Nykänen was named a notable translation of 2012 by *World Literature Today*. London divides his time between Helsinki and Seattle.

Joe L. Murr

JOE L. MURR was born in Finland and has lived on every continent except Antarctica. His fiction has been published in numerous anthologies and magazines such as *Beneath Ceaseless Skies, ChiZine,* and *Noir Nation*. He currently divides his time between the Netherlands and Finland.

Sami Kero

JUKKA PETÄJÄ, born in Helsinki in 1956, has been a staff writer in the leading Finnish daily newspaper, *Helsingin Sanomat,* since 1988, serving mainly as a literary critic and essayist. He is the author of five novels and two nonfiction books. His latest crime novel, *Hiidenhyrrä (Diabolo),* is the first volume in a trilogy featuring the dry alcoholic detective inspector Pekka Suokko. He wrote his dissertation on American Jewish literature.

Svetlana Ilinskaya

DOUGLAS ROBINSON (translator), Dean of Arts at Hong Kong Baptist University, has been translating from Finnish into English since 1975, when he translated Aleksis Kivi's *Nummisuutarit (Heath Cobblers).* His translation of *When I Forgot* by Elina Hirvonen was reviewed on the front page of the *New York Times Book Review.* He has also written several books on translation including: *The Translator's Turn, Translation and Taboo, Becoming a Translator, Who Translates?,* and *Schleiermacher's Icoses.*

Andrea Walker

LOLA ROGERS (translator) is a Finnish to English translator living in Seattle. Her novel translations include works by Johanna Sinisalo, Sofi Oksanen, and Antti Tuomainen. She is also a regular contributor of translated fiction, nonfiction, and poetry to numerous journals and anthologies. Her translations of short fiction have been included in *Best European Fiction 2014* and *Words without Borders: The Best of the First Ten Years.*

JARKKO SIPILA, born in 1964, is a Finnish author and journalist. He has reported on Finnish crime for more than twenty years and has written seventeen crime novels. Five novels in his Helsinki Homicide Series have been published in English. *Helsinki Homicide: Against the Wall* won the Finnish Crime Novel of the Year Award in 2009. Through realistic characters and story lines, he explores current topics surrounding life in contemporary Finland. Visit www.jarkkosipila.com for more information.

Markus Schulte

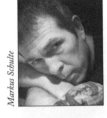

JAMES THOMPSON has lived in Finland for over fifteen years and has proven himself to be one of the most popular representatives of Nordic noir, with his work being published in a dozen languages. *Snow Angels*, the first book in his acclaimed Kari Vaara series, was one of *Booklist's* Best Crime Novel Debuts of the Year and was nominated for an Edgar Award, an Anthony Award, and a *Strand* Critics Award. *Helsinki Dead* is the fifth and latest installment in the series.

Lexa Saajasto

JILL G. TIMBERS (translator) grew up in Pennsylvania. She has lived and studied in Finland (Helsinki and Tampere), working there first as a bike mechanic after college and later as a university librarian, among other roles. Her translations from Finnish into English have appeared in many journals and anthologies. She and her Finnish husband have three grown sons and currently live in Illinois.

Toni Härkönen

ANTTI TUOMAINEN, born in 1971, was an award-winning copywriter before he made his literary debut in 2007 as a suspense author. In 2011, Tuomainen's third novel, *The Healer*, was awarded the Clue Award for Best Crime Novel and has since been published in twenty-seven countries worldwide. In 2013 his fourth novel, *Dark As My Heart*, was published in Finland to great critical acclaim.

Pekka Piri

OWEN F. WITESMAN (translator) is a professional literary translator with a master's degree in Finnish and Estonian from Indiana University. He has translated more than thirty Finnish books into English from a wide range of genres. Among these are two crime novels by Pekka Hiltunen, *Cold Courage* and *Black Noise*, as well as four mystery novels by Leena Lehtolainen. He currently resides in Springville, Utah, with his wife and three daughters.